LANCELOT'S GRAIL

LANCELOT'S GRAIL

NEW AGE TEACHINGS ON SELF AWARENESS AND ENLIGHTENMENT SET IN AN ARTHURIAN STORY

RICHARD GARTEE

Lake & Emerald Publications

Books by Richard Gartee

—Fiction—

Orgone Gizmo

Atlantis Dying

Atlantis Obsession

Lancelot's Grail

Lancelot's Disciple

Ragtime Dudes at the World's Fair

Ragtime Dudes in a Thin Place

Ragtime Dudes Meet a Paris Flapper

—Poetry—

Mountain Breathing

Watching Waves

Canyon Falls

Arbor Encore

—Non-Fiction—

Quest for Lancelot's Arthur

Skating on Skim Ice

The Hippodrome Theatre First Fifty Years

A complete list of currently available titles by the author can be found at www.gartee.com

This is a work of fiction based on historical characters.
Any resemblance to any person born after 550 CE is coincidental and unintentional.

Library of Congress Control Number: 2013910115

Trade Paperback ISBN 978-0-9895104-1-7
Published by Lake & Emerald Publications, LLC

Cover background: NASA
Cover Illustrations: Maryam Zahra

Typesetting services by BOOKOW.COM

for Gurudev

Acknowledgments

The extent to which this book (and my life) has been informed by my friendship with Mickey Singer is almost incalculable. Mickey not only introduced me to my guru but also to the many wise beings who visited the Temple of The Universe where he has lectured for over 40 years. I am ever indebted to him for all that he has given to me and the community at large.

I would also like to thank the many friends who read various drafts. Each of their comments helped me refine this work. Alena Aissing, Heather Beal, Kimberly Beal, Bruce Cornwall, Robert Garrigues, David and Judy Gold. Bryan Grossbauch, Barbara Harrison, Greg Jones, Brian Koss, Nell Page, James O'Dea, Dennis Shuman, Stacy Wagner and Erin Wilcox. Special thanks to Cindy Elder, Joyce Orr, and Felicia Lee for proofreading the manuscript and to Dave King – a most excellent editor.

For historical resources I relied principally on Sir Thomas Mallory, supplemented by Geoffrey Monmouth, Chretien de Troyes, and Dr. Monica Brzezinski Potkay. Climatic references included Procopius of Caesarea, Sir Joseph Norman Lockyer and David Keys.

Sources that influence Lancelot's spiritual philosophy are almost too numerous to name, but here are a few of the most important: Paramahansa Yogananda, Jesus, Buddha, Jianzhi Sengcan (Sengstau), Swami Muktananda, Ram Dass, Wayne Dyer, Eckert Tolle, and of course Mickey Singer.

HISTORICAL BACKGROUND

The period we call the Dark Ages began in darkness, literally.

A volcanic eruption so massive that it separated Java from Sumatra blotted out the sun worldwide for two years. The resulting freezes, droughts, floods, storms, and crop failures precipitated the collapse of empires and kingdoms across five continents. Britain was no exception. Camelot fell, King Arthur died, and the Knights of the Round Table dispersed.

The people of Britain had no knowledge of volcanoes in distant lands, but they witnessed the sun dim and feared it would never return. They saw their crops fail and felt the hunger that fed old superstitions.

Even when the sun burned bright again and the crops returned, the people's fears did not much diminish. Something had caused their world to collapse, and Sir Lancelot was an easy scapegoat. Many people already blamed his affair with Guinevere for the fall of Camelot.

According to Sir Thomas Malory, Guinevere entered the nunnery at Almesbury after Arthur's death while Lancelot became a hermit monk elsewhere. Malory describes miraculous phenomena surrounding Lancelot during this period of his life, which could indicate that he had found the Holy Grail and gained mystical powers and enlightenment.

Chapter 1

The August sun burned pleasant, evaporating any memory of the dark years. The sun was gold, the lawns were green and all the abbey gardens were abundant.

Alura was gathering rosemary and shallots in the herb garden near the Abbot's kitchen. She noticed her brother Frith crossing the distant vegetable gardens. He seemed to be playfully following the path of a sunbeam that capered in rhythm to the sway of tall trees. Where it veered from the walkway into the garden he ran after it, performing gawky leaps over the rows of vegetables.

Monks hoeing the beans and peas kept their eyes on the plants and pretended not to see that he crossed their rows instead of following the longer path around. Alura laughed. Frith had been the Abbot's personal attendant since he was a child and had a habit of doing whatever he wanted. Although he was grown now, the monks still indulged him.

Frith was making his way toward the Abbot's kitchen, where Alura had worked since her own childhood. Although the Abbey of St. Benignus wasn't a mixed house – all of the monastics were male – women were employed in the kitchens as cooks, bakers, and chefs. Assisted by younger monks, they prepared magnificent banquets and sumptuous feasts for the Abbot's guests. All but one of the women were married and lived in the nearby village – only Alura was single. She lived on the abbey grounds in a converted storeroom.

St. Benignus was located not far off the old Roman road. A small village with a market and a few tradesmen had grown around it. Travelers would stable their animals at the livery, and then inevitably ask where they could secure a meal and a night's sleep. The liveryman would shrug and point them toward the abbey.

Alura oft heard the Abbot say he wasn't in the business of running an inn; he was busy running a house of God. But safe places to take refuge along the road being rare, he thought it his Christian duty to offer accommodation to those who sought it.

Alura turned back to her task. She was pulling a few more shallots when Frith dashed up and pinched her. Alura emitted a startled squeal and whirled to slap him, but Frith caught her wrist in his hand and kissed her lightly on the cheek.

Alura glanced around quickly before embracing him. "Hello, little brother."

"Not so little; I am now taller than you."

"And none the wiser for it. Suppose someone had seen you do that."

"Well you do it to me."

"Not when anyone might see. I suppose you've come to tell me about the knight?"

"Knight! What knight?"

"The liveryman's wife says a knight has come, all bright and shiny in polished armor. The knight has left him care of a handsome steed."

"And is the knight handsome as well?"

Alura dimpled. "I haven't seen him."

"But you will."

"Oh yes! I'll arrange to be in the dining hall when the Abbot brings him to sup."

"What if he's married?"

"What if he's not?"

Just then Ethelburg, one of the kitchen ladies, poked her head out of the door. "Alura!"

Alura turned and held up her basket, "Just gathering shallots and herbs for the morrow."

"Is that Frith with you?"

"She has poor eyes," Frith said. "Tell her no."

"He has just come," Alura said.

"Frith!" Ethelburg said, "The Abbot is looking for you."

"I have finished my duties for the day," Frith said.

"That may be, but he wants you back."

Touching Alura's sleeve, Frith said, "Let me see what he wants. I will return as soon as I may."

"Don't hurry. I have to finish preparing supper before they will let me free."

"Frith!" Ethelburg called. "It's not tomorrow he wants you. It's now!"

Frith walked toward the building. "Coming, Madame."

"Wait, for me," Alura said.

Alura and Frith entered the Abbot's kitchen. Its tall conical ceiling, open at the top, provided a draft that kept three fireplaces blazing. The monks had a separate kitchen, similar in design, but smaller. This kitchen was dedicated to provisioning the Abbot's more important guests. The Abbot deemed it only fitting to provide richer hospitality to the noble guests who came to the abbey. They, in turn, filled its coffers with their generous donations and the abbey had become enormously wealthy.

Even if Alura hadn't known about the knight, the activity in the kitchen would have told her there was an important guest. There was venison roasting on one fireplace, a pig on the spit of another and several chickens in a great pot of vegetables on the third. All of this was to please the Abbot's guests. The monks lived a more frugal existence. They ate one meal a day, except during Easter. Each monk got bread, soup, two cooked dishes of beans or eggs, cheese and plenty of vegetables.

Frith snatched a sliver of meat off one of the carving tables and popped it into his mouth. The cook waved her cleaver at him.

"I moved here for the ample food," Frith said, grinning.

"You'd make a poor monk."

"I would never be a monk. I couldn't work around all this delicious smelling meat and have to eat a plain diet of vegetables."

"You'd eat well enough," the cook said. "Your sister would see to that."

Alura smiled at their banter. Her brother liked to joke that he sampled all the dishes to make sure the Abbot wasn't poisoned. The Abbot also imported a good wine. Frith sampled that as well.

"Besides," Frith said, "father sent us to the Abbot for jobs, not renunciation."

That was true. Back in the dark years, she and Frith were brought by an elder brother carrying a letter to the Abbot from their father. Their father in better times had contributed substantially to the church. He might yet again when better times returned. Thus Frith and Alura were not treated as novices, but as employees much in the Abbot's favor.

She remembered how hopelessly lost she had felt entering the gates of St. Benignus. She had seldom been off her father's estate and never to a church as large and impressive as this. The family said they were not abandoning them. They said St. Benignus was an important church. That meant they would live in a good moral environment, have plenty of food, and be safe from harm within its walled grounds. From her perspective, her older brothers and sisters had simply decided to get rid of the two youngest siblings. Her proof was that when better times returned, the family did not retrieve them. Further, she felt shocked and betrayed when she learned that there was no money left for a dowry, and thus no opportunity for her to get a husband.

The only bright spot in this crisis was that her best friend and playmate, Frith, was going to be with her. Alura had been one year old when Frith was born, and they had been constant companions from the time they were toddlers.

At first, Alura was given the scut work – gather vegetables from the gardens, fetch water, wash the vegetables, and feed the scraps to the chickens. These jobs, at least, gave her plenty of chances to run out of the kitchen and about the abbey grounds with Frith. That kept her loneliness at bay.

Eventually the two of them were given more responsibilities, but still they managed to finish each day with time to spend together. Over the years Alura learned to be a good cook. It was said she could turn out a tasty dish from whatever God provided, a skill that suited the Abbot's frugal nature very well.

In a sense, the abbey life was good. There was always plenty to eat, which was a blessing itself. Even better, the abbey was a main stopping point for travelers from far places. There were interesting overnight guests and interesting conversations for a girl to listen in on. She was intelligent, bright, and had a good mind, although she had learned that was not a desirable attribute for a woman in search of a spouse.

Alura believed Frith's lot was easier because the consequences of their abandonment seemed more severe for her than for him. Although she sometimes felt like women were chattel, sold for a dowry, bought for power, or to service a husband, the meaning of a girl's life was marriage. Wasn't it? By her age Mother had married and birthed her older brothers.

If only she had been returned to Father's estate... But no, she was stuck at the abbey and it seemed nobody back home was championing her cause. If she was to marry, she must do it on her own.

CHAPTER 2

Leaving the kitchen and its lovely smells, Frith crossed to the main building which held the cloister, scriptorium, library and the Abbot's office. A breeze danced up his sleeves tickling the newly minted man-hair under his arms. The carefree summer day made him feel as exuberant as a young colt. His work was done and soon Alura's would be too.

He made his way through the library. The room consisted of wooden cupboards filled with books. The Abbot had told him it was one of the largest in the land, containing more than just religious books, but also books on natural history, politics and the law.

He passed into the scriptorium where generations of monks had sat huddled in carrels, producing page after page of velum covered with ink. A few of the monks were illuminating the manuscripts with colorful illustrations. Frith quite liked those, but the rest meant little to him for he could not read. He liked the scriptorium though – it was the brightest, sunniest room in the abbey.

Leaving the scriptorium, he passed through a small, ledger-filled room where the abbey kept its records. Adjacent to it was the Abbot's office. Frith tapped gently on the door, and then entered without waiting for permission. Towering over the short elderly Abbot was a stalwart mass in chain mail. He turned toward the door as Frith entered.

Alura's source had been right; the knight was all polished and shiny. But God, he was old. Though he stood ramrod straight, he was balding. Where he had hair, it was graying. Still he was a knight. Here, before him, was a man who had lived the knightly adventures that Frith dreamed would one day be his own.

"Good lad, you've come," the Abbot said. "This noble knight is Sir Bedivere. Sir Bedivere, this is my man Frith."

Frith idolized knights, although this was the first time he had actually seen one. Men in his childhood were landowners and farmers, at the abbey they were monks, in the village were smiths and tradesmen, but this man was knight! He was so delighted that he almost ignored the fact that the Abbot had called him a man.

Frith bowed to the knight, and his eye caught on the knight's boots. They were clean as new, though they were clearly quite old. The boot leather was worn shiny on the inside calf of each, as if oiled by his horse's sweat and polished by its coat. The knight clearly spent many hours on horseback.

Frith noticed the knight's large broadsword. Its scabbard weighed on his wide leather belt, causing his stomach to fold over it. This made him look portlier than he was.

Rising, Frith admired the wondrous armor, a maze of interlinking rings so small and tight that they looked like a single, shimmering fabric. Each individual link looked like it had been lovingly polished and shone as bright as the cup and paten on the altar. It gave the impression that the man inside was the same.

Underneath the chain mail hauberk, Sir Bedivere wore a thickly padded gambeson to cushion the weight of it. In deference to the August heat, the knight had removed his hood and coif and laid aside his surcoat. Frith noticed he kept his left hand gloved, though in summer there was no need for it. The other glove was tucked in his belt near the hilt of his sword.

Frith's attention snapped back at the sound of his name. "Frith's entirely familiar with the area," the Abbot was saying. "He will guide you."

"I've already stabled my horse," Bedivere said. "I was told we can go there on foot."

"That's true. It's not far, merely hidden and difficult to find. As I said, it's close enough that he comes to Mass every morning. You could just wait for him to come to you."

Him? Him who? Frith wished he hadn't been distracted by the knight's marvelous kit.

"My business cannot wait," Bedivere said. "I need to see if it is really he as soon as possible."

"I've already said I'll lend you my man, Frith," the Abbot said.

"Can we go then?" Bedivere said.

"Forgive me, Sir," Frith said, "but where are we going?" Finally, a way out of his servitude at the abbey; a great adventure was looming and he was more than ready!

"Frith I want you to take Sir Bedivere to the cottage inhabited by the old hermit... you know the one I mean."

Frith shuddered. This was no adventure at all and the greatest of risk. Boys were warned not to play in those woods even on a dare. People of good sense avoided the frightening recluse who slipped like a wraith in and out of church in the morning's fog. Or so Frith had heard. He never went to early Mass to actually see the man himself.

"But sir," Frith said, "those woods are not permitted."

"They are if I say they are," the Abbot said. "And I do."

"Sir… you know what I mean. Many would say you would send him and me to our doom."

Sir Bedivere laid his right hand on the hilt of his sword. "Have no fear of wolves or even dragons in those woods, I have defeated both."

But the Abbot was chuckling quietly.

"It is said there is a thing far worse. Weapons cannot slay it," Frith said.

Sir Bedivere looked to the Abbot who shook his head. "You have nothing to fear. The superstitions of the ignorant fill his head. Living in the woods is the one you seek. He is certainly no threat – I know him well." Turning to Frith the Abbot said, "Whatever you have heard, discard it. You have no reason to fear that I would send you to harm."

But it was hard to set aside a fear that everyone in the area, monk and layman alike, shared. It was said the hermit brought misfortune to all who fell in contact with him. If that was true, why seek him out? It wasn't that he was afraid of being rent by sharp teeth, but being afflicted with some invisible… spirit that would bring ill fortune. How could a knight's sword defend against the unseen?

"But sir—" Frith said.

"Do not say 'but sir,'" Bedivere said. "Obey your Master! Abbot, have you no control over this man?"

Although normally a gentle man of God, the Abbot yanked Frith aside. His throat tight, he whispered hoarsely, "I indulge you. I allow you to run off and do as you please for the better part of the day. Now I need something from you. This is a knight of importance. Do not embarrass me. Do exactly as I say, and do it now!"

Frith saw there was no point in arguing. "Of course, sir, and I apologize. But if you must send me to my ruin, will you not lend me a sacred object to carry for protection?"

"You have no need of it, I have told you. The hermit is not cursed."

"A benediction then?"

The Abbot sighed. "I will give you a blessing for safe journey, for no holy man can refuse to do that. Kneel." Both Frith and Sir Bedivere knelt before the Abbot who made a sign over them, mumbled something brief in Latin, and then sent them on their way.

* * *

At the rear of the abbey there was a parcel of rough, rocky land that separated the woods from the walled abbey grounds. Not even suitable for sheep, it was overgrown with scrub and weeds as high as a man's thigh. At its far edge grew a hedge of thorny bushes. Frith pushed open a heavy gate and led the knight through the scruff, he kept careful watch where he stepped to avoid a snap of twig or rustle of leaves that would alert… whatever of their approach.

Frith's people were not pagan. He had been raised with the promise of the Christian world. But there was still this world to fear. The forest might harbor giants, wolves, or in its darkest hollows, terrible spirits. One did well to tread lightly there. He was comforted that the abbey gates were locked at night.

But his careful traverse was probably wasted. Behind him the massive knight strutted through the wasteland as though he were its king. Sir Bedivere was armed and had promised to defeat any wolf or dragon they might awaken. He had assured Frith they had nothing to fear. That would have been a comfort if all he worried about was badgers or bears. But Frith wasn't so sure how sword and armor would fare against bad fates. His only hope was that the noise the knight was making might drive away whatever evil spirits surrounded this place.

When they reached the thorny bushes, Frith noticed many of them still had good berries, but scolded himself – This was no time to think about food. They followed the hedge along until Frith found an opening. Though the hedge still appeared impenetrable, Frith easily slipped between two bushes and led them into the dense woods.

The forest was thick and dark. What little sun penetrated the canopy of leaves was filtered it into a dim green light. The forest floor was a sea of ferns with no discernible path. This gave Frith no comfort. He guided them in a general direction that he believed to be correct. Sir Bedivere would simply have to trust that he knew the way.

As the forest deepened Bedivere looked around. "Are you sure you know the way?"

"Oh, yes, sir."

"So you've been there before?"

"Do not say such a thing!"

"If you've never been there, how can you guide me?"

"I have been clearly instructed where to avoid. Trust me, good knight; I know where we should not be going."

A sudden sound overhead made Frith hunch and nearly dive for cover. He hunted through the canopy and saw a squirrel.

"Don't be so skittish," Bedivere said. "This is nothing lad, you should have seen the dark moors my master made me cross to return a sword."

Suddenly there was a crackle of old leaves on their left. Frith unsheathed his knife and whirled on it in a panic. A dark shadow moved low to the ground.

Bedivere was laughing. "It is only a hedgehog."

"It might have been any kind of creature," Frith said. "Sir, I am here in obedience to my master as I should. But many people say do not come here. I am… not a stickler for rules, but in this I obey."

"Therein lies the problem with our times," Bedivere said. "Since the fall of our king, men no longer stick to the rules, the code of chivalry. Yet they are in thrall to dark superstitions. We need the world to go back."

"How?"

"The restoration of the order of knights and our code is the first step to ending the darkness."

Bedivere seemed like a man on a mission, though these woods seemed like an odd place to pursue it. But right now Frith just needed to get the knight there and back without being beset by some curse. "You're the first knight I've ever known, and I'd consider it a great boon to learn knighthood from you. But for now we should proceed with silence so as not to alert any malevolent force to our presence."

"Nonsense," Bedivere said. "I'm not the slightest bit afraid in this forest. Thorns cannot penetrate my leathers, and neither sword nor teeth could penetrate this armor."

"Have you no dread for the unseen?"

"A knight has no reason to fear the spirit world. The chivalrous code, moral certainty, and Christian baptism protect us from anything profane. No, my only concern is, can I find my way back if you…"

Sir Bedivere had been striding along as he spoke. Now he pitched forward suddenly, throwing his arms out to break his fall. Then, some unseen force severed the knight's hand. It flew off his arm and landed in some rotting leaves.

Frith would have run then and there, if he weren't paralyzed with fear.

Bedivere seemed unaffected. He didn't even draw his sword. He simply scooped up his hand, pulled the glove over his wrist, and before Frith's eyes the hand magically grew back.

Thereafter it was silent between them. Frith couldn't understand why the knight didn't make more of the forest cleaving his hand. But at least the knight had seen for himself how the dark forces were at work in these woods.

They continued until they came to a fast-moving river. The water was not deep, but the banks were steep. It was good that they had come on foot, for a horse could not have forded here. Frith didn't relish descending the muddy banks, crossing the water, and climbing back up. However, that became unnecessary, for a short way upstream he found where an old fallen tree provided a natural bridge that he led Bedivere carefully across. In the slippery moss that covered the bark, they saw the first signs of human use ... a footprint here, a scuff mark there.

"There's an optimistic sign," Bedivere said.

CHAPTER 3

Not far past the makeshift bridge, they reached a clearing in the forest. A small yard of hard-packed dirt had been swept of leaves and debris. It was separated from the forest by a rough wattle fence. In Bedivere's opinion it was a poor fence, rotting back into the ground and sagging in places, but at least it had a gate.

The yard itself was a riot of colorful flowers, organized in groomed and tended beds. Not accidental patches of wildflowers, but bearing the mark of the gardener's touch, the work of someone who knew what a courtyard garden should look like. Scattered around the garden were several pieces that resembled furniture. A tree trunk had been hewn into a bench. A great slab of bluestone had been squared and assembled into some kind of an altar.

Beyond the gardens was a cottage – though cottage would be a generous term for it. It was poorly thatched and barely large enough for a man. To Bedivere's eye, the addition of a tit-mouse would have made it overcrowded. He couldn't believe the lad had led him to the right place.

Since the fall of Camelot, Bedivere had roamed the countryside, searching for a leader who could resurrect the remaining knights to their former glory. Bedivere did not want the role himself – he knew his own limitations. But he needed someone to stand beside, as he had stood beside King Arthur. He was a fierce and loyal knight, willing to fight anyone for what he believed in and to defend he who was to be their leader. But he knew he didn't have it in him – didn't have the charisma – to draw the knights together. He was sure the man he had in mind did. Bedivere was so enamored with this plan that he expected his enthusiasm would be catching – why just the gist of the idea should be enough for the man to pack up and accompany him.

Frith stopped timidly at the gate. "Here's the hermit's cottage, Sir."

Bedivere waited for the Abbot's servant to precede him. When he didn't, Bedivere prodded him, "Well, go on boy."

Frith shivered, though the day was hot. "I cannot, Sir. People say not to set foot here."

Bedivere snorted. "That's superstitious nonsense."

Frith did not move. "This hermit is cursed by some bad past deed that brings misfortune upon us."

God, the simpleton attitudes of these country people. The world needed the Round Table now more than ever. "Know you not who this hermit is?"

"I do not."

"Yet you are afraid."

"I… I am, sir."

He could stay and try to argue the boy out of his ignorant superstitions, but he had far more important things to do. Bedivere opened the gate himself and entered.

Frith held his palm out. After a moment, Bedivere realized he expected payment. Bedivere appraised the gawky lad, obviously only recently matured and not yet adjusted to the manly state. He would likely scamper back to the Abbot as soon as Bedivere's back was turned. Bedivere shook his head. "You've led me into a wilderness. If you won't come in, then wait here by the gate. You'll be paid when you guide me back to the abbey."

Frith sat on the ground, safely on the forest side of the fence. Bedivere turned toward the cottage. "A traveler, here. I seek the dweller of this wretched hut."

The cottage door opened and a man came forth, dressed in a tattered monk's robe. "Be away, leave me at peace."

Beneath his impoverished apparel was a man as vital and handsome as ever. Although he had aged and his hair was now fully gray, Bedivere recognized him at once. "Greetings, Sir Lancelot. Greatest knight that ever was!"

When Bedivere said the name, he heard a commotion behind him. Bedivere glanced back. The lad had still not followed him through the gate, but the boy was on his feet now, and definitely paying attention.

Lancelot bent down and pulled a weed from the flower bed, but said nothing.

"No greeting for your old compatriot, Bedivere?"

Lancelot straightened up and looked at him. "Sir Bedivere... There's a name from days long past."

"And grand days they were, before the fall," Bedivere said, "but bad days since the death of our beloved King. Everyone's scattered, Lancelot. For the last several years, I've been riding to and fro, trying to find who remains."

"And I've been right here or at the nearby abbey," Lancelot said.

"I know. This boy has just brought me from there. But what brought you to this low estate?"

"The grace of God, though I didn't know it," Lancelot said.

Bedivere looked at the shack; looked at Lancelot's poor dress. "The grace of God is treating you pretty shabbily, then. Your cottage is little more than wattle and mud. You deserve better."

"Why do you say that?"

"Lancelot, you cannot listen to what people say about you."

"Bedivere." Lancelot met his eyes evenly, with no hint of guilt but only a deep sadness. "Arthur wasn't simply my liege lord. He was my friend. And Guinevere was his wife."

"And he knew all, and still loved you both."

Lancelot simply shook his head. "After… everything, she became a nun, cloistered at Almesbury. I went to see her, you know. But she couldn't bear it and forbade me to ever come again."

"An attitude she should have taken while her king was alive," Bedivere said.

Lancelot looked off into the woods, toward the direction they had come. "Thinking penance her good example, I came to the Abbey of St. Benignus intending to take Holy Orders."

"Are you a priest now?"

Lancelot shook his head. "The Bishop wouldn't ordain me because… Well, you can surmise."

Bedivere nodded. "I suppose he could hardly do otherwise. Too many folk blame you for far too much."

Lancelot smiled then. It made him seem suddenly younger. "Yes. Isn't it absurd to think the sins of two humans can blot out the sun? Even the most ignorant couldn't really believe that."

"Yet they saw the sun dim. The crops did not grow, Arthur died, and Camelot fell."

Lancelot's smile disappeared. "You know better. Neither I nor Guinevere brought the darkness."

"I do, but these are dark times we live in. So let's not debate that. Tell me why if you had residence in the abbey are you living in this wilderness?"

"Even in the anonymity of the church I was still the subject of rumor. This small cottage is near enough to church, but away from the petty and fearful."

"We can change all that!"

"I don't see how."

"Lancelot, you and I know firsthand what Arthur accomplished with Camelot. True learning and faith were not shut up behind abbey walls but were out in the world. Peace reined. The land was prosperous. And how was that achieved? Chivalrous knights worked together, fighting for the people."

"Yes…"

"Don't you see? If we could revive the Knights of the Round Table, restore the code of chivalry, the people will be restored, and the land will come back prosperous."

"I wish you well with that."

"But it is you who must do it! To succeed we will need a charismatic leader, one who can draw the scattered knights back to our cause. That is why I am here. You must ride with me to gather our flock."

"I doubt any will flock to my banner. When the sky grew dim, men's minds did as well."

"Not all," Bedivere said. "There are men in many places who remember you as their champion. Leave this wretched life as a hermit and travel with me. We'll find a flock."

"Old friend, I cannot. I'm sorry."

"Why be so quick? Hear me out."

"It's not what you believe. Since coming here to live in meditation I discovered… Well, nothing of our old life can compare."

"Only because you forget how great the old life was. When Camelot was in flower, when knights were chivalrous, didn't the world seem right?"

"The time we spent in tournaments and with damsels cannot compete with the mystical visions I've attained here."

"It's not for me to question a mystic's visions. But the rest of us not living on your humble estate have need of you."

Lancelot laughed now, though there was no humor in it. "The rest of the people do not want me. I've become like Eve blamed for the fall of Eden."

"Then maybe you owe the people. How can you be sure we're not all paying for your sins?"

"Because that's not how God plays the game."

"How can you claim to be a holy man, yet diminish God by suggesting he is playing?"

"Bedivere, if you could hear Him, you'd know He does nothing but play."

"What? Are you hearing voices? Having conversations with God out here in your hovel?"

"Yes."

"I see." Bedivere hesitated, afraid to say aloud what he was thinking. Finally, he did. "Lancelot, are you mad then?"

"Bedivere, how many years did we ride in quest of the Holy Grail?"

"Many more than I can recall. But why are you changing the subject?"

"Because when you find the Grail, it leads you into direct communion with God."

It took a moment for the full meaning of Lancelot's words to hit Bedivere. "You have found the Holy Grail! Where is it?"

Lancelot spoke in a voice so quiet, Bedivere had to strain to hear him. "It's not some distant treasure. It's the nearest of the near."

Bedivere looked around at the primitive surroundings. "The Grail is in this place?"

"Not here," Lancelot said with a dismissive gesture at the flower-bedecked yard. "Here." He tapped his forehead.

Bedivere didn't understand, but he didn't let that hinder him. "If you've truly found it, then ride with me. Lancelot, this is exactly the news that will give the knights new hope."

Lancelot shook his head. "No thank you. There is peace here. I have seen enough of the world to know there is no peace out there."

"It's true, there is no peace," Bedivere said. "The kingdom is in disarray. That's why I have given every day since its fall to finding a leader like you to pull the knights back together. To bring peace."

"Bedivere, to seek peace out there is an illusion. Besides, there is no great Lancelot left, just a quiet man of God before you."

"If you have truly found the Grail, give the people a taste of what we can become."

"I have tasted a bit of the world and it has bitten me back. The people have abandoned their hero."

"Come with me, for just a fortnight. Surely all your saintliness won't leak away in so brief an outing."

"I'm not worried for my saintliness," Lancelot said.

"Then why fight me?"

"For your own sake, old friend," Lancelot said. "Your life is a constant struggle to recapture the past. Look at my life, it is tranquil and calm. You can have this as well."

"My life is about helping others. Yours is wasted in the woods helping yourself."

"There's more to it than that. But I'll keep my solitude, thank you."

Bedivere's jaw tightened. Had Lancelot forgotten his own sacrifice? He held up his gloved hand. "I gave my hand for king and country. Surely you can sacrifice your solitude."

"Bedivere, I don't want to diminish the value of your contribution, but face facts. Camelot is gone."

"And you can bring it back!"

"No, I couldn't. Even if I agreed, you couldn't get fifty knights to follow me."

"Come out of this hermitage and see for yourself. Let your own eyes persuade you."

"There's no one here to persuade. I'm not a knight anymore, only an ascetic who is willing to show you a different path."

"What are you talking about?"

"You've fought enough battles, man. Don't you recognize there is one more to be won inside you?"

"What battle?"

"Do you not hear the voice that is talking, telling you every thought you have? That voice is not you. You are the one listening to it."

"That's just… clever word play."

"No, it's not. It's a battle going on inside your head, right now."

"There is nothing going on in my head!"

Lancelot started laughing. After a moment Bedivere realized what he had said and had no choice but to join in.

When their laughter subsided, Lancelot said quietly, "My old friend, that battle is there. It is in your head. It was in mine. Our internal… ongoing argument has mesmerized us for so long that we've forgotten that we are the listener. And the results are not even as meaningful as we believe."

"What do you mean?"

"Our mind forms all of its conceptualizations based on our past experiences, but you and I have not had the same experiences, so what our mind thinks it knows is really limited by our individual experience. Therefore what one man thinks is right, another man believes is wrong, and each is based on difference in experiences."

"Now you've gone too far. I know what is right and wrong."

"Wouldn't you like to finally be at peace and free of it?"

"I would much rather our countrymen be free from darkness and want. Peace will come when things go back to the way they were."

"We can't go back to the past. As surely as all rivers flow into the sea, all time flows into the now. Trying to get back to the past is like an oarsman rowing against the current. It's wasted effort. The minute he puts down the oars, time is going to carry him into the now."

"But using what we know from the past can't we mend it?"

"I'm going to tell you a wonderful secret about the past which you can use to free your mind…"

Bedivere waited.

"It's over… gone… done. Not one minute of thinking can ever change what already was."

"But we can move forward, can't we?"

"Absolutely. The past is only an indicator of the course we have come by, not the only course that exists. I've said the mind's conventional way of knowing is limited. But suppose there was another way of knowing, beyond the mind… intuitive knowing. It comes from reaching a place that we saw in Arthur's court when the Grail appeared."

"Oh, I don't doubt you have found it. I can sense a holiness about you. Although you didn't bring the darkness, you may be able to bring some light. Why not come and show the other knights?"

"Bedivere, you have a mind like a bear trap. When it snaps shut on something, it won't let go. Even when someone leads you into a different way of thinking, your mind instantly snaps right back."

Bedivere turned his head away and swallowed hard. He had forgotten the Grail quests all those long years ago. "No, you misunderstand me. Now that you've reminded me about the Grail, I believe it makes our cause even more important. Why not come and remind the others?"

Lancelot sighed. "You have not understood a word I said… Perhaps this cannot be taught." Lancelot turned from him and walked toward his cottage.

"Wait," Bedivere said.

Lancelot turned. "I think we have said all that can be said, haven't we?"

Bedivere was not one to give up easily. It was apparent that this was not going the way he had hoped, but in any battle there might come a time to disengage and come back with reinforcements. "All right, I'll leave you to your peace. But please don't close out the idea completely. Let me take measure of what knights I can find that will follow you and report back."

"Can you not understand? There is no knight here to convince, only a hermit tiring of this argument."

"Promise you'll reconsider it when I return?"

"The only promise I can offer you is my benediction. Peace will be with you." With that Lancelot made a sign of blessing and retreated into his cottage.

CHAPTER 4

And to think, when Frith first arrived, he had been tempted to leave. He'd only decided to stay in hopes that he might gain employment in the knight's service – it couldn't hurt to show you were brave enough to remain in the fearsome woods. But Frith's fears were forgotten from the moment he heard Bedivere call the hermit by name.

Lancelot.

Lancelot was the idol of his youth, his feats the legends of his childhood.

Now that Bedivere was leaving, Frith started talking as soon as he stepped outside the gate. "You knew King Arthur!"

Bedivere seemed to grow taller; his bearing became more erect, his chest pushed at the links of his chain mail. "It was I whom King Arthur entrusted to return his sword, the mighty Excalibur, to the Lady of the Lake when he was dying."

"And this recluse who's been disparaged by our village, is he really the great Sir Lancelot?"

"You've heard of him then. I thought you didn't know this hermit."

"Who has not heard of Sir Lancelot? But I'd have never guessed that this is what became of him."

"He's hiding from the world. He might claim his heart was broken by Guinevere, but I think it was broken when he was abandoned by his adoring public."

"Then have you come to restore him?"

"I hoped my long search was ended when I learned Lancelot was here," Bedivere said. "He could be our savior, lead us on a great quest and restore the sense of purpose we once had. But… you heard him. He rejects my pleas to resume the knightly life."

The cottage door burst opened and Lancelot stuck his head out. "You may think me God-mad, but do not think me deaf. Can you not leave in peace?"

Bedivere looked chagrined and motioned him forward, as though it had been his fault they had tarried.

"Sorry for the disturbance, we're leaving. I shall return in a fortnight," Bedivere said.

Frith's mind was spinning, working out a plan for his future. When they had gone a little ways he sought an opening to discuss his idea with the knight. "What will you do now?"

"I'm discouraged but not despairing. I'm going to the south where I've heard there are a number of knights. When I pass back this way I'll bring Lancelot a tally of those knights. I believe that if I can show him that there are knights willing to follow him, he will come to his senses and leave the hermit life."

"I understood him to say no one will follow him," Frith said. "Why?"

"Well it's not slander to tell a well-enough-known tale," Bedivere said. He almost seemed to be speaking to himself, as if he were trying to work out why his arguments had failed. "Lancelot fell deeply in love with the wife of his mentor, our King. And she with him."

"Queen Guinevere?" Frith said.

Bedivere nodded. "The King's evil son Mordred exposed their affair and attempted to force the King to burn her at the stake."

Frith paled. How could someone burn a Queen?

"Then while the King was wracked with the agony of his dilemma, Mordred attacked."

"That all seems to be Mordred's doing. How's that Sir Lancelot's fault?"

"The things people do in the name of love can have terrible consequences. Lancelot and Guinevere disrespecting the sanctity of marriage provided Mordred with the leverage to bring down Camelot."

"So you're saying he was at fault?"

"Most folks point the finger at one of the two of them. I'd never speak ill of the Queen... I was ever loyal to her."

"Then you blame him?"

"I cannot step in that moat because I'm depending on him to save us. I'm willing to forgive Lancelot his past transgressions, for we have greater need of him than he believes. Now, I must be off to find enough knights to change his mind."

"Do you think he will… change his mind?"

"He must. Our land is in disorder. We're entering a dark age. The way back to the glory of Camelot begins with the revival of the Round Table."

"But, if he's an outcast, blamed for these years of hardship, perhaps he's right. People will not follow him."

Bedivere waved his hand dismissively. "Knights are not the common folk. They respect his past feats of courage and will forgive his flaws. They will follow such a knight."

"But will they follow a cursed mystic who frightens villagers and children?"

"He won't frighten his fellow knights. Many of us spent years questing for the most sought after object in history. I've known several who attained that greatest gift. Lancelot is not faking. He has truly found something holy. I sense it. But that doesn't mean he should keep it hidden."

"What should he do?"

"He should share it as Galahad did. He should end his isolation and bring his spiritual gift to the world for the betterment of those who haven't had his good fortune. There's no point in having a realization then keeping to yourself out in the woods."

They were nearly back to the abbey lands. Frith couldn't let his opportunity slip away. "Sir Bedivere, do you need a squire to ride with you?"

Bedivere stopped short and stared at him. "I thought you were bound to the abbey."

"Not by oath. I hope my future is elsewhere. I would very much like to lead a knightly life. I could help you rebuild the Round Table."

"Have you a horse, equipment, training?"

"No, but I'm anxious for adventure."

"It takes years to become a knight," Bedivere said. "You should have started already. I was age seven when I began as a page in service to the knight who was my master, learning how to care for weapons. Then, still younger than you are now, I became a squire. It was during this training I learned to use the weapons I'd once kept care of. I accompanied my master to tournaments and battles. In doing so I gained skill as a horseman and a groomsman as well."

"A groomsman?" Frith thought of the men who shoveled out the stables on his father's estate.

"The success of a battle or a tournament depends on the strength, agility, and bravery of the horse every bit as much as the man who rides him. A knight's horse is his most valuable possession."

"But my sister said you've given care of your horse to the liveryman. Where are your squires?"

"It is a different time now. I used to travel in a great company of knights. Now I ride alone, like an old stallion cut from the herd. Not that I was abandoned by the others, but rather that they have abandoned the ideal of Camelot."

"Then you should take me with you, as your knight in training."

"My cause is vital; my mission is serious. I'm sorry I can't take on an apprentice."

CHAPTER 5

Alura picked up two bushel baskets and headed out the kitchen door. "I'm leaving to get carrots and beets."

"You'll never be able to carry both baskets when they're full," said the cook. "Take a couple of the scullery boys to help you."

Alura wanted to find Frith, and she didn't want company. "Thank you, no, I can carry one and I'll get one of the monks to help me with the other." Without waiting for an argument she was out the door.

The fields Alura desired were a good distance from the Abbot's kitchen, near the part of the abbey where she was most likely to find Frith. Yesterday, when her brother had returned with the old knight, he had sought her out straight away, beside himself with a need to share what he had found. He told her the old hermit, abandoned and living alone in the woods, was one of the true heroes of their time.

Frith's story had filled Alura's head with an excitement that stayed with her through the night. Imagine, Lancelot, the most handsome and romantic of all the knights, living so near. Frith planned to return the next day to see this great knight. Alura planned to go with him.

Slipping away from the abbey with Frith sounded like a delicious and dangerous escapade, but she hoped to make it something more. This was her chance. Possibly her only chance. When they first arrived at the abbey, she had been a leggy girl without skills – her mother and sisters had never found time to teach her to cook or sew. Her principal job at home had been to keep her little brother occupied and out of the way. After a decade at the abbey, she had built up all the skills necessary to be a good wife, but was surrounded by men who were sworn to celibacy.

When she'd first bled, there was no mother or older sister to explain. Finally, an old crone in the kitchen told her about her "monthlies," but nothing of that bother explained the feelings she experienced when a groomsman smiled at her or the way her tummy tingled when she served a handsome traveler. There were many strange things going on with her, but the only person she could talk to was Frith. And what did he know about being a woman? He hardly knew about being a man.

She suspected that most of the abbey staff assumed she would now want to become a nun, having grown up in the abbey. However, Alura wanted to be like her sisters, married and full of babies. Granted, she wasn't quite clear what celibacy required her to give up, but she knew she wasn't interested in giving it up, whatever it was. In fact the more boys she saw, the more boys she liked. She didn't know why, but boys were what she thought about most.

Unfortunately for her, the famine, followed by some stupid battle, decimated the population of single males. Literally every man living in her world was either already married or a monk. When Frith told her that he overheard Lancelot say his lover had died, she had realized that the great man who lived nearby was single.

Alura followed the path around the gardens until she saw Frith in the distance. He was alone, waving the handle of some garden implement in imaginary sword play with an invisible foe. She dropped her baskets and started to run toward him, when a group of postulants, most younger than himself, rounded the corner and asked him what he was doing. She halted and retrieved her baskets.

Alura set the baskets down between two rows of beets and meandered through the garden, inspecting the vegetables, plucking a fat one now and then. She made many trips, taking one beet at a time to the basket, placing it carefully. She made a process of it, stalling, waiting for the young monks to leave. She worked her way few rows closer so that she could overhear their conversation.

"So I said, were you really a member of the famous Round Table?" Frith said.

"Was he?" one of the novices said.

"One of the original hundred knights who brought the Round Table to Camelot."

"The actual Round Table?"

"Well, Sir Bedivere said it was a gift to King Arthur from Queen Guinevere's father."

"What did the Abbot say about you running off with a knight?"

"Oh, he gave us his blessing. He told Sir Bedivere I was the man to lead him."

Alura could see Frith was enjoying this far more than he should. She knew he had always wished the young men in the abbey could have been his playmates, but they mostly never had time to play. Most were from poor families who couldn't feed them but also couldn't make substantial contributions to the Abbey, as her father had. There were so many, the abbey couldn't take them all. So they were made to suffer a test, to show they had sincerity and stamina. Boys who came to the abbey had to stand outside and knock at the door for days before they would be admitted. Once they became postulants they were made to work, and work hard. There was no time for games or horseplay.

Of course, they had chosen their vocation. She and Frith had not. He had often said that he would leave the Abbot's service as soon as she was wed. Although it was marriage she craved, she could not imagine a life without him as her principal confidant.

Brother Fastidious came upon the group. Fastidious was slightly younger than Frith, but had been at the abbey longer. The fact that he was perpetually serious made him seem older than they were, but he wasn't. She remembered that even when he was a boy he had been resistant to join the others in any fun.

"What are you doing here?" Fastidious said.

"Frith is telling of his adventure with a knight."

"You're squandering time better spent on work or study," Fastidious said.

"Don't act like you're the Abbot," said a monk who was much larger than either Frith or Fastidious.

"I didn't say I was," Fastidious said. "Frith can do as he pleases, but we have to obey the rules of our order."

"There's no harm in their hearing about him," Frith said. "He's just about the most important knight to ever come here."

"It's a distraction. Frith, you haven't chosen this life, but don't stand in the way of those who have."

"If you mean did I inherit servitude by virtue of my birth, no, I didn't. I am from a landed family."

"So you have told us," said one of the postulants.

"Well, soon I will improve my station," Frith said.

"Not everyone here sees service as a bad thing," Fastidious said. "We are men who chose to serve God."

Alura noted the slight emphasis on *men*. She had stretched her task out as long as she could. Her baskets were full, and it looked like she would have to go back before the monks decided to leave. Instead, she resolved to make her own opportunity. She approached the circle of young men, who when they saw her, stepped away. She thought they might. She had noticed on other occasions that the monks Frith's age had a difficult time even meeting her eyes, as though their renunciation enjoined them from having feelings.

"I have two large baskets of vegetables that need to be taken to the Abbot's kitchen," Alura said.

The monks looked at each other.

"They are just too heavy for a mere girl."

They stepped further from her, as if by mentioning her sex she had stripped bare.

"You don't want to be seen walking with a single woman, is that it? Fine, I'll wait here with Frith. Can two of you be of some service to your Abbot and carry his vegetables to the kitchen?"

To her surprise, it was Brother Fastidious who volunteered, "I'll carry one. Brother Thomas, you take the other. The rest of you get about your duties."

The monks walked away and Alura stepped close to Frith. "Well, that was unexpected."

"What? That he didn't miss an opportunity to be annoyingly pious?"

"No, that he was the one who volunteered… So, were the others impressed with your adventures?"

"Some were, but some of them didn't believe me."

"About Sir Lancelot?"

"About Sir Bedivere. I didn't tell them I found Lancelot."

"Why?"

"That's our secret. You're the only one who knows."

"The Abbot and Sir Bedivere know."

"Obviously, but the Abbot doesn't talk about Lancelot. He hadn't even told me who the hermit was. And Bedivere's gone."

"I never even got to meet him."

"He said he'd be back. But for now, it's just our secret."

"But explain why you didn't tell them you met the greatest knight that ever lived. That seems like a rather important omission."

"I have my reasons."

"Like what?"

"First, they're too judgmental. Even when I told them same story I told you last night – what I saw happen to Sir Bedivere's hand – they didn't believe me. They said, 'Ha, Frith, in your mind.'"

"I believe you," she said. "You should have had a witness. What else?"

"Sir Bedivere said there are many who blame Lancelot for our bad times. I'm going back out there, and I don't want them to tell anyone who might try to stop me."

"When?"

"Today, as soon as the Abbot has no further need of me."

"Take me," Alura said.

"What?"

"I want to go with you. I want to see Lancelot."

"You can't."

"Why not?"

"I want to persuade him to teach me, and I've never even met the man. He won't take me seriously if my sister's clinging to my sleeve."

"What do you mean you've never met him? Where were you yesterday?"

Frith looked at the garden, the abbey, anywhere but her eyes.

She couldn't understand. He wouldn't lie about a thing like this. "Tell me Frith."

"Only Bedivere went in. I waited outside."

"I thought you saw Sir Lancelot."

"Oh, I did, but I was never introduced to him. Today I am going in there and meet him. Sir Bedivere has shown me that there is much I need to learn."

"So take me, I'll gladly watch from outside his gate. It'd make me so proud to see my brother with Sir Lancelot."

Frith swelled a little in his tunic, but then he hesitated, "No, it won't work, it's not the same situation."

"Why not?"

"There was no social obligation for Sir Bedivere to introduce a servant waiting at the gate, but I couldn't very well have you standing there without making an introduction. He would think me extremely rude."

"Is there a place to hide?"

"Hide?"

"Yes, some bushes or some place of concealment where I can watch the two of you, but he can't see me?"

"Of course, he lives in the midst of a dense wood."

"Good, then I can go. Hide me when we arrive, and I'll be your witness should any ever doubt that you have kept company with the greatest knight that ever lived."

Alura knew if she kept at him, especially his pride of manhood, seldom would he refuse her anything. "Frith, you are my protector, you'll worry if you leave me behind. Take me along and you can spend time with this knight without fretting that I'm unguarded." Her logic was absurd, but she knew Frith.

"Can you leave soon?" he said. "I want to get started as soon as the Abbot releases me. I'm anxious that my arrival for our first meeting should not be ill-timed."

"Oh yes! How shall we do this?"

"When your tasks are done and there's nothing left that's your responsibility, make as if to go to your quarters. Continue past your room to the rear of the abbey. There you will see a thick gate in the wall. That's where I'll meet you."

She could have kissed him with delight, but they were in the very public abbey gardens. Instead she ran to the Abbot's kitchen, where she hurried about doing every task asked of her so that she indeed finished early.

Chapter 6

The luxury of summer light in Britain was that it lingered, extending the evening hours. This would afford Frith ample time to get to Lancelot's and back before dark. But that knowledge didn't make him less impatient to get started.

Frith waited at the rear of the abbey for Alura. Last night, Frith had relayed to her every detail of the conversation he had witnessed and most of what he and Bedivere had discussed. Frith omitted only his failed proposition to serve Sir Bedivere. He knew she would hate knowing he had tried to leave her. They both knew too well how it felt to be left behind.

The forest that had scared him yesterday now seemed a friendlier place, knowing there was a great man in its midst. His new plan was that the greatest knight in the world would be his mentor.

He saw Alura coming and walked toward her. She carried a basket on one arm.

Frith greeted her with a kiss. "What's that for? At first I thought you brought something to eat, but I see that it's empty."

"We're going to pick the blackberries that you said grow at the edge of the woods."

"No, we're not."

"You, my young brother, are allowed to go where you will. I may be asked to account for myself. Therefore, my pretense is that we have gone for berries."

Frith was keen to get to Lancelot's, but when they reached the hedge she insisted he wait while she picked some berries. "I'm as eager to see this great knight as you, but I shouldn't return with an empty basket, should I?"

When the basket was half full and her fingers purple he said, "That's enough, let's be on our way."

"A few more."

"Let's go now or it will soon be too dark!"

"How'll I explain being gone long, but returning with little?"

"Wipe a berry or two on your lips and they'll think you ate what you picked. Here, I'll do it." Frith chose a plump one and smeared it on her.

"Maybe you need some too." She grabbed his face and rubbed it with her purple lips. It was less a kiss than a torment.

Frith vigorously rubbed his mouth with his sleeve. "No thanks! You want Lancelot to think I look like a child?"

Frith led her to the opening in the hedge. Before entering he picked up a hardy walking stick.

"Why the staff?" Alura asked. "Have you gone lame?"

Frith waved it about, brandishing it like a swordsman. "A precaution, should we meet any peril or creatures."

"I thought you said it was safe."

"Better to have a stout stick than an empty hand. Hold to me." He took her hand and they entered the woods.

Frith led Alura swiftly the same way he and Sir Bedivere had come. Their trail of yesterday, barely discernible, was the only sign of human passage through the woods. But Lancelot had to walk this way twice every morning to attend mass. It was as if he treaded so carefully that he never crushed a flower or a plant.

He was going to meet Lancelot. It felt so strange to even think the thought. This time he was not afraid of the hermit, but he needed to hide Alura. She would be silent witness to his meeting with the man Sir Bedivere rightly called 'the greatest knight that ever lived.'

When they got to Lancelot's, Frith pointed at a large clump of bushes to the left of the gate and silently motioned for Alura to hide there. Frith waited impatiently until she was well concealed before going to present himself to the knight.

He tried to unlatch the gate, but the staff got in his way. Afraid that it would make him appear lame or that Lancelot would think it a sign of weakness, he backtracked and left it with Alura. He didn't imagine she'd need a weapon, but she would have it just in case.

CHAPTER 7

Lancelot was tending the lady-slippers when he saw Bedivere's servant step gingerly through the gate. The boy obviously didn't see him for he called out toward the cottage door, "Sir!"

"No longer Sir," he said. "Just a man."

Frith jumped at the sound of his voice and spun toward him. After a moment, he said, "Are you not the famous knight Sir Lancelot?"

"Sir Lancelot was a man of another time."

"But it's right to call you Sir."

"It would be easier if you would simply say who you are and what you want. Though I should warn you, most live their entire lives without knowing those particular truths."

He saw Frith's brow wrinkle with confusion.

"My name's Frith. I think you are a man who has seen the things I want to know of."

"I recognize you," Lancelot said. "Sir Bedivere brought you."

"With respect sir, I brought him."

Lancelot looked toward heaven. "I have left the world. Why won't the world leave me? First Bedivere, now you—"

"But Good Sir, I see before me one of the heroes of our time. Won't you grant me a word?"

"Does your mother know where you are and who you're talking to? For none of the people in this countryside think well of me nor would they think well of you for being with me."

"My mother need not know where I go. I'm not a boy at home. I am a man already employed."

"By Sir Bedivere."

"No, I'm at the abbey just over there." Frith pointed in the direction he had come.

"If you're a monk, then why aren't you wearing a robe?"

"I've taken no vows. I serve the Abbot personally."

The gangly young man before him brought back memories of when he had struggled to get the world to acknowledge that he was a man. "I apologize. In my isolation, I don't see many young people. There are very few of your years, after the years of hunger. You are lucky to have survived."

"You say luck, but it is the curse of my family... six older sisters, five who live with their husbands on father's land, and six brothers. I'm the youngest."

"If you're not a monk and your father owns land, then why are you working as a servant?"

"Father has a large estate but the dark years took their toll. He had to send my sister and me to the abbey."

"The dark years have passed, the crops grow again. Why did you two not go home?"

"My eldest brother doesn't want responsibility for us when father dies and he inherits. And since there is no money for my sister's dowry, they've kept us at the abbey."

"If you're employed by the Abbot, won't he notice your absence?"

"My duties are light, and that old Abbot won't care."

"Speak kindly of the Abbot," Lancelot said. "He sheltered me and gave me work when I was cursed and rejected elsewhere."

"The Abbot let you live there?" Frith said.

"For a time, I worked as a scribe."

"You worked at the abbey?"

"Since I was versed in Latin and Greek, I was set to copying the Holy Scriptures."

"Oh, how tedious."

"No, it was a blessing," Lancelot said. "What do you know of scripture?"

"As good as any man my peer… I'd guess."

"Which is only what's said aloud at Mass. The average man has never read the scripture, but in my task I was given to see the whole of it."

"It would not serve me to see it, for I cannot read."

This was looking more and more like a waste of time. "You say I've seen things you want to know. Tell me then, what knowledge have you come for?"

"Why to learn about the life of a knight. That should be self-evident."

Oh God!

"If you've come for tales of fights and jousts, then you waste my time."

"But if I learn from the greatest knight, I can escape my situation."

"I'm sorry, but I have long since traded all interest in knighthood for the pursuit of God."

Frith's face betrayed his disappointment. "Oh, religion. I get enough of that at work. I came to you looking for a way out."

"The way out is within."

"Huh?"

"The secret of the Grail knights was not their strength at jousts but their pursuit of the spirit within."

"If that's the secret of being a knight, why don't you teach it to me?"

"Each day has trouble enough for itself. I'm not…" He circled one of the flower beds, mumbling to himself, "But if you've been sent…" Lancelot paused to observe his own resistance. What was going on here?

At Lancelot's hesitation, Frith jumped in. "Do you see another who has dared to cross to your side, who dares to speak to you?"

"What does that matter to me?" Lancelot said.

"Sir Bedivere says you have lost all fame."

"Gained infamy is more like it, but fame is a chattel worth less than a breath."

"Sir Bedivere says you're troubled, being abandoned by the world."

"If I'm abandoned, then why does it pursue me? Just go back to the abbey."

"Sir Bedivere says you're a holy man, but I've never seen you keep company with the other monastics."

"They prefer it that way," Lancelot said. "As do I."

"You like living out here alone, having no one but yourself to talk to?"

"There are none who would even know of what I speak."

"But I'd like to try," Frith said.

"That does not seem… likely."

"But nothing is impossible for one such as you."

"Flattery? I'm no longer subject to the adoration of young men who want to be knights."

"Sire, I see you are clever in speech. Won't you spend a pittance of your wisdom on one who wants to learn?"

Lancelot considered the boy a moment, all eagerness and ignorance. Too ignorant, in fact, to know how little he knew. "Let's say you win your point. What would you want me to tell?"

"You were at Camelot. Why not tell me about King Arthur?"

Warm memories flooded Lancelot. His voice suddenly became reverent. "Arthur, that great being! What one perceives in spirit cannot be spoken of in a common way."

"Spirit? You see your King's ghost?"

"No, that is just more childhood superstition. I refer to his spiritual life. He was a great master."

"King Arthur? Religious?"

"I know, the people saw him as the great warrior who united us," Lancelot said. "But we saw him a spiritual leader, a student of Merlin, a student of the universe."

"I'd love to hear about him as a great warrior."

"The battles of legend are not his only accomplishment. The real meat at Arthur's table was the quest for the Grail."

Frith smiled broadly. "You're talking about the Knights of the Round Table?"

"The same. At Arthur's court, many were called to the great quest."

"And did you go on many quests?"

Lancelot thought Frith already knew the answer. It was almost amusingly transparent how the young man was trying to steer the conversation in a direction more pleasing to his interests. "The quest of Arthur's court was for spiritual enlightenment, and I uphold that to this day."

"Sir Bedivere says you've found it, but he says there's no point if you aren't going to share it."

"Sir Bedivere says… Why do you keep citing Bedivere?"

"He's a knight sir, of the Round Table, trusted by King Arthur. Besides, I overheard your conversations with Sir Bedivere. You can't keep the Grail for yourself."

"Sir Bedivere is not wrong in that. I face an essential conflict…"

"What's that, sir?"

"I see the divine in all men yet distrust their behavior."

"But doesn't that compel you to do something for others?"

Lancelot shook his head. "I've no desire to become a public figure again. Not leaving this hermitage means not facing the world."

"I want badly to learn the true nature of a knight. I could come here, and you could teach without having to go back out into the world."

Lancelot was about to dismiss the notion out of hand, but after a moment of watching his own reactions, he realized he distrusted them. There might be something to the lad's arguments. There was something here he still needed to understand. "I could ask you to go away and come back tomorrow, but if you'll indulge me, I will meditate on this matter now —"

"Oh, gladly please do."

"That way if the answer is no, you can leave me in peace and have no need to interrupt my solitude again."

"But if the answer is yes?"

Lancelot saw Frith's eyes were filled with hope. "Be still now, I'm going within for a while." Without another word, Lancelot sat down among the lilies and folded his hands in his lap.

* * *

Frith's mind was afidget. He tried not to move, so as to earn favor from this hermit knight. He fixed his eyes on Lancelot as if to prevent his chance at knighthood from escaping. He had sometimes seen the brothers pacing slowly around the ambulatory, telling their beads. And old Brother Caedmon sometimes sat on a stool in the courtyard and closed his eyes for long periods of time, though Frith assumed he was just warming himself in the sun. Now Lancelot was perfectly still and made no prayer with his lips or his voice, but after a time some of the light streaming through the leaves made Lancelot appear to have a glow.

Frith rubbed his eyes and briefly looked away. He saw his sister standing up from her hiding place, exposed. He wanted to warn her, but dared not speak. A beatific expression on Alura's face gave way to astonishment, almost fear. She then motioned toward Lancelot with her eyes. Frith looked back. Scared and unsure of his own senses, he thought he could feel the light emanating from Lancelot like a beam of sunlight at midday.

After a time, he saw Lancelot slowly open his eyes. Alura ducked back behind the bush.

"I see you are right," Lancelot said. "It may be time for me to—"

"Sire! My eyes disbelieve what they have witnessed."

Lancelot slowly stood up. "And what is that?"

"Your body seemed to become spectral."

"Did it?" Lancelot turned his back on him. "Well, I didn't mean to frighten you. Despite what Bedivere might have said, I'm not deluded. I really have found a higher spiritual state."

"Oh, Sir Bedivere believes you're real, Sir. He just wants you to use your powers to restore Camelot. Are you going to teach me how you gave off light?"

Lancelot turned to face him. "You know, I'm sorry you saw that. It's another reason I prefer to do my spiritual work away from the abbey. People are so easily distracted. Don't seek the Grail for phenomena."

"Phenomena?"

"I don't want to get drawn out into the world, yet it seems clear it's time to pass this knowledge on. You came looking for a great knight to lead you out of your current life. Perhaps I can do that. But true knowledge is the goal, not spiritual tricks."

"Does that mean you're willing to teach me?"

Lancelot hesitated. "I don't know if this can be taught... But I have been long without company, so come again if you like." His tone became firmer. "But if you come again, come only to learn the secrets of the Grail, not to hear about jousts or magic."

"Oh, thank you, sir. But I'm here already. Will you not tell me about how the knights sought the Holy Grail?"

"All right, one story. But there are several stories you need to hear before we get to the Grail, for without them the tapestry will not be whole. Today I'll tell you the first. You may as well sit."

CHAPTER 8

Frith took a seat and looked up at Lancelot expectantly. Alura rearranged herself into a more comfortable position. As she did, the branches made a rustling sound. Lancelot glanced toward the gate. That was no animal. Someone was hiding there.

Lancelot felt a tug on his robe. "I'm ready for you to begin Sir," Frith said.

Lancelot decided to ignore the person in the bushes. He'd agreed to allow the boy here. He might as well get used to it.

"This story happened before any of us ever went on a quest for the Grail," Lancelot said. "It was Pentecost and the Knights of the Round Table had come from everywhere to celebrate it with King Arthur."

"I thought the knights lived at Camelot."

"Not all. But perhaps you don't know this – nearly every Knight of the Round Table was a king or prince in his own fiefdom. King Arthur organized and ruled these men of strong bodies and even stronger opinions. He did so by being fair and just, but he demanded fairness, justice, and chivalrous conduct from his knights. As a king he was accustomed to making demands and having his demands met. When it came to God, King Arthur made demands of Him too."

"In all the Masses I've ever attended, I never heard such an idea. A man can pray, but how dare he demand of God?"

"By fasting. At Pentecost it was King Arthur's custom to fast until God granted him a vision of wonder."

"And God would do this?"

"On this memorable Pentecost, I saw God grant him three," Lancelot said. "None who were there will ever forget that Pentecost... Someone outside called for the king to come see his wonder delivered. We ran out to find a great slab of marble floating on the river. It was inscribed with a prophecy and impaled with a sword that Arthur recognized at once. He said it had once belonged to Sir Balin."

"How could a rock float?"

"Merlin made it do so."

"Merlin! You knew Merlin?"

"'Know' isn't the right word. I saw him at court several times."

"I like this story very much. Did you see Merlin do magic?"

"No, but I saw the stone float and read its words. 'Never shall man take me hence, but he be the best knight of the world.'"

"Sir Bedivere said you were the greatest knight."

"Sir Bedivere says many things... So the King made a contest. Gawain, Percival, and many other knights attempted to pull the sword, but it wouldn't budge for them," Lancelot pantomimed the knights' struggles to draw the sword from the marble block.

"Weren't those knights worried about ill effects from such a sword?"

"What do you mean?"

"Can't a man be cursed from handling objects tainted by magic?"

Lancelot could see the ignorant had done their work, filling the boy's head with superstitions. "The sword of Sir Balin was not a product of the dark arts, but a measure of a pure knight. You see Arthur knew the sword had once belonged to Sir Balin because he remembered the day a Lady appeared at court with it girded over her groin."

"A woman wearing a sword? To this day women do not bear arms."

"You're no more bewildered than those knights were. She was the first Lady the knights had ever seen heavily armed."

"But *why* was she wearing a sword?"

"As a test. She said only a knight pure of heart could pull the sword from her loins. Every man tried her, even King Arthur, but only Sir Balin succeeded."

"Arthur failed? I thought he could pull a sword from solid granite."

"It was said he once did, but that was before my time. Different sword, different stone. In any case, kings are subject to the laws of destiny just like the rest of us. Certain swords have intended owners. Arthur already had Excalibur, so this sword could not be his."

"You're saying it was destined to be Sir Balin's?"

Lancelot nodded. "Until his death. After Sir Balin died, Merlin embedded the sword in marble, inscribed a prophecy and sent it afloat towards Camelot."

"So who finally pulled the sword out and fulfill the prophecy?"

"That part doesn't come until later in our history, but you needed to know about the sword to understand the next story."

"Oh, please tell it."

"It is a long story, and it's already dusk. You must start back to the abbey now if you're to reach there before dark. Perhaps if you come another day …"

"Oh Sir, I shall come every day that you allow. Your abandonment is over."

"You may come again if you like, but that is enough for today."

His abandonment? As the gate closed behind Frith, Lancelot couldn't help but ask God, "What have you done to me now?"

CHAPTER 9

At Mass the next morning, Lancelot lingered uncharacteristically. It had been his custom since moving out into the woods to attend the earliest service, be first in line for Eucharist, and leave as soon as he had received the sacrament. He felt sure the other monks did not mind that he was served first; they were probably glad to be rid of him. But today he lingered so that he was served last.

When everyone else had gone, Lancelot caught the Abbot's eye and made a jerk of his head toward a small niche. The Abbot met him there. The Abbot lit a candle and crossed himself. Lancelot did the same. The Abbot smelled strongly of incense. It permeated his robes and wafted off from him.

"Reverend Father, I thought you endorsed my solitude," Lancelot said.

"I do."

"Then why have you sent this cavalcade of visitors my way?"

The Abbot shrugged. "I thought you might welcome the company of an old friend."

"I welcome the company of God."

"Don't we all?"

"With respect, holy sir, I thought we had an understanding concerning my anonymity."

"And so we do. But I thought there would be no harm in telling Sir Bedivere. He is a knight of great importance and he said you were old friends."

"Oh, we are well enough acquainted."

The Abbot studied a loose thread on sleeve of his alb. "I was only trying to do right by that knight... I thought you would be pleased."

"But it's not he alone that has come."

"Oh, Frith. Well, someone had to show Sir Bedivere the way. Your hermitage is not easy to find."

Lancelot tried to keep his voice casual. "Tell me about the boy."

"He's a good enough boy."

"I got the impression that he had to overcome great fear to come there."

The Abbot smiled. "I'm sure he did. Frith grew up without the benefit of manly service."

"What do you mean by that?"

"He was too young to be in the field with the men, so he was left at home ... surrounded by women who thought he could do no wrong."

Lancelot decided to get right to it. "And you are his spiritual guide?"

"One could hope. But in truth he has no heart for abbey life. He runs my errands in exchange for his keep, but that is the extent of it."

"No hope for him at all?"

"I have hope for every man," the Abbot said, "but Frith has not yet embraced his manhood."

"We've all been at that difficult age."

"Too long ago for you and I to recall," the Abbot said. "Now about your visitors?"

"I apologize. I should not have bothered you about it."

"No, let me apologize," the Abbot said. "I will send no more."

"Oh, let them come or not. If any come, then it must be the will of God."

"What about Frith? If Sir Bedivere returns shall I send a different guide?"

"No need. Frith may come if he likes."

Lancelot had heard enough. The Abbot had not awakened Frith's spirit, he certainly shouldn't object if Lancelot tried. Frith might act younger than his years, but the Abbot's description of his upbringing explained a lot. Lancelot had more hope for him now than he had yesterday.

Chapter 10

Frith paced around the Abbot's room, waiting to help him out of his vestments so he could begin the day's errands. But the Abbot was not back from morning Mass. How could he finish early if he started late? He was also hungry. If the Abbot's errands took him anywhere near the kitchen, he might beg a bit of something to eat.

Frith stepped out of the Abbot's quarters to find out what was keeping the Abbot when he recognized a man in hermit's robes walking out the back of the abbey. Frith called out in a loud whisper, "Sir!" but Lancelot kept going.

What should he do? It wasn't smart to shout at this hour of the morning and he certainly couldn't call Lancelot by name. So he went after him.

The old hermit moved with a smoothness and grace that looked leisurely but was faster than Frith expected. Frith chased him all the way to the edge of the abbey gardens without catching him. He watched Lancelot go through the back gate and was about to follow when he heard the Abbot call his name. He hesitated. The Abbot called again, louder. Obviously, the Abbot was not worried about disturbing the morning quiet. He didn't think the Abbot saw him, but someone would surely tell on him if they saw him run out of the abbey and into the woods. Frith turned back.

The Abbot was standing in front of his quarters, still in his vestments. "Where is that man? He is always disappearing when he should be here."

Frith crept up behind him. "I *have* been here, sir. I just started to look for you. You took so long this morning, I was afraid that something happened."

"You watch out for me like a son," the Abbot said.

"Shall we go in, then?"

He followed the Abbot to his room and helped him remove his vestments and store them in a chest. After the Abbot was back in his robes, he said to Frith, "I need a good batch of quills."

"Quills?"

"To write with. If you can, find some that have already been tempered, if not, just bring feathers. I can temper them myself."

"Where shall I find them?"

"Use that intelligent mind that God gave you, Frith."

"The scriptorium?"

"Good lad, now be on your way."

Frith left for the scriptorium. This was going to be an easy day. Get the quills, bring them to the Abbot, and then subtly stay out of his way until it was time to go to Lancelot's. Frith was sorry he hadn't caught up with Lancelot this morning. He thought about the sword of Sir Balin. Now that was a story that would impress the Brothers. They would probably be weeding the garden today. He would look for them as soon as he fetched the Abbot his quills.

Maybe he should practice the story first. Frith held out his foot, pretending to brace it on the block of marble, pretending he was the knight who pulled the sword out. The sword that would make him the best knight in the land. He struggled with it a bit. He had to loosen it before it would come free.

"What are you doing, Frith?"

It was old Brother Theodoric, come up behind him.

"On my way to the scriptorium for the Abbot, sir."

"Are you trying to hop there on one foot?"

"No sir," Frith said.

The old monk just shook his head and continued on his way. Frith stopped telling himself the story and went into the scriptorium.

Sunlight streamed in tall windows, lighting the carrels where monks with stained fingers and bent backs were at work. The place was too quiet to suit Frith; no talking, just the sound of nibs scratching ink on parchment or vellum. The only variation, the occasional sound of a blade scraping away an erroneous letter. Frith preferred the Abbot's kitchen. The boisterous banter of the ladies as they worked felt warm and delicious. This place felt arid and somber. Frith cleared his throat.

A monk looked up from his work, "Yes, Frith?"

"I have come for some feathers."

"I'm afraid we don't have a surplus."

"They're not for me," Frith said, "I cannot write."

"I know that. But even if you could, we haven't any to spare."

"Not even for the Abbot?"

"Not even for him. Look..." The monk picked up his knife and a scrawny quill the length of Frith's hand. "Every five letters, the end must be re-cut." He reshaped the tip with his blade. "Soon enough, there is nothing to hold onto." He grasped the quill between ink stained fingers and showed him.

Frith didn't care; his only goal was to satisfy the Abbot and be done with it. He pointed to a carrel where there were several nice long pheasant feathers. "What about those?"

"No, you can't have those. Those are for the colored lettering and each color ink requires a separate quill."

Frith eyed the rest of the carrels trying to spot any extra plumes. He had to admit every feather he saw was as scrawny and sad as the one the brother had showed him. "Where do you keep your supplies?"

"You won't find any feathers there; our stores are depleted. Look about you – you will notice that most of my brothers have resorted to making quills of reeds."

"All right. Do you have more of those?"

"Yes, take as many as the Abbot needs."

The reeds were about the diameter of his little finger. Frith took as large of a bundle as he could fit in one hand, thanked the monk, and returned to the Abbot.

The Abbot pushed the reeds away. "Frith, if I wanted to write with these, I would have sent you to the river."

"This is what they are using in the scriptorium."

"Have we no geese? Or better yet, swans? Those make the best quills. Return these where you got them and find me some feather quills."

Frith returned to the scriptorium and handed back the fist of reeds. Then he wandered back out into the open air, away from the oppressive silence. Where could he go for feathers?

His stomach rumbled.

The kitchen was a good idea. They often dressed birds there. Frith couldn't remember if they had served any geese or swans lately, but maybe…

When he arrived, Alura was away, so he probably wasn't going to persuade anyone to feed him. But he still had to find the Abbot's quills. He found the cook in the storeroom.

"Sorry, Frith, whenever we serve goose, we send the long feathers to the scriptorium, and the ladies take the rest to make bedding. We never keep any here."

"What about swan? The Abbot said goose or swan…"

"Oh we haven't killed a swan since I don't know when," the cook said. "If you go to the river, you might find swan feathers. Of course, you'd have to go in the woods to get there. That might not be wise."

Frith didn't fear the woods anymore, but he doubted if she was right. He had been there twice already and had not seen any sign of a swan. But he had seen many geese. They wandered all over the abbey. "What about the geese here?"

"What about them?"

"Isn't it about time to cook another goose, don't you think?"

"For whom? The brothers? There is not a great need for meat unless there is a festival or a special guest."

"You could roast one for the Abbot's dinner."

The cook laughed. "He wouldn't thank us for that. No, we never kill the geese that live here."

"But you've served goose many times."

"Yes, but the goose on our table usually comes from outside the abbey."

"Why, when we seem to have so many"?

"It's a strange thing about geese," she said. "When one of the gaggle is killed, the others get sad, almost as if they're mourning – like a wife who has lost her husband in battle."

Frith thought quickly, "Couldn't I just pluck several goose feathers without killing one?"

The cook laughed so hard that her ample bosoms swayed like church bells. "I think you'll find live geese resist that."

"How hard could it be?"

She laughed again. "Tell me after you catch one."

It couldn't be that difficult, they're only stupid birds. However, this was going to take a while. He might as well eat first. "If I'm going to be chasing down geese – in service to the Abbot – I'll need something to sustain me."

"I suppose I could give you some soup and bread." She ladled broth and vegetables into a large bowl and tore a loaf of bread in half.

Frith accepted it, looked into the bowl. "No meat?"

"None to spare."

He wished Alura was there. "How about a good portion of cheese to go with my bread?"

"Oh, if you must." She cleaved a thick slice from a block of cheese and gave it to him. "I've three boys at home who eat just like you, and believe me, they never get their supper before it's time. I have no idea why I give in to you."

"Your sons are fortunate to have you." He gave her is best boyish smile.

She blushed and shooed him away with the back of her hand, "Go."

Frith took his meal into the adjacent banquet hall. It was deserted. He ate alone. When he finished, he returned the bowl and spoon to the kitchen and went looking for the geese. The cook had to be wrong, it shouldn't take that long. Geese wandered all over the abbey grounds. In fact, they used to follow him when he was younger.

Frith located the geese in a fallow field beyond the storehouses. But he had to chase them until he was sweaty before he cornered one against a stile. He picked it up and the crazy bird tried to beat him with its wings. They were wickedly harder than his goose-down pillow. Frith snatched a wing feather. The goose honked with pain, kicked him furiously, tore his blouse, and got mud all over him.

Frith was holding the goose at arm's length, trying to avoid its thrashing feet while he figured out how to get his next feather, when a gander and several geese rushed him, snapping at his ankles and buttocks. Their stout beaks bit hard and he kicked at them to make them stop. Before he could get another feather, the goose he was holding broke free.

The rest of the geese got between Frith and the wounded bird. They put their heads low to the ground and made a hissing sound that was too easy to interpret. He tried to retrieve the fugitive bird, but the other geese attacked again and began chasing him.

Frith heard a small boy laughing. The gaggle reversed course and went in the other direction. Frith turned to the postulant, maybe eight years old. "Brother, I need your help. Can you lay hold of that goose?"

The boy looked at the feather in Frith's hand. "What are you trying to do?"

"I'm in the Abbot's service, and he has need of a good number of fresh quills."

"Don't you know anything? You can't take them all from one goose or he won't be able to fly."

"You're very impertinent," Frith said. "But I admit the only thing I know about geese is they've scattered all over the place. Come and help me."

The boy glanced behind him, toward some brothers hoeing nearby. "I don't want trouble, I'm supposed to be weeding the garden."

"You won't get in trouble. I'm the Abbot's man and he would want you to help me."

"What's your name?"

"Frith, what's yours?"

"They call me Little Thomas."

"All right Little Thomas, how do we catch these geese?"

"It would be easiest if we had some grain."

Frith obtained a large earthenware bowl and led Little Thomas toward the abbey granary. Along the way Frith began to tell him the story of Sir Balin, but as soon as he mentioned Merlin, the boy paled and warned him against witchcraft. Frith needed the boy more than he needed to tell the story, so he stopped.

After acquiring the grain they found the geese again. Frith approached, holding the bowl out to them.

"Shake it so they can hear the grain," said Little Thomas.

Frith did so, but the geese ran away honking. Then Little Thomas took a handful from the bowl and cast it toward them, calling for them to come. The bravest crept forward and began eating. The others followed.

"Now you do it," said Little Thomas, "So they will know the food is coming from you."

Frith tossed some grain near his feet, but the geese kept their distance. They were still wary of him.

"Gently," Little Thomas said, "Keep feeding them, move slowly, talk nice to them."

"How do you know so much about geese?"

"I raised them at home, before I joined the abbey. Didn't you?"

"I don't remember much about home," Frith said.

Frith worked his way closer, holding the grain bowl in front of him, and was nearly upon them when suddenly an aggressive gander came running from behind and bit at his butt. Frith jumped away and threw the bowl at them. "Here, take it all!"

The whole gaggle disappeared.

"I think they ran down in the lower garden," Little Thomas said.

Frith was about to simply give up the whole project as a bad idea. But the thought of returning to the Abbot with only one feather was more than he could manage. So he let Little Thomas lead him to the lower garden.

On the way, they met up with Alura. She had seen where the geese went and offered to help. Frith introduced her to Little Thomas, who seemed to like her right away.

"There is another Brother Thomas," Alura said.

"I know, but he is much bigger, that is why they call me Little Thomas."

Little Thomas didn't seem worried about being seen in the company of an unmarried girl the way the older boys did. Perhaps he was too young or too new, Frith thought.

When they found the gaggle, the geese formed a picket line, putting their necks out and heads down. The geese begin hissing at all three of them.

"What's wrong with these geese?" Alura said.

"They're mad at Frith," Little Thomas said.

"I may have upset them a little." Frith handed Alura his feather.

"What is this?"

"The source of my humiliation," Frith said.

Alura studied his torn blouse and nodded. "Geese are very protective. You've made yourself their enemy. You better make up with them, for our sake."

"What do you mean?" Frith said.

Alura put her head close to Frith's so Little Thomas could not hear, "They're going to make a loud fuss every time we return from Lancelot's. To pacify them you will have to apologize."

Frith sprang away from her, "You want me to apologize to a goose?"

"Oh, what a good idea," said Little Thomas. "Apologize to the one you wounded. Pick it up and pet it, tell it you're sorry and the others will forgive you."

"Pick it up? What have we been trying to do this whole time?"

"We've been bullying them," Little Thomas said. "We have to approach them gently, with respect. We have to bow to them,"

"I've already had enough humiliation. I'm not bowing to a goose."

"If you don't, they'll see you as a threat. Let me show you how it's done."

"Will you catch the goose as well?"

"If he lets me pick him up, I'll hand him to you. Stay back for now. They have rules about how you are supposed to approach them."

Little Thomas bowed his head and walked toward them with his hands held behind him. "See all that head bobbing they're doing? That is their way of greeting. When I bow to them, it shows I'm a friend."

One of the geese came toward Little Thomas, head up, not hissing. He stroked its neck for a few moments, and then picked it up. He whispered a few words of encouragement, let it down, and patted several others. Finally, he picked up the bird with the missing feather, stroked it and spoke soothingly. The goose seemed happy being held.

"Here Frith, come and take him... Not like that! Be courtly, be humble. Pretend you're bowing to the king."

"Let Alura do it."

"I'm not the one who ripped out its feather," Alura said. "It has to be you."

"I've already been bitten. Thrice."

"Then you should be used to it by now." Alura gave Frith a nudge. He looked around, hoping no one would see him bowing to a bird. But he did it. Eventually, he succeeded in getting the wounded goose into his arms. Although he felt foolish, he followed Thomas' advice and apologized. He put that bird down and petted a couple of others. When all seemed right in the goose world, he took his feather and went to the Abbot's office.

Frith entered the Abbot's office. As soon as he closed the door behind him, the Abbot looked up from his work and laughed. Frith did not see anything funny. His day had been wasted making friends with geese and he only had one feather to show for it. He handed it to the Abbot.

"One?"

Frith opened his mouth to explain but the Abbot shushed him. "I don't want to hear how many geese you had to chase or how you got dirty, I just want you to succeed. Now go back out and try again."

Frith stomped out of the Abbot's office and slammed the door. Right now, he envied Alura. She got to eat whenever she wanted. She didn't have to do what the Abbot said. All Alura had to do was wait to be taken for a wife. He had to figure out what to do with his life. But whatever he did, it wouldn't have anything to do with geese or abbeys – or a wife for that matter. Leave that up to Alura.

At this point in his life, he had neither time nor money to think of marriage. It wasn't that Frith didn't like girls; he did. He wasn't a eunuch. Frequently he was stirred by the handsome sight of one of the kitchen women doing something provocative. But they were all married, and he generally appreciated them for their food more than their looks. He found single girls in the village very appealing, but he became fumble tongued around any that he particularly liked. The only unmarried woman he could talk to was his sister.

Besides if he stayed here, he would never be able to garner enough to marry. He paced the abbey courtyard. Once he became a knight he wouldn't be afraid to talk to women. And he'd be able to support one. That would be the time to think about a wife. He simply couldn't be the Abbot's lackey forever. He had to go out and make a man of himself.

The thought of leaving of the abbey gave him an idea. He could try the village for goose feathers. Frith went out of the abbey gates and into the market. He immediately found a stall with a goose hanging upside down. Using the Abbot's name and an appeal to charity, he convinced the poulterer to give him all the wing feathers.

Frith returned to the Abbot with a bundle of feathers, feeling very pleased with himself. He waited while the Abbot sorted through them. Casting the short ones aside, the Abbot kept about a dozen of the long ones. "These will do nicely."

"Thank you, sir."

"I hoped you haven't stripped the geese bare before winter."

"No sir, only the one I brought earlier came from our geese."

"I heard a lot of honking."

"That was me making friends with them."

The Abbot didn't inquire further about that, and Frith was glad for it.

CHAPTER 11

With the geese settled and the Abbot happy, Frith felt free to go to Lancelot's. Again, Alura tagged along and, again, he hid her in the bushes outside the fence. When he called out, Sir Lancelot promptly came out of his cottage. Frith had already decided what he wanted to hear about – he had hardly been able to stop thinking about Merlin since he'd heard the story of Sir Balin's sword. "Sir, could you please tell me more about the great wizard?"

Lancelot scowled. "I told you if you're only coming for tales of jousts and magic, don't bother me."

"But sir, we did talk about Merlin last time. It was you that brought him up."

The scowl disappeared. "You're right, I suppose I did." Lancelot sank fluidly to a cross-legged position on his rough-hewn bench. "You know ordinary men either fear or are fascinated by spiritual power. Only one man in a thousand would have ever asked Merlin, 'Where does this power come from?'"

Frith settled himself on the pathway between flower beds, at the great knight's feet. "I'll be that one man. Where did his powers come from?"

"Spiritual powers come naturally to those who grow more enlightened," Lancelot said. "Remember Jesus' disciples had powers. He told them, 'These and even greater works shall you do also.'"

Frith slapped his forehead. "Sir, I ask one thing and it seems you answer another."

"That's only a seeming, not the truth."

"I asked you about Merlin, and you tell me about Jesus. I asked about magic, and you say spirit."

"Because that is the answer. Merlin drew from the source which all knowledge comes. A Christian would call it Holy Spirit."

"But Christ did miracles, not magic. Isn't it heresy to compare the two?"

"Jesus didn't turn water into wine to put the vintners out of business, did he?"

"Of course not."

"No, He turned the ordinary into the extraordinary to open men's minds to newer possibilities. Merlin's purpose was similar."

"But Merlin wasn't a Christian, was he? I heard that he was of the old religion."

"Well, it's not as simple as that… No, he was not a Christian, but he went far beyond that old religion as well. Religions are made by man."

"Religion is made by man?"

"Spiritual knowledge comes by Grace, not from following the rules of an order."

Frith looked around quickly, struck by an irrational fear they might be overheard even in this deep woods. "Are you speaking against the Church? Are you not the holy man Sir Bedivere believes you to be?"

"No, no, no. I'm as Christian as you are. Didn't you see me leave Mass just this morning? But I've found that spiritual power comes through us from within, not from without."

"Did Merlin teach you his magic?"

Lancelot got up from the bench and studied one of the flowering plants, turning its leaves this way and that. "Tell me, should I just send the young man back to the abbey until he grows a bit more?"

"Oh, no, please Sir."

Lancelot stood and walked over to the blue stone altar. He removed a fallen leaf and brushed the smooth stone with his hand. "I've told you, Merlin was Arthur's teacher, not ours."

Frith wondered if the altar had once been used for some magic rite. "Was King Arthur secretly a magician then?"

"King Arthur was a Wiseman, not a magician. He was the best of all souls. Arthur had spiritual powers, but unlike Merlin, he kept them hidden. He taught us by example in the way he conducted himself. He treated every knight with equanimity, as if addressing the soul inside, not the men at our table."

"You're talking about the Knights of the Round Table?" Perhaps Lancelot would move onto the subject of the knight's adventures.

"Yes, of course."

"You say that at the Round Table all men were equal, but Sir Bedivere told me otherwise. He said there was a select inner circle?"

"Ah, Bedivere. To be fair, that doubtless seemed true to him, but let me explain. We were equal as knights, but in spiritual realms equality is measured otherwise. Arthur taught us all high thinking and right action. He sent us all, equally, to quest for the Holy Grail. But it seemed some were chosen by the Grail."

Religious stuff again. Perhaps he could change the subject. "You were part of that quest?"

"I was. Percival, Galahad, Gawain, and I were among the chosen."

"So isn't it time to tell me how a knight quests?"

"Frith, you know you are as transparent as still water."

Frith looked down to see if his body was still solid.

Lancelot gave him a thin smile. Frith didn't know why.

"You're trying very hard," Lancelot said. "You are desperate to find your path, your manhood. But your time is just beginning, while mine is nearing its end. For now our fates have overlapped, and we have this brief window through which I think I will be able to point you toward the path by which I have already found my way. If you attend me, I may be able to impart the knowledge Arthur found, the wisdom he gave to us, and that state I now experience. But I am not a sheep you can drive toward what you want to hear. You must let me be the shepherd. You must hear what I want to tell you or not come at all."

Frith felt his cheeks grow hot. He tried to look away but somehow Lancelot's eyes didn't let him.

"I chastise you only that we might make better progress with what time we have. You may come tomorrow if you wish to learn, but I will go no further with you today. You must first learn to behave."

Embarrassed, Frith went to the fence where he fooled with the gate. He burned to leave, but he needed to wait for Lancelot to look away so Alura could come out of hiding. Lancelot turned his back to them and stooped down near a patch of Eyebright. "It is easy to love plants," he said to the cheerful little purple and white blossoms. "You do not talk back. It is harder with human beings; they so often misunderstand even the best that we intend."

CHAPTER 12

Frith wasn't sure if what Sir Lancelot was teaching him about knights was going to be of much help. He had been hoping to acquire some skills before Sir Bedivere returned, but who could he learn fighting from inside a monastery? Recalling what Sir Bedivere had told him, he decided he should master horsemanship. For that he would need a horse.

Frith carried a tray to the Abbot's chambers and entered without knocking. He had been waiting for just the right moment. The Abbot had just risen from his midday nap. "I thought perhaps a little afternoon refreshment, sir."

"Why thank you, Frith. A cold cider is just what I need."

The room was dark and stifling. Frith pulled aside the heavy drapes that had blocked the afternoon sun for the Abbot's nap. A cool breeze blew in the open window and ruffled the old man's hair.

The Abbot lifted the goblet from the tray and took a long cool sip. He looked at Frith. "What's on your mind, lad?"

"You, sir."

"Me?"

"Yes sir, I was thinking that a man of your importance should have a horse."

The Abbot set the goblet down. "Why would a humble man of God such as me need a horse?"

"Why… to visit the Bishop or… to call on other abbeys or…. to make pilgrimages."

The Abbot laughed a deep hearty laugh for an uncomfortably long time. That wasn't the reaction Frith had hoped for.

"I don't know what gets into you sometimes, Frith," the Abbot said, still laughing. "We have no place in the abbey to stable a horse. And who would take care of it?"

"I would, sir. It would be good practice. I could learn to be a groomsman."

"A groomsman?" the Abbot said. "That is so far below your station—"

"But I would be learning a vocation."

"A vocation that would not please your father. In fact, he would be furious if he knew that I had you training for such a lowly position. Now if it is a vocation you want, let you consider the priesthood. Your mother would be very pleased, and that *is* something I could help you with."

"But sir, it is you that I wish to help. I think a man of your station should be a man with a horse."

"Why? I never travel, but should I ever need to do so, God will provide one."

"How, sir?"

The Abbot waved his hand dismissively. "I'm sure one of the local noblemen would lend their priest a horse, and there's always the livery stable."

"But that would involve some delay. Should you suddenly need a horse for some urgent church business, you should have one at hand."

"Frith, have you ever even ridden a horse?"

"Twice, sir. When I was small, my older brothers put me on a horse and struck it on the rump. They were greatly amused when I bounced up and down all over the field. To avoid a repeat of that humiliation, I decided to learn on my own. When an opportunity came and my keepers were distracted, I jumped on a mare and rode her bareback."

"Well, that was nothing if not brave. What was the result?"

"When she perceived that I had no training, she took her head. She tore down the lane, and turned suddenly to the left whilst I continued straight. I landed squarely on my head."

"You're lucky you weren't killed."

Frith was chagrined. "My brothers had to go and find the horse. Thereafter, I was left in the care of my sisters while the men went out."

"If that's the sum total of your experience with horses, why do you suppose that I'd want to get one?"

It suddenly occurred to him that perhaps the Abbot was not himself a horseman. "Sir, you wouldn't have to ride yourself. You could get a cart … and let him pull it."

"Like a prisoner or livestock? Men ride on horseback, Frith, even holy men."

"No, forget I said that; forget the cart… We could learn together, both of us."

"What makes you think I cannot ride? Of course I can ride. I was not born an Abbot, you know."

"Then why should the Abbey of St. Benignus not have a horse for its Abbot? A horse is a sign of prestige."

The Abbot laughed again. It was disconcerting how often he did that. "Do not think that God put me here to enjoy prestige."

"But the abbey attracts prestigious guests."

"When we offer opulent feasts to the noble and wealthy, it's to increase the size of our abbey, not my stomach." The Abbot patted his rather rotund tummy as he said this.

"But the knights and the nobles all have horses. Why shouldn't we have one as well?"

"Frith, tell me the truth. Why is this important to you?"

"For the experience, sir. Sir Bedivere says that horsemanship is a prerequisite to being a knight."

"A knight? Frith, I don't think that's your destiny. If it were, your family would've given you into a knight's service instead of sending you here."

"They didn't care. They were just trying to get rid of me."

"Oh, I'm sure that's not true."

"But it is," Frith said, "for myself, and Alura too."

The Abbot clasped his shoulder. "Your family entrusted me with your service. Do not think badly of them. Life is service. An apprentice has to serve his master; a squire has to serve his knight. Every man has to serve some other man. Except a holy man, he serves only God. Think about this as you consider your vocation."

"But you answer to the Bishop."

"I do, and he the Cardinal. But I am not the Bishop's servant, nor he the Cardinal's. We are all only servants of God."

Frith left the Abbot's chamber feeling he'd gotten nowhere. Two knights and an Abbot in his life, and none of them seem willing to help him. Alura had the better situation. All she had to do was wait for a man. He had to figure out how to be one. Apparently, on his own.

CHAPTER 13

Lancelot found that he did not mind the company as much as he pretended. Too long had eyes turned aside when he came to church. Too long had women gathered small children behind their skirts when he passed. It was nice to actually speak to someone who sought his company. Even if that someone was immature and undisciplined.

Frith came through the gate and walked meekly over to him. "Sir, I am chastened. I shall be glad for you to direct our course. But you did promise to tell me how the knights sought the Holy Grail."

He gave Frith a smile. "Soon, but we still have one story before. You'll remember we were at Camelot for Pentecost?"

"I remember."

"On the evening before, a damsel had appeared at Camelot and asked for me by name. Though a stranger to me, she said she was sent by King Pelles. She asked me to accompany her into the forest."

"You'd leave King Arthur's court to go with a woman you didn't even know?"

Lancelot glanced at the gate. Someone was out there again today. He gave Frith a knowing look. "One should not leave a damsel in the wilds alone."

Frith's eyes darted to the forest and back to Lancelot.

But he shouldn't be playing games with the boy. "The damsel took me to meet Sir Bors and Sir Lionel," Lancelot said. "They were waiting with a handsome young man that they asked me to knight."

"You are empowered to make a man a knight?"

"I was. Though we had to answer for the knights we made, so we did so sparingly. But this young man… well, I did not hesitate." Reliving the memory, Lancelot acted out the motions of touching the man's shoulders with his broadsword. "I dub thee Sir Galahad."

"And he became a knight – just like that?"

Lancelot could see where Frith wanted him to go, but he stuck to the story. "Knighting Galahad was even more significant than I realized when I did it, for it soon brought fulfillment of the Siege Perilous—"

"I'm sorry, the what?"

"The perilous seat. On the Round Table, a knight's name was inscribed at each seat but one. At that place was inscribed a warning of peril."

"A warning?"

"That if any but a true Grail knight sat there, he would be instantly struck dead."

"Dead?"

Lancelot drew his finger across his neck like a knife. "But that Pentecost, when we came to supper, all of us were in wonder, for the inscription had changed."

"How?"

"No idea. But now it read that it was time for the seat to be filled." Lancelot adopted Arthur's voice, "'By God, fair fellows and lords, we have this day a marvel,' Arthur said to us. He was about to break his fast, but before we could eat, an elderly knight entered with the young man I had knighted the evening before."

"Sir Galahad!" Frith said.

Again he changed his voice, becoming the old knight speaking to King Arthur, "'I bring this young man who is a descendent of holy Joseph of Arimathea.'" Lancelot found he was enjoying this. "The old knight led Galahad straight to the perilous seat and sat him there."

"And he didn't die?"

"No. As Galahad was seated, all the candles suddenly blew out and the thunder rumbled. In a ray of light appeared the Grail, hovering under a cloth of white silk."

"You saw it?"

"As I say, it was veiled. But we didn't have to see it. Every knight, damsel, king, and queen in the room felt its wonder. Without even touching it, each person was elevated by its presence, according to their own nature."

Frith scratched his head. "How do you mean, sir?"

"For the gourmet, it was as if they were having the best food and wine they'd ever tasted. Those who craved beauty saw the beauty in each other. For the more enlightened, it was as if their souls levitated, lighter than their bodies."

"And you, sir?"

He closed his eyes and remembered the moment when the spiritual world opened to him. "For me it was as if I lay my head on the feet of the divine and floated in absolute peace."

"Was that when you attained the holy state you now possess?"

"Oh no, I had a long ways to go. But it was the moment when I first knew that state was possible." He paused. Frith waited. When Lancelot spoke again, his voice was soft. "I did not achieve that first experience of the Grail on my own, but because my son, young Galahad, experienced it."

Frith's mouth dropped open. "Galahad was your son?"

"I never knew. I only discovered it that night."

"But how could Galahad's experience create yours?"

"Plotinus, a philosopher much admired by my Greek tutor, said that all of creation flows from God down through various lesser beings, like a cascading waterfall. I think it was like that. Galahad's ecstasy was such that we could not possibly comprehend it, but it overflowed from him into the rest of us. Surely he fully achieved his realization in that supper. It was… it was…" Lancelot began to re-experience that evening in a vision. His eyes turned upward involuntarily.

CHAPTER 14

Alura found herself standing with a beatific smile on her face. Shafts of sunlight penetrating the canopy of trees created an aura of light encompassing all three of them. Well-being permeated Lancelot's garden like a golden light. The sense of wonder she had experienced the first time she saw Lancelot meditate overtook her. She forgot that she was supposed to be hiding.

As the experience faded she heard Lancelot resume his story. "We did not understand then what I understand now and hope to impart to you – well, hello."

Her eyes met Lancelot's and she realized what she had done. Alura immediately ducked back behind the bushes, but it was too late.

"You there, girl in the bushes, you know I saw you."

Alura moved a branch and peeped out.

"Come… come out. I've known you were there for days. Stop hiding."

Their secret was exposed now. What should she do? Frith came over to her. He kissed her lightly on the cheek and she felt reassured. He took her hand and helped her rise.

Frith led her into the garden, but in Lancelot's presence she suddenly felt shy. She hid behind Frith, and wrapped both arms around him for security, peeking around him. This first meeting was not the romantic encounter she had imagined. Then she found Lancelot's eyes. She experienced a sudden thrill of passion that embarrassed her. For no reason at all she nervously kissed Frith on his ear and ducked back behind him.

"Do I find you here without chaperone?" Lancelot reached over and gently touched her hand where it embraced Frith. A sensation passed through her arm and into her body. Lancelot pried her hand from Frith's waist and looked at it. "Frith, your wife has no ring."

"Not wife, sir. This is Alura, my sister one year elder."

She felt Lancelot pull her hand further toward him. He drew her out from behind Frith. "Your sister? I thought wife because you two were acting… What's a tactful term for it… familiar?"

Forced to stand before him without Frith for a shield, she somehow felt braver. This was her chance. "Sire, I have no husband and no prospects for a betrothal."

"I know that few boys your own age have survived, but surely other men desire you," Lancelot said.

Alura pressed her lips together, but they quivered. "Sir, there are no single men in my world, 'cept those who are already monks."

Lancelot let her hand drop. "What then do you do?"

"I'm stuck at the abbey like my brother, 'cept I work in the kitchen. With no dowry, I await some soul so wealthy or so merciful as to take me out of there."

"Well you are here now. Since you've been listening in on our conversations these past several days, what do you take as the meaning of my story?"

Alura knew this was a test, but she was amazed at how her fear vanished in the face of it. "The meaning of your experience, if I understood you correctly, was that the real Grail was not the cup under the veil, but the holiness Sir Galahad saw within."

"Ah, you've spoken well, Alura." Lancelot said. "Do you see Frith? Understanding is not limited by gender. Alura, don't hide in the bushes anymore, you are welcome here."

"Oh thank you, good sir," Alura said. "May I, in kind, do some service for you?"

Frith clenched his fists and stomped his feet like a child.

Lancelot looked at her brother with a slight sparkle in his remarkable eyes. "Yes, thank you. This talk has made me thirsty. You will find a well just over there. Please fetch me some water."

Alura danced off in the direction Lancelot had indicated, feeling like a child given a treat.

* * *

As soon as she left Lancelot said, "I have sent her to the well because I see you have something to say."

"Sir, you cannot openly include my sister in these lessons."

"Why not? I know people in this day say women cannot learn, that they are only here to serve men. But that is not true. The queens of old had great skills of comprehension, and like those queens, your sister—"

"Well this is not the old times. It's forbidden to educate women."

"Don't concern yourself about that."

"But we shouldn't risk it."

"You seem curiously concerned with breaking the rules all of a sudden. Is there some other reason for your resistance? Say, that you are unwilling to let her share in my teaching? Surely you're not like men who try to control women by keeping the source of knowledge to themselves."

Frith crossed his arms and stood there, mute.

"Aren't you the one who brought her here?"

Before Frith could respond, Alura returned with a cup of water and handed it to Lancelot. This simple act seemed to fill her with joy. Lancelot saw Frith clench his jaw.

"It is not me, but you who could be in trouble if she's caught," Frith said.

"Unless she becomes boastful, there's little danger that anyone in this village would ever ask a woman if she has an education."

Lancelot handed the cup back to Alura. "You understand what we're discussing, don't you? Promise you will neither repeat what is said here to others nor puff yourself up and thereby give us away."

"I would never do anything to expose you. I would adore you and be forever grateful."

Frith spat on the sand and then ground the spittle with his shoe.

"No. Adoration is unnecessary," Lancelot said.

"Sir, learning from you is important to me," Frith said. "If you're found out it would be the end for us all."

"Let me be the judge of that. And don't be petty about sharing me with your sister; be a man."

Lancelot looked back and forth between Alura and Frith. "This conversation is finished," Lancelot said. "I'm reminded why I enjoy solitude."

Frith had a look of panic.

"Go now, both of you. Come back when you can do so as equals." Lancelot turned, went into his cottage and shut the door, leaving them standing in the yard.

CHAPTER 15

Alura could think of nothing else to do, so she took Frith's hand in hers and pulled him toward the fence. His feet followed her lead, and soon he caught up with her. By the time they reached the gate he was ahead of her.

Lancelot's eyes had been so warm and inviting, her brother's so angry and cold. What had got into him? This whole adventure was his idea.

Frith sulked all the way to the old log they used for a bridge. Then he stalked across it ahead of her. Alura crossed more carefully, the moss was slippery and if she started to slide Frith was too far away to catch her. When he reached the other bank and was beyond Lancelot's hearing Frith spun around to face her. "What were you thinking, standing up like that?"

"Why are you so upset? I thought we were of like mind about this, but you turned into a complete ass when he said I could stay."

"When I came with Sir Bedivere," Frith said, "I didn't intrude on their conversation, I just waited in the bushes. Why couldn't you have done the same?"

"Frith, I didn't expose us on purpose," Alura said. "It was as if Galahad's experience just lifted me off the ground. Suddenly I was, standing. I can't explain it."

Frith just shrugged.

"Look, I tried to hide again. He summoned me, and told me to stay."

"After you showed yourself."

The memory of the feeling that had lifted her off the ground came back. She felt suddenly… aware, as if she were only just noticing how miraculous the smallest things were. The feeling had brought her to her feet —

she felt she was on the point of dancing. It was fading now, but at the time… "You felt it, too. Wasn't he wonderful?"

"Yes, he was. But then you started acting like… *that* with him. Why?"

"Hiding in the bushes I didn't realize the kind of power he emits, but when he touched my hand…"

Frith snorted.

"Don't belittle it. I know you sensed it too. I think he could be the one…"

"Which one?"

"One who will take me without a dowry."

"He's a monk."

"Is he? He's not at the abbey anymore. Maybe he's left the order… I do think he likes me."

"Alura, Sir Bedivere says Lancelot will never love anyone but Guinevere."

"Who is dead."

"Yes, but his love for her isn't."

"We'll see about that."

Frith suddenly quickened this pace. Because of his longer legs she had to take twice as many steps to keep up with each of his. If she didn't, he was going to leave her behind. Frith was acting like today was a disaster, but to her it was wonderful. No more hiding in the prickly bushes, no more cramps in her calves from trying to keep still. Lancelot had freed her. Alura didn't know how a woman would go about winning the affections of one such as he. But at least she was in the yard now, not stuck outside the fence.

A light rain started to fall. She couldn't feel it yet, but sound of the drops hitting the leaves overhead was plain enough. Frith stayed ahead of her. Sunset was nearing, and although it would still be daylight once they reached the field, it was growing quite dark in the woods. She should know her way by now, but still...

"Frith! Quit running away from me."

"We're about to get a downpour, you'd best hurry."

"Oh, I agree, so why are you leaving me behind?"

"I think it's you who will run off with the first man you can find. I'm the one being left behind."

So that was it. Could Frith really be so stupid? He had to know that someday, somehow, she must be wed. They were only few hundred steps away from the clearing that led to the abbey. At this pace, she knew there wasn't much time left. She needed to convince him now.

"Frith, I will always be your dearest sister. Even if he takes me—"

"Oh don't be daft, he'll never take you."

"Don't be so sure," Alura said, "But if he does, there is no reason we cannot take you as well."

"You think I'm afraid of losing you?"

"I'm just saying, you worry for nothing."

"I'm not worried."

"Then wait for me."

Frith gave her a chance to catch up. She put her arm around his waist. "Frith, there were always many risks in this venture. Sneaking off somewhere we're not supposed to go, spending time with someone we aren't supposed to talk to, learning things that are questionable, if not heretical —"

"And now he wants to break the rules by teaching a woman."

"You heard him say it wasn't forbidden to the queens of old."

"I heard him tell you not to puff yourself up and give us away."

"In my experience high minded men think they're so above women they'd never ask our opinion, and the small-minded would never imagine a woman could be learned."

"Alura, you'll surely get all three of us in trouble."

"I won't."

"You won't be able to resist showing up one of those old ladies in the kitchen once you have an education."

"Yes, I will."

"But will you be able to resist him?"

"Why would I want to?"

"Sir Bedivere implied he had a very immoral past."

"He seems moral now. More than moral. Holy."

"How can you possibly see him clearly when you're acting so... like a girl?"

"I am a girl. That's not a fact I can change. I wasn't doing it to make you feel bad."

"When I saw you trying so hard for his attention, I just felt... I don't know ..."

"Jealous?"

"Oh, God no, I know as a brother it should be my duty to help you find a husband, but..."

"You're sure?"

"Look." Frith was speaking softly again, gently. "I know you'll marry someday, just not now. The prospect of losing you feels a lot like getting sent away did."

"You ninny, I'll never abandon you."

"Am I going to regret taking you to Lancelot?"

"Frith, this is our adventure. We're in this together." She kissed him on the cheek to make him feel better. Everything was going to be all right.

CHAPTER 16

When Frith came to the hermitage the next day, he and Alura came openly together. He held the gate and let his sister enter first. Once they were in Lancelot's company he found it surprisingly easy to discard any remaining shards of awkwardness or discord from the previous day.

Lancelot immediately picked up his teaching as if he had never been interrupted, as though the disharmony with Frith had never occurred and as though Alura had always been party to their intercourse. "As soon as the Grail left our presence, Gawain said we should quest until we saw it fully. For what we had seen, however holy, was obscured."

"By the white cloth?" Frith said.

"By our wants," Lancelot said. "We only saw partially, for our preferences clouded us as though we were seeing it through a gauze curtain. Arthur said that we would ride out the next morning to quest after what we thought was a holy relic."

"I'm confused. Isn't it the most holy relic?"

"It wasn't what we thought it was. So for years, knights have looked for the wrong thing, in the wrong place. That's why I've allowed your visits; that I might show someone the real Grail before I die."

"You have it?" Alura said.

"Legend said the Grail was the cup used for communion at the Last Supper, but it's not."

"It isn't?" Frith said.

"It's not that kind of cup. It is the cup that runneth over in Psalm 23, the place of communion where you meet God in yourself."

Not religion again. But having been chastised before, this time Frith used a gentle rein. "The plan to ride out the next morning, sire…"

"Yes… As we readied to leave, Arthur realized Galahad didn't have a sword. He sent him to the river to fetch Sir Balin's."

"And Galahad pulled the sword out?"

"With ease," Lancelot said. "That's why I told that story first, to show that we knew early on the measure of Galahad."

"By the prophecy that he'd be the best knight of the world."

"Good, you remembered."

Frith was pleased with the compliment, but troubled by a detail. "What about his shield? In stories, knights always have one."

"Five days into his journey, Galahad came to possess a powerful shield that had once belonged to the son of Joseph of Arimathea. In fact, later Percival and I didn't recognize him because of that shield."

"You didn't recognize your own son?" Alura said.

Frith wondered if his own father would recognize him. He was no longer the small boy they'd sent away and forgotten.

"When a knight is ready for battle, his body and face are covered with armor," Lancelot said. "Friends or foes are identified by the symbols on their shields. We'd never seen the shield Galahad carried, so we didn't know him."

"Weren't you all riding together?" Frith said.

"No, the King sent us in small groups, searching in different directions. What we didn't realize then, but which I realize now, is that Arthur sent us on different paths because each knight had different obstacles to overcome."

"Like what?" Alura said.

"On a quest there are many opportunities to see one's faults. You rise above them or fail," Lancelot said. "Take for example Melias, a young prince of Denmark, who traveled with Galahad as his squire. He asked to be knighted and Galahad complied—"

"Wait," Frith said. "You knighted Galahad. Galahad knighted Melias?"

"Yes, but then Melias became distracted and took off on his own. One must keep single-minded focus on the quest, for there will be many pretty diversions along the way. In seeing them, we know what our imperfections are, but we must not stop for them."

"But not you," Alura said. "Surely you did not fall along the way."

"Almost continuously, and most grievously, for my fault was lust for a woman who was forbidden to me."

Frith whispered in his sister's ear, "He means Queen Guinevere."

Alura made a face that Frith recognized, the one that meant 'you're being annoying.'

"You might think that God leads a knight through a life of action," Lancelot said. "But his real battles are spiritual battles between what he's attached to and what he should be free from."

"But you didn't give up love," Alura said.

"I did not," Lancelot said. "Here's how the quest led me. Percival and I were searching for Galahad. Percival stopped to rest, but I continued on alone. Late in the day I came to a church, where I removed my armor to sleep for the night. In the morning I awoke as a wounded knight was carried in. He must've been a worthy knight, for the Holy Grail appeared and healed his wounds."

"You saw the Grail a second time?" Alura said.

"I saw it, but I was paralyzed in its presence and could not move or speak."

Frith wasn't skeptical, but he had had dreams where it seemed like he was awake when he wasn't. "Maybe you were still sleeping..."

"No, I was completely awake," Lancelot said. "Its power was so great I could neither stir my limbs nor tongue, even when the knight's squire found my armor and gave it to his master. I could not move until they rode off – with my armor and horse."

"Thieves! Did you catch them?"

"As it happens, I did later recover my belongings," Lancelot said, "but that's not what's important here. My lesson that night was that to change, you must give up what you are holding to."

That made no sense. "Give up your armor?"

"It's symbolic, Frith. The armor we use to protect that which is holding us back."

Frith just shook his head.

"From there I traveled on foot until I met a hermit sitting wake for a holy man. He made me understand that I would never find the secret of the Grail if I kept giving in to my carnal desires. The hermit gave me the deceased holy man's shirt and I repented. When I had vowed to be chaste for life, he sent me on my way with new armor and a horse."

Frith noticed that his sister had somehow edged quite near Lancelot. Now she gave Lancelot a seductive smile. "And did you succeed? ...in remaining chaste?"

"I failed, more times than I succeeded," Lancelot said. "No... I failed until I succeeded."

Frith couldn't believe Alura's brazenness. Was she so desperate to get a husband that she was trying to seduce a holy man? Besides, didn't she know she was disrupting the story?

Lancelot gently pushed her away. "I see that you have learned to flirt with men. Saintlier men than I have fallen off their pedestals. Do not make me one of those."

Alura scooted back with her eyes on the ground. "I'm sorry."

Frith was glad Lancelot had put her in her place. "Please go on."

"I came to a river which I could not ford and which had no bridge. The only thing to do was to wait for guidance. Soon a voice told me, 'Board the next boat that passes.' That ship took me to Sir Galahad. We sailed together to Corbenic Castle. There I had my third experience of the Grail, but when I craved to see more I was struck by the Holy Spirit. So powerful was the experience I could not move or speak."

"As before?" Alura said.

Lancelot nodded. "This time I lay twenty-four hours until King Pelles found me and took me to his court."

"The Grail doesn't seem to be a particularly good thing," Frith said. "Twice you were struck as though dead by its mere presence."

"It is good. It just depends on whether you're ready for it. The Holy Spirit overpowers all men when it awakens. Some regret to ever leave it and some, though awed, hope to never have the experience again."

Alura was looking at Lancelot starry-eyed. "What is it like?"

"Imagine starting a fire by striking a flint, but instead of a spark, you got a bolt of lightning."

"So that was when you achieved your holiness?" Alura said.

"Oh my no," Lancelot said. "Again, I only experienced it because I was in Galahad's presence as holiness flowed through him. But for many years I thought that experience was the highest state I was ever going to achieve. Even after such an experience, we may again become caught up in trivial jousts with life and spend our days as if they have no end."

Frith could not shake the fear of paralysis. "Explain what is achieved after you are turned still as a stone?"

"For Galahad, everything, the highest of the high. Just as when the Holy Spirit came upon the disciples of Jesus and they could heal the sick and lame, so was Galahad transformed. Whilst I returned to Camelot, he traveled throughout Britain healing the sick and blind."

"Where is Sir Galahad today?" Alura said.

"After he had done this work for several years, Galahad looked deeper into the Grail. Therein, he witnessed the final secret."

Frith felt they were finally on the verge of learning something important. "What is it?"

"I cannot say it. You must see it for yourself."

"We can do that?" Alura said.

"It is entirely possible," Lancelot said. "Now to conclude Galahad's story ... With his prayers answered, Galahad prostrated himself before the altar and died."

"Died?" Frith said. "Now I'm completely confused. What's the point of acquiring the Grail if you're just going to die?"

"You think that when you reach spiritual union you live forever?" Lancelot said. "The Grail leads you to experience your own soul. It is available to every person, but it is only fully realized by those who give themselves to the quest."

"Like the knights?" Frith said.

"Knights quest for the Holy Grail, but what a knight understands in the end is that the journey is the purifying experience."

"You could make me a knight."

"I could make you something greater."

"What about me?" Alura said.

"Ah, yes. You do have your own quest. When you lose your want of love, you will find yourself in the hands of love."

"But losing Guinevere broke your heart," Alura said.

"It did. But that time of sorrows showed me how attached I was. It wasn't until after her death, when I left the abbey to live here, that I had my fourth experience of the Grail. And the first one of my own"

"But this Grail seems a fearful thing," Frith said. "It hovers like a disembodied soul."

"Oh, it's not disembodied. It's a portal to your own soul. The quest for the Holy Grail is the quest to find your own Self."

"I'm not lost." Frith tapped his chest. "I'm right here."

"Frith, nearly all men are lost." Lancelot gave him a thin smile. "In my bereaved silence, I realized the mysteries of life and death. One day, the Holy Grail appeared to me. It said 'I shall take you to the Holy Spirit.' I realized the truth of the Grail was that it led to our innermost self."

"But we could never hope to attain what you have found," Alura said.

"I've just told you, you can. I shall teach you. The scripture says, 'Be still and know I am God.'" Lancelot pointed toward the gate. "It's time for you to go back to the abbey now. But while you're there do as the monks do... spend a little time in stillness each evening. Then you will see into the Grail."

Lancelot looked at each of them. "The quest itself teaches self-mastery. You cannot be spared going through the experiences you will have in the world, but if you do so, then one day you too will experience the Holy Grail for it is within the reach of every man." Lancelot gave Alura a wink. "And woman – But keep that to yourself."

"Thank you, sir. We shall come every day it pleases you."

Taking his sister's hand, Frith led her out the gate. Behind them, he could hear Lancelot talking to himself. "Pleases me? Trading my knowledge for their admiration may risk what I've attained more surely than being Sir Bedivere's show piece."

CHAPTER 17

Frith and Alura seldom fought, at least not seriously. But the next afternoon, they argued all the way to Lancelot's. It started when Frith complained that he was bored with religious topics. He wanted to learn about things that applied to knights and becoming a knight.

"Don't be immature," Alura said.

"Not being interested in his choice of topic does not make me immature."

"If you're not interested in what he's teaching, then why go?"

"You know why," he said. "There is some effect, some good feeling in just being with him. Even when he's sermonizing."

"I agree, I feel strangely uplifted while I am there. I really don't care what he teaches us. I just crave to hear him."

"But I care. Why won't you support me in my desire to learn about knights?"

"He's already admonished you about that. If you keep pestering him, he'll send us away."

When they arrived at Lancelot's, Frith didn't see him anywhere. He walked over to the cottage and started to knock on the cottage door.

"Wait. I've found him," Alura said.

Lancelot was lying on the bench, still as a stone.

"Sir," Frith said.

Lancelot didn't stir.

"Do you think he's dead?" he whispered to Alura.

"He's not dead."

"Well, he is pretty old."

"He's not that old," Alura said, "Maybe he's paralyzed by the Grail again."

Frith doubted that. He looked around and didn't see anything floating around – veiled or unveiled.

Then Lancelot turned in his sleep, and they both breathed a sigh of relief.

"Should I wake him?" Frith said.

"I don't think we're allowed," Alura said. "What if he is having a vision?"

Lancelot wasn't having a vision. He was dreaming. Although Lancelot extolled the virtues of a still mind and opposed dwelling on the past, reminiscences ran roughshod over the present. Talking with Frith and Alura had brought Guinevere to mind, which made him weep for the past. That in turn had fatigued him and made him sleep in the middle of the day. His nap filled with bad memories from a most distressing time.

Lancelot first dreamed of the time when he returned to Britain and learned that his most noble king, Arthur, had been overthrown. He grieved that his men had arrived too late to help Arthur.

Next, Lancelot dreamed of when Sir Gawain died and he was called to Gawain's requiem and wake. It was during those days of mourning that he heard that Queen Guinevere, suffering too much emotional pain, had fled west. Lancelot told the other knights, "If all others abandon her, I myself will ride and seek Guinevere."

Sir Bors warned him against riding alone, saying he would find no friends in the realm; saying there was much hatred for him and the danger was real. In spite of Bor's dire warning, Lancelot made it all the way to the Almesbury nunnery without a challenge or a duel. But there his heart was pierced when he saw Guinevere dressed in black and white. Queen Guinevere had made herself a nun.

When Guinevere saw Lancelot at the cloister gate, she swooned. The postulates around her, thinking her stricken by some malady, had to hold her upright. When she could finally speak, she said, "It is from the sight of that yonder knight that I am faint."

Lancelot's anticipation of a joyous reunion dissipated when he made to come through the gate.

"Sir Lancelot, forsake my company and return from whence you came," Guinevere said.

"But, my own heart, I just arrived," he said with all the love he could.

"Come no closer. You can see the life I've chosen from my dress."

"Yes, I see you've put on religious habit, but why?"

"I am set on such a path as to heal my soul."

"There is no need of it. You are already a Goddess to my eyes."

"Do your eyes not see that our love destroyed the flower of kings and knights?"

"Lay that disaster upon the bastard son, who tried to take the throne."

"But we gave that demon leverage against our king."

"It is said that love conquers all. Mordred may have destroyed our kingdom. Let him not destroy our love."

"Lancelot, I did love you then, but it will not serve me to love you now. I pray continually that I may make amends for our mis-living."

"I am as saddened as you, even beyond words, for the death of our king. But don't you see, we no longer need to sin. Remove your habit and let me take you to my kingdom as my legal wife."

Guinevere bowed her head. "If truly we have ever loved, then I should want what is best for the beloved. Therefore, Sir Lancelot, go back to your realm and take a wife. Live with her in joy, and may the two of you pray for me occasionally."

"Never!" Lancelot said, "How can I wed another? How can I be false to all my love for you?"

"Then I beseech you, for all the love that ever was between us, that you go and see me no more."

"Oh! I cannot bear it!"

"Am I still your Queen?"

"Ever, my own heart."

"Then I command you to forsake my company. And if you will not have a wife, then follow my good example and spend your days in Holy Communion."

"I see penance by your good example. The same destiny that you've chosen I will follow as well."

"Your change of mood seems sudden."

"I will forsake all the vanities of the world. I will renew my quest for the Sangrael with all my thought and will and heart."

"Do you mean it, truly?"

"If I had done so when our king was alive, I would have passed all the knights in quest of the Sangrael – except Galahad, of course."

"Yet, that is itself vanity."

"That was not my intent," he said. "I take note of God in you, but you are my earthly joy. Since you are not disposed to join me in my own realm, I will take to yours."

"Meaning?"

"You have undertaken to right our imperfection. I, too, must take up the quest of perfection. I assure you that if I find any monastery that will receive me, I will take to penance and prayer while ever my life lasts."

"If you will, then prove it by leaving me in peace."

"In my departure, I pray you one boon."

"What is that?"

"Kiss me once more and we never will again."

"No. I am cloaked and abstain from such intimacy. Hold to the promise that you will never return to my world again. Now go."

He departed and rode into the forest. Although renewed in his quest, he felt alone and abandoned to the depth of his heart. When he was a good distance from the nunnery where he could not be heard, he stopped his horse and threw his arms apart crying out, "Alas! Who may trust in this world?" He continued riding that day and all the night weeping.

Lancelot felt the wetness on his cheeks and the rough wood against his back. Where was he? He heard voices and struggled to shake off the sorrowful memories.

"We should go," Frith said.

"No, let's wait a bit longer and see if he wakes on his own."

Lancelot opened his eyes, sat up slowly, and looked around his garden. Frith and Alura were there, watching him wide-eyed. He wiped his face with his sleeve. "I… must've fallen asleep. Have I kept you waiting?"

"Not long," Frith said. "You seemed to be dreaming."

"And not a pleasant one either," Lancelot said.

"You, sir?" Alura said with disbelief.

Lancelot chuckled. "Are you surprised? Even though I know the past is no longer – only the now is real. Being done with the past doesn't mean you forget the past."

"What do you mean, sir?" Frith said.

"Threads of past thoughts are tied like little strings to the heart. When something pulls on one of them, they all begin to tangle. The best you can do is to let go of it as soon as you recognize what has happened. But even then, they may come again to haunt your sleep."

CHAPTER 18

In the morning Alura began making venison stew. Yesterday some archers gifted the Abbot with a small stag they'd killed. Its tender haunches had been the centerpiece of last night's feast. The rest of its meat had been cut into cubes and soaked overnight in buttermilk. Today it was stinking but tender.

Alura went to the garden to gather vegetables. As she did so, her thoughts turned to Lancelot, as they had so often lately. It was plain by his solitary life that he was unmarried, and since Guinevere's death, there was none to whom his heart belonged.

She pulled some parsnips and carrots. The onions were still small, but she pulled six or eight of them. Mother used to call them 'boiler' onions, fitting for a stew.

Taking her knife from her skirt, Alura cut a stout leek and a stalk of celery. Yes, he was twice her age, but wasn't King Arthur old enough to be Guinevere's grandfather?

Back in the kitchens, she laid the vegetables aside and fetched a large bucket of water. Next she hung the medium cauldron on the fire and melted some pork fat in it. The deer had been lean and wanted for a bit of grease. Some might say he was too old for her, but where would she find a man her age as fine as Sir Lancelot?

When the drop of water she flicked into the cauldron danced on the hot grease, she plucked the cubes of venison from the bowl with her fingers, swished them in water to rinse off the buttermilk, and dropped them in the hot fat to brown. She paused at intervals to stir the meat with a large spoon, and then resumed adding cubes until there were no more. Now that she had come out of hiding and finally met him, what should she do to win him? To make him love her?

She swung the cauldron away from the fire and let the meat simmer from the heat of the iron pot while she went to get fresh water. She also dumped the buttermilk into the hog trough. It smelled awful, but the pigs wouldn't mind. She was glad to have it out of the kitchen.

She washed the vegetables in the new water and peeled the onions. They were very small so she threw them whole into the pot to simmer next to the meat. She took the leek and sliced it very thin. She also chopped the stalks of the onions and added both to the stew.

She cut the carrots in pieces the width of her thumb, but sliced the parsnips a little thinner. Next she chopped the celery. She threw the chopped vegetables in the now quiet cauldron and swung it back over the fire so it could start to heat again. Her older sisters had often said the way they appeased their men was through their stomachs. If that was true for them, it should work for her as well.

At the edge of the third fireplace, they kept a stock pot. She ladled out several good measures of broth which she added to her stew. She returned an equal amount of water and added all of her peelings to the stock pot. She was a good cook. Perhaps she should make him something delicious to eat?

Alura went to the herb garden and thought about flavors. She spied the chervil. It would give the stew a subtle anise flavor that would work well with the gamey venison. It was a nice sunny morning, and it was best to gather chervil on sunny days. The flavor of chervil leaves dissipated if overcooked, so she would use them as a garnish when the stew was served. The roots, however, could be boiled and retain their flavor. She would add those as soon as she went back in the kitchen.

Growing next to the chervil was coriander. It had gone to seed. The seeds could be used for many recipes, but the roots could also be boiled. She pulled up the whole plant. She would use the root for her stew and save the seeds.

Alura returned to the kitchen taking also two small handfuls of rosemary and thyme. She thought the stew was going to turn out well. Perhaps she would fill a clay pot with stew and have Frith give it to him on their next visit. If Lancelot did not already know her reputation as a cook, he would taste her worth in his own experience.

Alura never made a dish the same way twice, but her advantage was that she would make something wonderful out of whatever there was at hand. For example, there was plentiful unused meat from the deer carcass, and here she was making a lovely stew out of it. The Abbot would like her stew. Alura doubted that he knew her name, just that she was Frith's sister, but the Abbot liked her cooking. He said so.

She chopped the herbs fine and added them to the stew. She thought about peppercorns, but they were expensive. She wasn't sure the deer warranted it. Instead she substituted a small measure of crushed juniper berries. Finally, she added two bay leaves. These she would remove before serving.

Suddenly, Alura remembered that except for the Abbot, the monks ate no flesh. And since Lancelot once lived here, perhaps he still abstained. If so, a pot of meat stew wouldn't be the best way to impress him. She would have to find out what he liked, and then bring him his favorites. She would surely win his affection at first bite.

Alura thought about Lancelot as she moved on to prepare the next dish, and the next. Her ruminations on how to get Lancelot for a husband continued throughout the day, ignoring the fact that he had pushed her away. After all, hadn't he as much as admitted that he might fall for her?

CHAPTER 19

Later the same day, when the cooking was finished and she could get away, Alura and Frith went to Lancelot's. She was not paying much attention to the forest as they made their way, nor to Frith, who was nattering on about something, probably knights. Inwardly she was working out a plan. Silently she rehearsed her speech in her mind, imagining what she would say, what he would say…

Suddenly they were there.

Lancelot was waiting for them. "I thought I heard voices. Here again? Six days in a row?"

"Since you are willing to teach us, we feel obligated to come as often as you'll allow," Alura said.

"Won't they become suspicious at the abbey?" Lancelot said.

"Not shirking my work, Sir," Frith said.

"Frith, you're not getting my meaning," Lancelot said. "We don't want them to come looking here…"

Alura understood his meaning and she had a solution. Shyly at first, then gathering confidence as she went, she said, "I see your point. I bring greater risk to you. It's also more difficult for me to get away from the abbey than Frith. But I've an idea that could protect both you and me. Will you hear me out?"

Lancelot nodded.

Alura swallowed the lump in her throat. This was what she had been rehearsing. "It would be easier if you would keep me here."

Lancelot shook his head emphatically.

A definite no? So quickly? "I beg you sir, ask the Abbot to let me serve here."

"Alura! You too?" Frith said. "Would you abandon me at the abbey like the rest of our family?"

She ignored Frith, and began throwing her carefully-rehearsed words at Lancelot in a rush. "I'm a most excellent cook. I can grow a fine garden of vegetables and butcher your meat –if you eat meat. I'll sleep anywhere and I'll feed you well."

"I cannot deceive the Abbot," Lancelot said. "I have no use for you here."

Tears welled in her eyes. He thought she was of no use. Her whole plan was collapsing.

Her brother, however, looked immensely relieved. The dolt.

Lancelot touched her sleeve. "I see your feelings are hurt. I'm sorry if that sounded harsh. It wasn't meant that way."

This simple kindness on Lancelot's part was enough to turn Alura's tears into sobs.

"Will you let me tell you a knight's story? It will help you understand."

Alura sniffled and nodded.

"Is this more of the quest?" Frith said.

"Not mine own, but Percival's. When he first told it, I could scarce believe him, but from my own experience, I now know that what he witnessed was true."

Alura continued to sniff. She pulled her sleeve down over her hand and used it to wipe her tears.

"Weren't you traveling together?" Frith said.

"No. At that time we were on separate quests. Percival wandered a long distance in a wasteland until finally he came to a mighty river. He followed its banks but found nowhere to ford. It was nearing dusk when he finally spied three men in a small fishing boat.

"Percival hailed them, but they were anchored far out in the current. This made it necessary to converse by shouting across the water. Percival called out, 'Can you tell me where there is a bridge, or at least a ford?'

"'Not for twenty leagues in either direction,' one of them shouted back. 'No ferry, either, not that can carry a knight and his horse.'

"Now Percival, still a youth, new to the trials of the quest, was losing hope. He knew there lay nothing behind him. So when the oldest fisherman took measure of him and offered to lodge him for the night, he agreed. 'Ride up there by that cleft in the rock. When you reach the summit you will see a valley ahead and at its far end the dwelling where I live.' Percival, glad for the invitation, followed the old man's directions and rode off at once.

"His elation soon dissipated. For when he reached the top of the hill and looked out there was no cottage, nor house, nor even a hut as tiny as mine. Being young, he thought the fishermen had been making a sport of his situation and tricked him into riding away. He cursed them for their practical joke.

"Then, at the far end of the valley, he spied the top of a tower. He rode down into the valley and along its hollow. As the distant tower drew nearer he could see it had turrets and was in fact a substantial castle. It was hardly the humble fisherman's cottage he had been seeking. He regretted the bad thoughts he'd been having about the men and repented deeply. The fisherman was in fact ruler of this land, known to his people as the Fisher King."

Alura had never seen a castle. "What was it like?"

"Percival said it was wondrous, constructed of massive stones. Beneath the tower stood the great hall, and in front of it the living quarters. Percival said the great hall could seat four hundred knights. In the center of the hall was a great blazing fire and over it a chimney of heavy bronze supported by four magnificent columns. That night Percival was served a sumptuous feast. Yet his host the Fisher King ate only a wafer of Holy bread."

"What ailed the king?" Frith said. "Why would any man not eat his fill?"

Alura had to laugh. Her brother would never imagine eating less than he was permitted.

"The king was not ill," Lancelot said. "He simply lived without any food except the Eucharist."

"That little bit of bread?" Alura said. "No man could live on just that."

"Percival said it was so. The king proved the scripture, 'Man does not live by bread alone, but by that which proceeds from the mouth of God.'"

"Isn't that just an expression?" Frith said.

"I assure you it is more than that," Lancelot said. "A few months ago, after I returned from burying my beloved Guinevere, I was without appetite. The only solace to my grief was my meditation. Of course I continued to attend daily Mass. After several weeks I realized that I myself had been living on only the communion elements... and a little water."

Alura filled with awe. "Are you the Fisher King?"

"Lord help us, no, I'm the man you see. But I've realized something. That which causes creation into being is the true force keeping us alive, not our daily supper."

"If the Eucharist is now your only sustenance, why'd you leave the abbey?" Alura said.

"After Guinevere's death, I never resumed my duties there. I felt it wasn't right to occupy a cell for which I didn't work. Since I no longer needed any meals I moved here."

"If you have no need to keep livestock, then why have a fence?" Frith said.

"It was left behind by the previous owner."

Alura had been around his gardens for days. This was the first time she noticed there were no vegetables – only flowers. "And you never eat, but just a bite of Holy bread?"

"And a little wine—" Lancelot said.

"This is why you don't need me to prepare your food?" Alura said.

"Now you understand the whole of it."

"I don't understand any of it," Alura said.

"Be that as it may, while I cannot accept your service, I will accept your company if you continue to come with your brother."

"Sir, you *are* saying Alura should stay at the abbey, not here?"

Alura wasn't ready to give up yet. "But sir, my insides are so stirred by your presence. I want to feel what you feel, be as you are. I could achieve so much if you would keep me here."

"The abbey is a safer place."

"Would I not be safe here as well?"

"Since I've no use for a cook, asking the Abbot for your service wouldn't be very truthful, would it?"

"But I want to learn from you."

"And you shall. I've already said I will teach you."

"But what if I'm caught? You'll surely get in trouble."

"I am teaching whom God has sent. He will protect this work, I'm sure. Besides, who would catch me? No one else has ever come here."

"Sir Bedivere has," Frith said.

Thank you for pointing that out, Alura thought.

Lancelot waved his hand in a dismissive gesture, "Bedivere's an old knight, too interested in reviving his past to pay attention to what we're doing here. I don't think we need worry."

CHAPTER 20

After they had been going to Lancelot's for many days, it seemed to Frith that Lancelot had begun to take him seriously. It felt like they were no longer just visitors at his hermitage. He was teaching them in earnest. Sometimes Lancelot used stories from his past, sometimes fanciful analogies. Frith found Lancelot to be a wonderful storyteller. He used different voices for different characters and often played out their actions.

Frith sometimes worried that he asked too many questions, but Lancelot didn't seem to care. Lancelot had once told him, "Questions are part of learning. You must ask question after question until you fully understand the answer. But that's only one kind of understanding, a limited understanding. Real understanding comes in the form of experience that courses through your being like blood. When you feel the presence of the Grail, then you will find yourself beyond the realm of questions."

Today Frith felt he was ready. "Will you tell us about the Holy Chalice?"

"If you like... Legends say that when Joseph of Arimathea founded the first church in Britain, he brought with him certain holy relics, including the Holy Chalice. But if the Chalice was ever here, it has since been lost."

"But you know where it is," Alura said.

"No. I know where the Grail is."

"I meant the Holy Grail," Frith said. "Isn't that the same thing?"

"Many knights have made that mistake. Although the Chalice is a holy object, it is just an object. It's the cup for Elijah into which Christ poured the Passover wine that He shared with His disciples at the last supper. The Holy Grail that I have found is not an object."

"Then how will you show it to us?" Frith said.

"When you're able to see it, you will," Lancelot said.

"How?" Alura said.

"Only by changing how you see. Everything I am going to teach was known by the ancients. As Merlin taught Arthur, as Arthur taught us – change the way you see, then you might see the Grail."

Hearing the names of Arthur and Merlin made Frith's heart pound. "Oh I'm ready to learn."

Suddenly, Lancelot seemed very serious. "What we discuss here must not be spoken of elsewhere. If you tell of it at the abbey, you'll be excommunicated at the least or treated severely at the worst."

"Is it… Merlin's witchcraft?" Frith said.

"No, Truth with a capital T," Lancelot said. "But they'll burn you as quickly for speaking beyond their beliefs as they will for speaking against their beliefs."

"Not against Mother Church!" Frith said.

"Not against it, but transcending it – beyond the homilies of small-minded priests. Christ Himself taught his disciples to transcend the rabbinical teachings of the Sanhedrin – and you know what happened to him."

"How should we begin?" Alura said.

"At the beginning," Lancelot said. "Where did you come from? Where are you going? Why do you believe what you believe? How do you go beyond your beliefs?"

"What could be beyond a man's beliefs?" Frith said.

"Have the priests not read these words to you at Mass, 'I and my Father are one,' and 'Through me you shall become as I am'?"

"Meaning that we too can know God?" Alura said.

Frith thought Lancelot looked pleased with his sister. Frith was not. "Know God? I thought we were going to know secrets."

Lancelot turned on him. "What greater secret could there be! Inscribed on the temple of Apollo in ancient Greece it was written: 'Know thy self and thou shall know all the mysteries of the Gods and the universe.'"

Frith took a step back.

Lancelot stepped toward him and put his hands on Frith's shoulders. "To know this, you must see yourself in a new way. From a new place. But as I say, let us start with the basics. You know you have a body."

"Of course."

"But do you think this is you?"

"Who else would it be?"

"You'll see. Is your body you? Or is it something you possess, like this tunic?" Lancelot tugged on Frith's shirt. "When your arm is hurt you say 'my arm is hurt.' The same as you say 'my shirt is torn.' Your very speech shows that you intuitively know there is a difference between you and your body."

"But I can take my shirt off."

"And one day you'll take your body off too." Lancelot abruptly grabbed Frith by the shoulders and shook him vigorously. "The problem is you have worn this *garment* so long you have mistaken it for yourself. You have forgotten that you are the owner."

"How can you say this?"

Letting go of Frith's shoulders, Lancelot grasped Frith's wrist, bending his arm at the elbow. "Look, your body did not move. I moved it. Now, hold your arm still. Don't let me straighten it."

A tug of war ensued. Frith swelled with pride when Lancelot could not force him to straighten his arm. "Ha! I am the stronger man."

Lancelot released his hold. "You see, your body did what you told it to do. You are a rider, in command of your animal."

"All right... But what good does it do to know this?"

"I'm getting there," Lancelot said. "How do we know what's around us?"

"We see it," Frith said.

"Or hear it," Alura added.

"Or smell it, or touch it, or taste it," Lancelot said, finishing the list. "Yes we know this world through the five senses. But there are things we know are there that cannot be seen."

"Like ghosts?" Frith said.

Lancelot chuckled. "No, I mean emotions. You are aware of what you feel; sometimes you are even aware what others feel. For instance, Frith, show me anger."

Frith squinted his eyes and bared his teeth.

"You are showing me a fierce face, yet I know you're not really angry. How do I know this?"

"You can feel when people are really mad," Alura said.

"Exactly," Lancelot said. "And you can feel love when you give it."

"And when you receive it," Alura said.

"Just as our senses tell us about the physical world, we have similar senses of the emotional world," Lancelot said.

This was all new to Frith. "Where?"

"You tell me," Lancelot said. "When you are nervous or very afraid where do you sense it?"

Frith thought for a moment. "In the pit of my stomach."

Lancelot reached over and gently touched his sister. "Alura, when you feel so much love you are going to burst, where do you feel it?"

Frith saw a little tremor go through her at Lancelot's touch. "In my heart."

"Yet there is a third way we know what we know," Lancelot said.

"By thinking?" Frith said.

"Good answer!" Lancelot said.

Frith beamed.

"How do you know what you think?" Lancelot said.

Frith thought for a moment. "I hear it. I talk inside my head."

Alura nodded.

"Good! Now, if you know your thoughts because you hear your mind talking, who is listening?"

Frith was not sure what Lancelot was asking. "I… am?"

"Yes! Now, can you remember that?"

"Remember what?" Frith said.

"That you are the one who hears your thoughts."

"Of course I am," Frith said.

"You say that, but it's easy to get so lost in them and forget you are just hearing them. Thoughts are something you have, not something you are."

"Wait, please," Alura said. "Up to now, I thought I understood you, but what are you saying? Thoughts are things?"

"You have a blouse. You have a skirt. You change your blouse. You change your skirt. You change your thoughts, just as easily"

Alura laughed. "It's not always so easy to change what you're thinking about."

"Because what happens in front of your senses stimulates them," Lancelot said.

"Imagine a trader from far away is traveling our road. Along the way he's thinking about how to improve his business, about his wife back home, about… many things. He seeks shelter for the night at our abbey. A beautiful young girl from the kitchen brings him his supper.”

Lancelot gestured at Alura. She practically purred. Frith stifled a snort.

“She smiles flirtatiously as she serves him… He is no longer thinking about his wife or his business. His thoughts have changed,” Lancelot snapped his fingers, “Just like that.”

Alura affected innocence. “They have?”

Lancelot grinned at her playfully. “You know they have.”

The byplay between Alura and Lancelot was… troubling. She already had vivid enough dreams about snagging him as a husband without him encouraging them. “But thinking to improve his business was useful,” Frith said.

“There is nothing wrong with what he was thinking. But the real you is the observer not the thought.”

Now Frith was even more confused. “I’m not what I think?”

“No more than you are the body or the shirt that you wear. You are the one who is seeing the thoughts.”

Lancelot must have some mystical power, he didn’t know about. “Can you see thoughts?”

“Everyone does, all the time. Close your eyes, both of you.”

Frith and Alura closed their eyes. Frith expected something wonderful to happen. Instead Lancelot only talked.

“Visualize a… sword. Really see it. Can you see it? Describe what you see.”

“A powerful broadsword with a magical aura – Excalibur!” Frith said.

“A strong knight wearing a heavy sword… its scabbard weighs down his belt… He is quite handsome,” Alura said.

"Open your eyes," Lancelot said. They both opened their eyes. Frith looked at Lancelot, still expecting some miracle.

"Where are your swords?" Lancelot said.

Frith was disappointed. "Gone."

"Yet you really saw them, didn't you?" Lancelot said. They nodded decisively. "You were seeing a thought, formed at your command and dissolved at will. We do this all day – about everything."

"We do?" Frith had never before noticed.

"But surely not you," Alura said.

"I have thoughts just like anyone else. But they do not break my inner peace because it is unconditional."

His sister seemed to be trying to curry favor with Lancelot. Frith needed to show that he was just as clever as she was. "Inner peace must be really inner excitement. If it weren't, it would be boring."

"That is just your mind talking," Lancelot said. "It never wants to be still, so it says being quiet would be boring."

Oh. Frith wished he could take it back.

"When Christ spoke of 'a peace that passes all understanding,' he meant it was beyond the mind's ability to comprehend that peace can be unconditional."

"Frith ought to do well with this," Alura said, with a mischievous look.

"Alura!"

But Alura just laughed. "His name means peace. That was mother's little joke."

Yes, their mother's joke, picked up by all of his older siblings and repeated until he was long past tired of hearing it.

"Mother already birthed twelve children," Alura said, "so she named her last Frith – meaning Father should give her peace thereafter."

Frith turned crimson as Alura giggled.

But Lancelot didn't laugh at him. "The name may be auspicious. To hear God's voice, you have to go someplace really quiet."

Frith glumly scuffed the dirt. "Everyplace here is pretty quiet."

"Someplace really quiet within," Lancelot said. "Where you can see that the duel between your thought creation and real creation is the cause of your delusion."

"A duel?" Frith said, with renewed interest.

"I will show you how to see the duel of thoughts that is causing your distraction," Lancelot said.

"Not a real duel?"

"One moment your mind says one thing, another moment it says something else. You see something and then you have a feeling. From that a thought springs up."

"I thought you were going to show us a secret?" Frith said.

"The secret is Self-awareness, and that is known to very few. The first step is simple, really. Don't try to stop your thoughts and feelings, but do try to notice you are the one observing them. Every moment you can perceive yourself as the watcher of your thoughts, you are one step closer to the Grail."

"We are?" Alura said.

"Realizing you are the self who is observing is going to help you realize that you are greater than all the things you think you are."

"So then who am I?" Frith said.

"Ahhh! The very question you must start with. I would say you are the one who hears your thoughts, watches your feelings, and directs this body. But my saying it is no good. You must see it for yourself.

"One day each of you is going to experience the Holy Grail. Do not worry, I promise you that. If you have learned anything from me these many days, it's that you don't find the Grail by going to a particular castle or cottage. It's found because you have mastered yourself."

Lancelot patted Frith's shoulder in a friendly manner. "I think we have actually made some progress today, but I think that is enough until the morrow. Keep notice of who sees you see, who hears you think."

CHAPTER 21

Their schedule on Sundays could go either way. Sunday was a feast day for the monks, but they had their own kitchen. If there were no travelers at the abbey, Alura sometimes got off early. But if there were important guests or pilgrims, Frith's presence would be required to serve the Abbot's needs and Alura's to prepare and serve a feast. So neither of them would get their day of rest.

This Sunday the abbey was crowded with guests. Before they could finally leave for Lancelot's, it was almost too late to go. Nevertheless, they slipped away from the abbey and into the woods as soon as they could, even knowing that it would soon be dark. This would have to be a very short visit.

Although the monks said Lancelot came regularly to the early Mass, Frith and Alura had not encountered him at church. In fact, only once had Frith ever seen Lancelot away from his hermitage. Therefore, they were quite surprised to find him waiting by the fallen tree that served as a bridge.

"I'm sorry we are so late," Alura said.

"Stay there. I'll come over," Lancelot said. "It's a nice day for a walk. I want to show you the river."

"We see it every day, sir," Frith said.

"I doubt that," Lancelot said. "When you're walking here, you don't notice the river, do you? You're not thinking about the trees in the woods or the birds in them. You're thinking how you can get me to talk about what you want to hear, or how to avoid an unpleasant topic. You don't see much on the walk here. Mostly you see the thoughts created by your mind."

Lancelot crossed the fallen log and began to lead them back toward the abbey. However, instead of following the path they had come on, he took them along the river's edge. When they came to a place where the depth and quietness of the water let them see to the stream's bottom, they paused.

"The problem is we become engrossed in thoughts and forget our seeing of them." He pointed to where a school of grayling was swimming. "For example, fish live so immersed in the water that they can't see that it is water. But standing on the bank, we can see the water is a river in which the fish are swimming."

"But fish can't live out of the water," Frith said.

"No they can't," Lancelot said, "but every once in a while you'll see a fish leap out of the water to catch a fly. That fish, for a brief instant, realizes there are two things, water and air."

"Does that fish retain its realization when it's back in the water?" Alura said.

"Who knows the mind of a fish? But you understand the analogy. When you observe yourself thinking, you realize that you and thoughts are separate things. If we forget we are separate, our awareness drowns."

"Drowns?" Frith said.

"When we become immersed in our thoughts, they begin to swirl about us instead of going away."

A few fallen leaves dotted the surface, swirling in the currents, moving down the river. Lancelot went to the river's edge where some rocks caused a natural cascade. "If I plant my foot into the river just there, what do you think will happen? My foot will become like a dam to the water, won't it?"

"Don't do it sir," Frith said. "The water is deeper downstream and the rocks here are slippery. You could be swept away."

"The natural tendency of thoughts is to flow by, like these leaves going down the river." Lancelot put his foot in the water between two of the rocks. The leaves on the river surface began to cluster around his ankle. "Tell me what's happening."

"Is it… our immersion in thoughts that keeps us from letting them go?" Alura said.

"Well done! When enough thoughts have accumulated around us, we don't see the world as it is, but rather a layer of thoughts about the world."

"Like the veil you said covered the Grail?" Frith said.

"Now you are getting it," Lancelot said.

CHAPTER 22

On Monday they were able to slip away after noon. As they approached Lancelot's gate, Frith suddenly remembered the gift. His sister had the idea that they somehow needed to gift Lancelot for all he was giving them. "Did our family send it?" he asked.

"It arrived this morning. I have it hidden in my skirt," Alura showed him the outline of it wrapped in the pleats of her skirt.

"Do you think he'll like it?"

"It's the only thing we could offer. But you take it. I can't give it to him."

"No, actually you should. This was your idea," Frith said.

"I know, but just the brush of his hand, just his glance, makes me tingly."

Frith's ears reddened and his heartbeat quickened. "What do you mean?"

"Like when your arm falls asleep and then it wakes up tingling – only this is in my lips, my nipples, my tummy–"

"You've told me enough, thank you."

Lancelot came out of his cottage and greeted them.

"Sir, Alura has you a gift." Frith nudged her and whispered, "Do it."

He saw her blush and she whispered back, "No you."

"Just do it," Frith said.

Giggling, Alura pulled a stoneware cruse from the folds of her skirt and offered it to Lancelot. "Sir, since you only partake of the holy elements, we have brought you a fine wine."

Frith saw that Lancelot was truly surprised. "Not purloined from the Abbot's kitchen, I hope."

"No it's ours – from father's estate."

"I was making a joke because I didn't know what to say, but... thank you."

"I shall pour you some," Alura said.

"Very little, but pour what you will for yourselves," Lancelot said.

"Oh, no. We brought this for you."

"And what kind of host would I be if I didn't share? Alura, search out three cups."

Alura found three simple, carved-wooden goblets and poured. They commenced to make toasts, each taking a turn. After they had been drinking for a while, Alura and Frith became playful and inattentive.

Alura sat down on the bench. "You've told us stories about many knights. Won't you please talk about love?"

Lancelot looked into Alura's eyes. "True love doesn't fill you up, but empties you out. For real love only wants to give, not possess. In thinking only of the beloved, you cease thinking about yourself."

Frith watched Alura's nostrils widen and a trickle of perspiration run into her cleavage. He stepped between them. "More wine?"

Lancelot shook his head no, but Alura waved her empty goblet. Frith poured more for her and some for himself. They were not yet drunk, but were on their way there.

"We've heard so much talk like this," Frith said. "Today won't you tell us one of your adventures as a knight?"

"No, tell of loving Guinevere, please!" Alura said. It came out a little slurred.

Lancelot threw his hands in the air. "All right, I can see this day is lost to wine – a story to accommodate you both."

"Oh, thank you!" they roared in unison.

Lancelot set his cup down. "One time Melegant, the mean-spirited son of King Bademagu, kidnapped Queen Guinevere. Sir Kay was the first to give chase to the vile kidnapper, but was badly wounded by him. Thereafter, Kay languished with Guinevere in a prison tower at Bademagu's castle."

"What a scoundrel!" Frith said.

"Sir Gawain and I rode to their rescue, but we became separated along the way. Gawain was stranded, and thus I arrived alone to fight Melegant for her freedom."

Suddenly, Alura jumped up on the bench. "Let's act out to your telling. I'll be Guinevere. This will be the tower. Frith, you be Lancelot."

This seemed like a fine idea to Frith. He joined with merry enthusiasm. "Let me get my lance." Frith picked up a broken tree branch. "Sir Lancelot, the battle was not just to free Guinevere, but Sir Kay as well?"

"That was the result but not the reason. I was so in love with Guinevere that I would've left Kay if it meant freeing her."

"And she was so in love with you." Alura looked at Lancelot with doe eyes.

"But she could not show it, for she was married," Lancelot said. "In fact that day she broke my heart."

"Never!"

"Oh, the heart is a fragile thing, even when wrapped in a suit of armor. After I won the day, the King presented me to the Queen. 'Lady here is Lancelot, who should really please you,' but she acted offended."

Alura pretended to be young Guinevere. "Please me? He is nothing to me."

"That's about right. The king, dismayed and confused, said, 'But my lady, he has put his very life at risk for you this day.' But she turned away and closed her chamber door." As Lancelot spoke the words, Alura turned her back on Frith and pantomimed closing a door.

"I could have died then and there, for I thought my love lost," Lancelot said.

Frith waved his lance at Lancelot. "You skipped the whole battle."

"Frith is right," Lancelot said. "I haven't told the battle."

"Start again," Frith said.

Lancelot nodded. "Overcoming many challenges, I made my way to King Bademagu's. The King had heard reports of us and our feats as we rode his way. He feared for his son and tried to get him to make peace, but Melegant was having none of it."

"He was a fool to fight you," Frith said.

"He was a fool who delighted in doing the opposite of his father's wishes. In battling me, he was struggling against his father's will. His father tried throughout the day to get him to stop, but that only made him more adamant."

"Tell the battle—" Frith said.

"Yes, of course. At dawn we set our chargers upon the field. From the tower window Guinevere could see the contest below. The king went to the tower to watch with her."

Frith, tucked the branch under his arm like a lance, prepared to charge. Lancelot went to him and adjusted his grip, showing him how to hold it parallel to his forearm. It was the first time Frith felt like Lancelot had shown him anything about actually being a knight. He tried to mimic Lancelot's instructions precisely.

Lancelot walked back to where he had been. Following Lancelot's every word, Frith and Alura played out the scene. "A great assemblage had come to watch. The attack began."

Frith pretended to joust with the lance.

"The crowd shouted, 'Lancelot, look who sees you from the tower!'"

Alura waved from the bench.

"My eyes fixed upon her."

Frith fixed his eyes on Alura.

"I tried to fight without looking away. Melegant attacked me again and again. While I, mesmerized by love, was getting the worst of it. Finally, my queen spoke to me, 'Lancelot, if you won't avert your eyes, at least maneuver him so you are facing the tower. Then you can parry his charges.' What sweet, sound advice from my beloved. I began to circle my steed forcing Melegant to turn with us."

Frith galloped in a large circle.

"And thus turned the battle," Lancelot said. "Quite literally."

While keeping his eyes fixed on Alura, Frith pretended to make several charges at an invisible opponent. This was fun!

"Finally, in a blow so mighty it broke both lances, we became unhorsed." Lancelot took the tree branch from Frith and broke it over his knee. "We took to swords in a furious attack."

Frith picked up one of the broken pieces and began flailing it around. This time Lancelot did not correct him. That's a shame, because swordplay was what he needed to learn the most. He probably looked like a serf beating a mule.

"Not with feints, but with mighty blows, I drove him back toward the tower," Lancelot said. "'We were so close to the tower wall that I lost sight of her. I stepped back into her view and he lunged toward me. I beat him about with fierceness, but I hardly noticed, for I myself was burning with the fire of my lady's love."

Frith, whose eyes had remained locked on Alura's, began to understand Lancelot's passion. Lancelot, now fully engrossed in telling his memories, appeared to have forgotten they were there.

"The king saw Melegant so overwhelmed that surely his son would lose his honor if not his life. He called for a respite, but Melegant was so full of himself he would not stop. The king turned to Guinevere and said, 'While my son has kept you here, I have protected you from his advances and treated you with respect. I now ask that you call off Lancelot, as my boy is too stubborn to stop although he is clearly losing.' And in compliance my Guinevere said in a voice that could be heard below, 'I am willing that Lancelot should stop.'"

Alura parroted his words.

"Truly the lover does obey the beloved. Hearing her command, I ceased to beat him with my sword."

Frith dropped the sword to his side.

"But foolish Melegant resumed his thrashing attack. As numerous as stars in an August sky were the blows I suffered, but I did not fight back."

Frith began acting as though he was being struck, ducking and weaving to avoid Melegant's imaginary blows.

"Until Guinevere called out, 'Defend yourself, Lancelot.'"

Frith immediately resumed his swordplay.

"The king sued for peace. Guinevere spoke again, 'Rest your sword my knight.' And I did so, but again I fell victim to Melegant's terrible rage."

Frith dropped his sword to his side and pretended to protect his head with his other arm. He was beginning to think the best way to be a knight was to avoid love entirely.

"Shamed by his son, the king rushed from the tower, saying, 'Is this any way to behave, hitting him when he does not answer back?' That broke through Melegant's rage and ended the fight. I rushed to my beloved, but she treated me as I described earlier."

Frith rushed to Alura, who, falling out of character as Guinevere, whispered to him, "I would never treat you so."

Lancelot overheard her. "But she did. Pained as I was by the moment, she later gave me to understand her pretense. For in public, illicit love must hide under the cool aloofness of affectation."

Frith also stepped out of character to ask Lancelot a question, "Sir Kay and Guinevere were free?"

"Yes, but Sir Gawain was still missing. I had to leave them for a few days to find and rescue him. Rumors spread that I died in the attempt, and the Queen showed her true feelings in her grief."

Alura resumed her playacting, performing a melodramatic fake crying. Frith again took up the role of Lancelot.

"When I returned quite alive, the lady was openly glad to see me. That night at the banquet, we ate together and spoke in guarded voices."

Alura sat down and patted the bench, motioning for Frith to sit next to her. They pretended to eat and drink, their heads close together.

"Sitting next to her at supper the heat between us radiated like hot embers," Lancelot said.

Alura did not have to act that part, her body was radiating heat. Frith could feel it. Perhaps it was the wine.

"I confessed to her, saying, 'I would have ripped my heart out from the pain of your rejection the other day.' And she responded, 'Come to me tonight at my window when everyone else is sleeping. It has bars so you won't be able to enter, but we can touch, and give form to our feelings without witnesses.'"

Lancelot was standing with his back to them by then, ignoring their play, his voice distant. "The hours between taking her leave and the castle going to sleep, dragged like there was no relief."

Frith and Alura rose from their seats. She again stood upon the bench, and Frith paced the ground in front of it, waiting for the castle occupants to sleep.

"Finally, when there was no one stirring, no candle lit, I went to her window. She, dressed only in a night shift, greeted me."

Frith stopped pacing and stood looking up at his Guinevere. She extended her hand through an imaginary window and they joined hands.

"Her lips lightly touch mine through the space between rough irons," Lancelot said.

Alura bent forward as though through a set of bars and Frith felt Guinevere kiss Lancelot.

"And sweetly following that kiss, those iron bars could not match the steel in my loins. I said 'If I could come in you, these iron bars could not keep me out.' But she said, 'These cruel bars are too stiff to bend, too strong to break.' And I replied, 'I have fought a dozen foes to be with you. Nothing but your word can stop me. Grant me your leave and it shall be accomplished.'

"Then Guinevere said, 'I am willing, but wait until I am back in my bed and don't make a sound, for it would be our undoing to wake Sir Kay or the others.' I assured her I could pull those bars apart without making a sound, and I did so."

Alura backed up on the bench, making room for Frith. He pantomimed pulling two sturdy bars apart. She pulled him and he climbed onto the bench as if stepping through a window.

"She held out her arms and I rushed to her embrace with the stealth of a cat. Hugging me in those perfect breasts..."

The young actors embraced.

Lancelot slowly began to turn toward them. His voice sounded like he was speaking from a dream. "Then her lips found mine and mine found delight in her perfect mouth."

Reaching down, Alura lifted his face to hers and kissed him more fully on the mouth than he had ever been kissed in his life.

* * *

Lancelot suddenly came to himself. And saw a drunken brother and sister enjoying a kiss such as brother and sister should never. "Enough!" Have these two no shame? No sense of right relations?

Startled, they stopped their play and Frith jumped down. He grasped Alura around her waist and lifted her to the ground, but then stood behind her so that he was hidden by her skirt.

Alura just stood there looking at him like she was completely innocent. "That's not the end of your romance, is it?"

Could these two really be that naïve – that childlike? "The end? No, that was the beginning – our first time together. But I think I've said enough."

"Please don't stop," Alura said. "I'm sure there must be more."

This was his fault. He had indulged himself, and it brought out a flaw in their upbringing. He needed to fix this, and they needed a lesson. "What did you take from this story?"

"That women can be alluring vixens," Frith said.

"Only if a man wants to be allured. Don't put it all on them."

The boy was twitching and shifting as if nature were calling. "Do you wish to be excused?"

Frith nodded vigorously and ran off into the trees.

With Frith gone, Alura moved closer to him than he had ever allowed. "Let me answer your question with a question," she said. "Is it that women have power, even when their gender might not make it seem so?"

"I admit I hadn't realized before today how much control Guinevere had. She could move me like a puppet. God, I was in love with her."

Alura's voice became softer and deeper, "Sire, I know I was only playing Guinevere, I could never be your Guinevere. But I'd gladly be with you as she was if you will have me."

Lancelot took a step back and tried to make his response sound cool and aloof. "I take your meaning, but I cannot take what you offer."

"Is your manhood not attracted to my womanhood?" Alura moved toward him. "Have I lost my allure so young?"

Lancelot pushed her away. "Do not doubt the power of your allure. It is such that a man might cry from desire for you."

She slouched onto the bench. "My spinsterhood comes already. There are no men to cry from desire but you. And you'll not have me, though I make my feelings shamefully plain."

"It is not you, dear Alura. I've put aside those drives that once raised me up. I've reined those passions for the good of your virtue."

"Why? No future husband awaits my virtue. I'll be like a flower wilting with age unless some fair knight takes it soon."

"I am no longer that knight, but rather a man of extraordinary experiences, suffering to follow the path they lead me on," Lancelot said. It didn't seem to help.

Alura stood up. "Isn't there a little hope?"

Lancelot decided no matter how old he got, no matter how young they were, he really didn't understand women. "These things we have spoken are not things I want to give into—"

"But that, sire, is my predicament. There's no man but you to give into. It is of my own will that I offer you my love–"

Frith returned from the forest.

"Become my master," Alura said quickly and quietly.

"I'm moved by your sincerity," Lancelot said. "But do you really understand words like love and will?"

"Let it be thy will, not my will that is done."

"Save that phrase for God."

"I am undone! Or rather want to be undone – can't I bend you to my will?"

"I wish I were above that, but I fear it is I who would be undone."

Frith inserted himself between Alura and Lancelot. "Then you have no lust for love left?"

"We cannot control the feelings of love that might arise."

"Wait," Frith said. "Sir Bedivere said loving Guinevere was wrong. Are you saying something different now?"

Lancelot moved away from them. "Love is never wrong, but I was wrong. I had great love for Arthur, as well, and he for me. I not only failed my king by having his wife, but I betrayed my higher self."

"But you wouldn't make that mistake again..." Frith looked back and forth between him and Alura.

"I was the person I was then, not the person I am now. These love stories are in the past. It took me twenty years to realize there is something above that love."

He felt Alura close in on him. "Remember the story you told Frith about how Sir Balin came to possess his sword..."

"Yes."

"Knights trying to get from a woman's loins something that she was willing to give. Isn't my proposition similar?"

"Not at all. As you just pointed out, women have power beyond their sex. The Lady was not offering her virtue, and the knights were not tempted by it. What the Lady gave and the knight received was validation of a pure heart."

"I'm pure," Alura said.

Frith tugged on Alura, but she stayed where she was.

"True love is not the romantic notions peddled by troubadours, but a higher realm," Lancelot said.

"Can you not share this love?" Alura said.

Lancelot was quiet for a long moment. "Go and stand next to Frith. I will try to show you both something higher than what you have… playacted today."

Lancelot took a deep breath and relaxed. He felt more in control now, more centered in his true self. "You know intuitively the heart is the source of feelings. You can perceive it just here…" He extended both of his arms and held his palms in front of their hearts. "But you can transcend even this."

Lancelot could feel warmth radiating from his hands. Even though he stood a good distance from them, he sensed that Alura felt it and he thought Frith did too. For him it was as if there wasn't any flesh or bones between his hand and their interiors. He felt a vast openness at its center in which he experienced a sense of well-being and security. "Saint Paul says love is the greatest of all spiritual gifts, but 'when that which is perfect comes, that which is in part shall be done away.'"

"Love is done away?" Alura said.

"Insecure, fleeting, love is replaced by a love that emanates from you. When you are free, you find yourself in the hands of love." Lancelot dropped his hands to his side. "Frith, a moment ago, just as you came back from the woods, Alura asked if I would become her master."

He saw Frith glance nervously at Alura.

"I see something in you two, it bears some thought—" A church bell in the distance interrupted him.

"Oh Vespers! I am late and it's my night to serve supper." Alura spontaneously kissed each of them and dashed for the gate.

Lancelot touched his lips. "Frith, you had best see your *sister* to the abbey."

Frith caught up with her at the gate.

Alura, called back to Lancelot, "Thank you *Master*."

"Not that kind of master," Lancelot said to himself.

CHAPTER 23

Frith would have liked to have gone to Lancelot's earlier on Tuesday as well, but he was waiting on Alura. He was loitering behind the kitchen, trying to stay out of sight when Little Thomas found him.

"You're supposed to report to the Abbot's office," Little Thomas said.

"I am? What for?"

"He doesn't confide in me. I'm just the messenger."

"Alura, I'll be right back. Finish up will you?" He dashed across the abbey grounds.

When Frith arrived, the Abbot didn't look happy. "Close the door."

Frith's heart hammered – the Abbot never asked him to close the door unless he was in serious trouble – but he did as he was told. The heavy wood shut with more force than he intended and sounded like a thunder clap. Frith jumped. The Abbot did too.

"I didn't say to slam it," the Abbot said.

Frith swallowed hard. "I'm sorry, Lord Abbot… I didn't mean to…"

"Something wrong?" the Abbot said.

Frith looked everywhere but at the Abbot.

"Frith, have you done something I am going to hear about later?"

Frith scratched his cheek. Did the Abbot know what they were up to with Lancelot? No, that was unlikely. "No sir."

"Then why are you acting so guilty?"

"I didn't do anything." That you could have heard about.

"You know that I already know don't you?" the Abbot said. "Are you trying to protect her?"

Who, Alura? Frith stopped breathing.

"Tell me you weren't a part of her transgression."

Frith shook his head no. It didn't count as a lie if he didn't say anything.

"Well, I hope not. I want you to handle this, so I don't have to get involved."

"What?" Frith said.

"You really don't know?" The Abbot's brow creased, his mouth turned down. He looked like he was going to cry. "Thievery."

"What?"

"The kitchen staff reported that Alura missed her duties last night. They found her drunk on wine."

"Oh," Frith said. He caught himself before he looked too relieved.

"Oh indeed," the Abbot said. "I can't ignore their logic... To be drunk she had to have stolen the abbey wine?"

"So you're not concerned that she was drinking? Only about the thievery?"

"It is a harsh accusation, but there it is. Now the women expect me to mete out punishment. I like your sister, I really do. But you see the position she has put me in."

How little could he tell the Abbot? "Sir, I do, but she didn't."

"What?"

"Steal. Alura would never–"

"I would have hoped not, but where else would a woman in Alura's position get wine?"

"Our family sent it – to help Alura with her troubles."

"Troubles?"

"The… forgive me, the monthly kind… they make her feel discomforted …"

The Abbot himself looked discomforted. "I wouldn't know. I try not to get involved in women's… workings."

"I am hardly expert myself, as you know, sir. Perhaps it is her time… perhaps she overdid it."

The Abbot took a deep breath and exhaled. "I can't tell you how relieved I am. Still, it's better if an Abbot just stays out of some things."

Frith nearly shouted 'Amen' but just nodded.

"Go. Find Alura and have her put these accusations right. Tell her to explain it to the women. Surely they'll understand such things."

"Yes, sir," Frith said.

"I feel so much better now," the Abbot said.

CHAPTER 24

Alura was washing dishes on the kitchen stoop. Her brother was pacing the patch of gravel in front of her.

"Don't you see what you've done?" Frith said. "I thought surely the Abbot had found us out."

"But he hasn't."

"No, but we shouldn't risk it again so soon."

"Do you realize how fortunate we are that he grants us a daily audience? We shouldn't fail to appear. It would be rude."

"But the women in the kitchen are already suspicious."

"They don't know where I was."

"The Abbot said to tell you to put it right with them… By the way, I made up some excuse about it having to do with your monthlies. You should use that."

"I'll talk to them, but I still say we should continue to go to Sir Lancelot."

Alura wiped her wet hands on her skirt and went inside. She used Frith's lie, which could easily have been true. It was nearly her time of month and she *had* felt a great wetness. That was the part she told them. But the old women had little care for her excuse. "We all have the same trials. What of it? We still get our work done."

Ethelburg, who was the nicest, took her aside. "We don't object if a sip of wine helps with the cramping, but don't expect others to do your work for you. Just finish today the work you missed last night, and the others will be pacified."

When she came back out on the stoop, Frith had changed his mind and was now anxious to go to Lancelot's. Alura looked at the pile of cauldrons and pots awaiting her. It was plain she would not get away with shirking her work twice. "You go ahead, brother."

"Aren't you coming?"

"I've got some penance to do. I'll follow as soon as I can."

"On your own?"

"We've been there and back a dozen times. I know the way like the lines on my own palm. It's not so far. Didn't we hear the cathedral bells from his cottage?"

"True, but I should wait for you."

"No, go ahead, so he'll know I'm delayed. I'll follow as quickly as I can finish here."

"Wouldn't it be wrong for me to let you traverse the woods alone?"

"The woods do not scare me, for the path we have made there is the path to our happiness."

She saw his hesitation. "Frith go! I am the elder and I am telling you I'll be all right."

"Since you put it that way, I'll go ahead to alert him to your misfortune."

"No, no, he doesn't need to know the whole story. Just tell him I'm delayed."

"I'm only going because you insist." He gave her a little kiss and skipped away. "Come as soon as you can."

Alura labored steadily, striving to complete her tasks so she could leave for Lancelot's. She was anxious to see him again. Her remaining work was not complicated. She poured water and lye soap in a large caldron and began scrubbing it with a twice-folded rag.

While her hands cleaned the giant pot, her mind was free to revisit yesterday over and over again. She had kissed Sir Lancelot! Only briefly,

as she was leaving, but still her lips had touched his. It was a bold act —
unmarried girls did not kiss unrelated men. It was her first kiss, except for
Frith of course, but he didn't count.

Maybe she would do it again.

She remembered the feeling as their lips met. Unconsciously, she touched
her fingers to her lips, imagining the sweetness of Lancelot's mouth. Instead she tasted the harsh soap and spat. She snapped back into the
present, applying herself to the last pot, knowing she would soon be on
her way.

She really did not mind that she would have to walk alone. She wanted
time to think. Kissing Lancelot had been monumental, but an even more
wondrous thing happened yesterday. During the play, she had discovered
a secret kept from her heretofore. Alura had known many assorted facts.
What she did not know before yesterday was that they had anything to do
with each other.

She was sure that no one had ever talked to her about sex. In her family,
women were not enlightened on the matter before they were married, lest
they should take it up. In some families, a mother would speak of it to her
daughter on her wedding day, but her mother believed it was the husband's
duty to instruct the wife. When she moved here, none of the old women
she worked with ever explained it to her.

Of course she and Frith knew about certain strange, physical acts. You
can't grow up on a farm without watching the ram mount a ewe or the
curs doggedly following the bitch round the yard until she finally relented.
Remarks she overheard suggested that this was how they got lambs and
puppies. But nothing in her upbringing ever gave her the thought that
people did that.

She knew her mother and sisters had babies, but her mind made no connection to what she had witnessed the animals doing. When she fantasized
about love, it was romantic, chivalrous — bowing and curtseying. Knights
risking everything for the sake of their ladies, the ladies showering them
with admiration. And kissing, much kissing. Alone at night in her room
she had practiced, pressing her lips to her hand.

Until yesterday, Alura's desperation for a husband had been merely to get out of her current situation and on with her life. But when Lancelot described his love scene with Guinevere, a thousand things she had seen and heard, that previously had made no sense, suddenly came together in an overpowering revelation. She realized he was telling her that this was how people did it. Now she understood that men had another purpose. It only increased her feeling that a husband was imperative.

Yet how was that to be? She had no one to throw her grand balls like they had for her sisters. She had no matchmaker shopping for a husband for her. She had only Frith, and she couldn't imagine what he'd come up with if she sent him to find her a suitor. She had to do it on her own.

As she came into her womanhood, she had made a self-discovery, one that suited her purpose. She noticed that sometimes something inside her gave rise to an almost uncontrollable feeling when she was around men. When this occurred, she discovered that, with a look or a smile, she could stir a similar thing in them. It was as if she were able to communicate what she was feeling to the boy or man she desired and awaken it in him. She didn't understand it, but she played with it as if she was an actor and the intended man was her audience. She did not do this with the monks of course, but she practiced on travelers and visitors to the abbey.

Still, what good did it do? What husbands were there to find? It was as if she had discovered the powers of the huntress goddess, but found herself confined to hunt where there was no quarry.

CHAPTER 25

Lancelot was pulling weeds from one of his flower beds when he saw Frith walk by, alone. Apparently Frith didn't see him, for he went straight to the cottage and knocked gently on the door. "Are you in there, sir?"

"Where's your sister?" Lancelot said.

Frith whirled around. "Oh, hello, sir – Alura will be along presently."

"She's coming through the woods on her own?"

"It's safe enough. You cross it every morning. Haven't you seen the path from our traffic?"

"I have."

"It was her idea that I come ahead – to tell you she is delayed."

"Still, one should not let a damsel wander alone."

"That's what I said, but she's the elder. She insisted. You know how head-strong she is."

Lancelot chuckled. "You're right about that. It won't do any good to send you back for her."

"No, sir. She'll come as soon as she can. She has to make up for last night."

"Last night? What happened last night?"

"She… missed her duties."

"Has Alura been caught?" Lancelot furrowed his brow. What would the Abbot say?

"I was afraid of that at first, but we fooled them."

"Fooled whom?"

"The Abbot and the kitchen women."

"The Abbot knows?"

"Not that she was here. She told the old women she was cramped up with her monthlies."

Lancelot shook his head. "Well, perhaps they believed that. But be more cautious. You said you didn't want her to get caught."

Frith nodded.

"Now, since we are alone we should have a talk – man to man..."

He saw Frith swell with pride when he called him a man. Good! Then let him take responsibility as one. "We need to talk about your conduct with your sister."

"What do you mean, sir?"

"Don't be thick. That little play you and your sister acted out went too far."

"We were just… caught up in the scene. No one was harmed."

Lancelot bit his lip. Frith acted as if this is a normal thing. And if it were … "You two seemed too… Have you played… at love before?"

"No sir," Frith said. "I think it was just too much wine. We got carried away by your telling."

Could Frith really be that naïve? Still, he was the master and they the students. It was he who permitted their inebriation and he who indulged them in his romantic memories. Perhaps he was scolding Frith as a way of scolding himself.

Still Frith and Alura were not totally innocent. The question was, how non-innocent were they? "Do not lay it all to the telling. I noticed from our first meeting an intimacy between you two." Lancelot took a deep breath to calm himself. "Although Alura is desperate to experience womanly love, it must not be with you. You know that it's a duty of a knight to protect maidens – part of the code of chivalry."

Frith's face broke into a grin. "Are you going to make me a knight?"

"I do not have to dub you for you to follow the code of chivalry."

"But teaching me the knight's code – isn't that a step?"

"What we're discussing is Alura. She should not be treated inappropriately by any man, but in your case, it would be doubly damned, for incest has far-reaching implications. Do you know the biblical saying, 'Ye shall reap what you sow'?"

"I'm a landowner's son. I don't need scripture to know that the seed predicts the crop."

"Not just fields of grain, but right and wrong actions, even if they occur by accident. Such was the case of Arthur."

"What? King Arthur would never do wrong!"

"Yes… Well, this is a part of the story that is not often told. As a matter of fact he did, and his father before him. You've heard that Camelot fell when Arthur was slain by his son Mordred. But did you know that Mordred's mother was Arthur's half-sister?"

"No!"

"A wicked girl named Morgan Le Fay, who plotted to conceive Arthur's child by deceiving him into thinking he was laying with his wife."

"Then it wasn't his fault," Frith said.

"No, but that didn't change the result. Mordred, begat by such a union, could not inherit his father's throne. But with such a father, he felt he deserved it anyway. In his bitterness, he tried to take it by the sword or deceit. So he attacked numerous times and in devious ways. Yet when they failed, Arthur, from guilt, forgave him. In the end Mordred was killed by his father, but Arthur died too – from wounds from a son he should not have sired."

"From a treacherous woman…" Frith said.

"No matter," Lancelot said, "The sins of the fathers are visited onto the sons, and the sons of sons, until we have a bastard like Mordred who destroys a kingdom. Though it is prudent for you to behave chivalrously with all women, it is especially important toward your sister. We don't want to create another Mordred."

"But why's it my responsibility? Alura is the elder."

"She has you by a year, yes, but you have her by gender."

"You're saying I am accountable because she is the weaker sex?"

"I would hesitate to call her weak. But we live in a land that gives women little control of their destiny. As you and I both saw yesterday, she has discovered she has the power to awaken certain feelings in men."

"I know, I know, Alura wants to marry."

"And those feelings are the only tool she has to get what she wants. But you know it can't be you, don't you?" Lancelot said. "You and I must commit to helping her without taking her for our advantage."

There was a rustling – Alura coming through the gate. She was wearing a broad smile. She gave a little curtsey, but let Frith continue.

"Then what man can she marry?" Frith said.

"A question constantly on my mind." Alura said.

"A question not befitting your obvious intelligence," Lancelot said.

The happy face she had been wearing disappeared. "Are you against marriage?"

"Not at all," Lancelot said. "But you'll either be married or not. You're not in a position to change that, so why squander your days pondering that issue?"

"Planning may make it happen. Besides, what other question should I ponder?"

"Who you really are!"

"The soul?" Alura said.

Lancelot reached out and laid his hand on her arm. "Have you experience of that, or are you just giving me the answer that will get you back in my good graces?"

"I didn't know I was out of grace."

"Have you forgotten about yesterday?"

Alura wrapped her hand over his and held him. "I think my answer is what you have been teaching us."

Lancelot slipped his hand from hers and looked at Frith. "Yesterday, Alura asked if I would become her master." He paused for a moment. Frith gave him a hard look. "I have decided to see if it's possible – not in the way Alura intended, but possible to transmit what I've mastered to both of you. If you're willing."

Alura dimpled. "Oh thank you, master."

"No more wine though." Lancelot shook his finger. "It only exacerbates passions and causes you to lose control of your better senses."

"Yes, sir," Alura said.

"Previously, I instructed you how to see your soul as distinct from your body, mind, and emotions. Have you been doing that?"

"I've… tried," Frith said.

"Are you able to watch yourself?" Lancelot said.

"Not so much so," Frith said. "But once or twice."

"It'll get easier. One thing that makes it difficult is that our mind, body, and feelings are interrelated."

"They are what?" Frith said.

"They're interwoven together. If the body gets really sick, the mind might not be able to think straight. If the mind is lost in thought, you may lose touch with what your feelings are. When you fall madly in love, the body may lose its appetite."

Alura brushed up against him. "I wouldn't mind."

Lancelot stepped away from her. "You think too much about men and women."

"Of course I do. You've known a woman, but I've yet to know a man. Why do you tell me that I shouldn't think about finding a husband?"

"Because it dominates your mind. I tell you the mind keeps us from seeing God. And it has since Adam and Eve."

Alura blushed, as if her desires betrayed her.

"Their story is not about sex," Lancelot said.

Alura's color deepened even more. "But they did... um... you know... They weren't... pure anymore."

"Yes, but that was a minor matter. It's the fornication of the mind that damns us." He saw them both blush at his use of this word. "Thoughts are like field mice, each one busy reproducing a litter, and each of those another litter. Soon we are infested with them."

"But I have not yet experienced that part of love," Alura said.

"I believe you, but neither of the men present here can give you that experience."

Frith got between them. "Sir, can we talk about something else."

"What I'm saying is that thinking too much about what we want keeps us from knowing who we really are. This is the real original sin."

Frith scratched his head.

"I see you know the story of Adam and Eve. Do you remember that God came into the garden and called 'Adam, where are you?'"

Frith nodded. "Adam answered that he was hiding."

"Now, if God and His creation are one, where could anyone hide from God?"

Frith looked like Lancelot had asked him why the moon came out. "I don't know."

"His mind," Lancelot said.

Alura furrowed her brow. "He was hiding in his mind?"

"Have you seen a toddler play the game of hide and seek? They just cover their eyes and hide in plain sight. The child assumes that, if they can't see you, then you can't see them. So it was that Adam imagined God couldn't see him. But it was Adam who lost sight of God."

"What does that have to do with original sin?" Alura said.

"Everything. Read the story yourself. The scripture does not say God accused them of having sex. That's a misunderstanding the priests encourage, because they want—"

"We can't read," Frith said.

Oh. Of course. "Right, but you know the story," Lancelot said. "When God found Adam wearing fig leaves, God said, 'Adam, why are you wearing that?' And Adam said…" Lancelot gestured for Frith to finish the sentence.

"Because I was naked."

Lancelot turned to Alura. "Then God said…."

"Who told you were naked?"

"The mind did," Lancelot said.

"What?" they said in unison.

"I thought it was the serpent," Alura said.

Lancelot shook his head. "If you could but read, you would see that nowhere in scripture did the serpent tell them they were naked. They decided that on their own."

"But they actually were naked," Alura said.

"Not until they thought about nakedness," Lancelot said. "Original sin was neither nudity nor sex."

"I remember now, it was eating from a certain tree," Alura said.

"Alura's right," Frith said. "The tree that gave knowledge of good and evil."

"Yes! And where does knowledge reside?"

"In… the mind, of course," Frith said.

"Exactly. They desired to eat of it, believing it would make them wise. But it didn't. It only started them judging. You see, the power they gained was not wisdom. It was the ability to think of things – like wearing no clothes – as either good or bad. That kind of thinking cost them paradise."

Frith scratched his head. "They were expelled from Eden for thinking?"

"Lost from it is more accurate," Lancelot said. "Tell me, how do our minds decide what's good or bad?"

Frith shrugged.

"By what we like or dislike," Lancelot said.

"Surely there is a real good and bad, though." Alura said.

"I'm not trying to debate the existence of evil. I'm trying to show you that what we personally decide is good is based on what we like. And what we don't like we think is bad. If you like sweet, then you think honey is good. If you hate sour, then you think vinegar is bad."

"I thought you were talking about something greater."

"I am. But it's easier to see how the mind works when you look first at small things. Once you learn to observe the mind, you'll see that it doesn't stop with honey and vinegar. We are dividing everything into what we like and don't like. It's an unending process. That's why God warned Adam and Eve that, 'Once you eat of it, in sorrow shall you eat of it all the days of your life.'"

"I thought paradise was lost 'cause they went into the desert." Frith said.

"It's symbolic. The desert's a place where nothing is provided, the opposite of paradise, where everything is provided. In the beginning they accepted everything as from God. Once they began to decide what was good and what was bad, that gift was lost to them. There was no more just accepting. They had to decide whether they liked or didn't like everything that happened. Adam and Eve could no longer see God – they had to think about Him."

"Huh?" Frith said.

Lancelot tapped Frith on his forehead. "By the sweat of their brow."

"Why'd they stay out in the desert?' Alura said. 'Why not go back?"

"Cherubim with flaming swords blocked the way back," Frith said.

"You do know the story," Lancelot said. "But so what if there are fiery swords blocking your way? Go through them!"

Frith trembled. "They might be burned or killed."

"They'll die in the desert, too. If they can get back into paradise, won't their wounds heal?"

Frith gave a reluctant nod.

"If you knew where paradise was, if you knew the way back, wouldn't you go through anything to get there?"

"Oh, I am willing," Alura said.

Lancelot smiled at her. "Yes, be optimistic. For if the way is guarded, it means there is a way back."

"What do you want us to do?" Frith said.

"First you must turn away from that with which you are obsessed, your own version of creation. We become so identified with this collection of thoughts and feelings surrounding this one body that we forget. The world we see now is not real."

Frith looked around involuntarily. "How can you say I'm not seeing reality?"

"Just as Adam and all of his descendants do it, by living so intently in a multitude of thoughts that we no longer see God's creation, but our own. We need to get back to Paradise."

"You keep ignoring the flaming swords," Frith said.

"Our fearful thoughts are our fiery swords. They make the way back seem insurmountable. We live in a world of our own thoughts, and most of them are about avoiding real or imagined pain. Every painful thought reminds us of a feeling that we want to avoid."

Frith clutched his stomach with his hands. "Isn't it natural to avoid pain?"

"Real pain. Getting unseated from your horse by a lance really hurts. A cook burning her hand – that pain is real. But painful feelings caused by a memory, those aren't real. Most of the pain we avoid is not real."

"I understand you're saying that painful memories are different from physical pain, but what about pain my heart feels. That's real." Alura said.

"It is real, but only when it happens. That's no reason to have it stuck in your mind forever," Lancelot said. "Certainly it hurt to have the queen break my heart, just like it hurts to be struck by a broadsword. The actual duration of those experiences is minutes, yet we hold onto them for years."

Unconsciously Alura shook her head no, whipping her hair back and forth.

"When our eyes see a thing, our mind does not show us just that thing. Instead, we see the thing overlaid with our fears and our schemes. The same is true of the heart. You don't experience feelings in the now because they are obscured by impressions from the past."

"Oh I think I see my feelings very plainly," Alura said.

"Do you?" Lancelot said. "When I examined my own life, I found that whenever I saw any person or object, I did not see it on its own, but also whether I thought it good or bad. Thus we repeat Adam's fault. This is our inheritance from him, to categorize everything in God's creation: do we fear it or desire it? A few we ignore."

Alura twisted several strands of her hair between her fingers.

"If it's something we don't care about, we quickly move on. If it's either fear or craving, a multitude of thoughts will rise faster than a flea can jump. How do we get what we want? How do we avoid what we don't want? The mind spirals away from the present into strategies to get it the way we want."

Alura put the twisted hair in her mouth and then pulled it out again.

"Maybe you have a saner mind than I, but that's what I saw when I observed my own processes."

"I don't mean to suggest I'm equal to your station," Alura said.

"I take no offense," Lancelot said, "You and I are equal before God. The difference is that I know it and you do not."

"You were going to help us deal with the swords," Frith reminded him.

"Ah, yes, the fiery swords that block our way by threatening pain. That is the second step. You must go toward the fiery swords knowing that passing through them may hurt."

"I would think that flaming swords would do more than hurt."

Lancelot could see Frith was becoming obsessed with the imagery. This teaching was harder than he thought. "How did Adam and Eve know the flaming swords were even real? Maybe they weren't. How would they know unless they tried to go past them? A squire in training who is knocked from his horse must remount and try again, or he'll never become a knight. He must overcome his fear of being hit or he'll never face a challenger."

"Is this how I become a knight?" Frith said.

"I tell you, it's how you enter paradise where you can commune with God as surely as Adam and Eve did in Eden. We could go there, but we're afraid."

"But there are many real things to fear," Frith said. "Doesn't the world have real dangers? I mean, Mordred really was treacherous."

"Of course," Lancelot said, "but deal with the dangers and be done. The only reason fears persist is because we keep them and continue to make more. Fears don't even have to be about something that actually happened, only about something that might.

"Fear is the result of original sin – of deciding what to like and don't like. From the moment we decide something we dislike might happen, we fear it and must avoid it. Even when we decide something is good, it makes us fear that we'll not get it or might lose it once we have it. Cease fearing to face thoughts that might hurt and you will see a gate to paradise is right within you. Give back to God the power to decide what you should and should not have, and you will cease to create new fears for yourself."

Frith and Alura were looking at him with eyes wide and their mouths open. "Never have we heard even the most learned priests say such ideas," Frith said.

"Well," Lancelot said, "we're just getting started."

CHAPTER 26

For the next several visits, Lancelot kept railing against the mind and its power to keep them from seeing the Grail. But Frith found that instead of diminishing their obsession with thinking, Lancelot's ideas had both him and Alura thinking harder than they ever had before. Even when they weren't with Lancelot, they were discussing his ideas. It was… amazing. Frith had never thought of himself as either a scholar or a saint, and Alura certainly would have agreed with him. But now they were talking about deep, spiritual matters like they were philosophers. And he was liking it!

However, there was an underlying hypocrisy that had been bothering Frith for a while. He made up his mind that today he would make Lancelot address it.

"Sir, it doesn't seem fair," Frith said. "You know the art of being a knight and the strategy of battle. You read and write several languages and have studied scripture. You're obviously a great thinker, yet you spend all this time lecturing us against it."

"I'm not against learning. In fact, am I not helping you learn?"

Frith nodded. "Well, yes, but that's my point."

"But recognize that there are two kinds of thinking. A cook knowing how much food to prepare for the number of guests at a banquet is a useful function of the mind."

Alura smiled that Lancelot had used her for an example. And he wondered if Lancelot would scold her for her pride.

Lancelot didn't. He just went on. "However, thinking about an argument after you've walked away from it, and then repeating it over and over in your head. How does that help? The conversation has ended, the other person has left."

Alura's smile disappeared. "But sometimes the old women won't listen to me, even though I'm right."

"That may be, but you'll find arguing won't really change them. You'll be more successful if instead of fighting back, you just put the argument out of your mind and go about your business. When they see your way is working, maybe they'll admit it."

"What if they don't?"

"Then that's their problem, not yours. The habit of petty thoughts – who said what to whom, who has what and who doesn't, who should be doing things your way – all of that is the mind I speak against. Until you get out of that mindset, it's the only thing you'll ever know."

He could see that really upset his sister.

Lancelot stroked her arm. "I'm trying to get you past all of that so you can see the next thing. I want to talk you out of being enamored with your thoughts so we can get on to something deeper, but it's hard. These habits of the mind are very powerful."

Alura nodded.

"Frith asked earlier why I talk against the mind? It's because you aren't going to see the Grail until you give up on the mind as the source of your knowledge. It's not. It's only one aspect of your being; stop thinking that it's right. Realize how much you don't know. Then you'll realize how little these thoughts are worth."

"I already know that I don't know," Frith said. "That's why I'm here."

"I know, and I know you're trying," Lancelot said. "Tell you what, you want to learn something practical? Shall I teach you how to read?"

Frith smiled. "Yes please."

"Take off your shoes."

That was a strange request. What did his shoes have to do with reading? Still, Frith did as he was asked.

Lancelot scooped up a handful of pebbles, brushed the dirt from them and handed them to Frith. "To read one must first learn the alphabet. This is how my Latin teacher taught us our letters. I am going to draw the first two letters in the sand. Arrange these stones in your shoes in the same pattern and then put your shoes back on without disturbing the stones. Wear them until tomorrow, when I shall give you the next two."

Frith positioned the pebbles in his shoes – three straight lines that looked like a little house, and a looping couple of curves – and then carefully put them back on.

"In twelve days, you will know all 24 Latin letters. I warn you it'll be an irritation, but you'll never forget them."

He gingerly put his weight on his shoes. The pebbles were annoying, but not painful. And he could feel the odd shapes imprinting into his flesh.

Lancelot turned to Alura. "Every person you meet, the majority of what you see, starts the mind talking: 'Oh, that's nice, I don't like that, I wouldn't like to have that happen, I wish that would happen to me, why can't that happen to me, how can I make that happen?' If you're observant, you'll notice that it always thinks about changing something outside of itself. 'How do I make someone or something in the world behave so that I'm more comfortable?'"

"Why?" Alura said.

"Because that's what it knows," Lancelot said. "The mind knows nothing of the Grail or of experiences beyond the Grail. It only knows the world it's seen. Its thoughts revolve about this world as a means to an end."

Alura pushed her hair back with her hand. "Isn't that what it's supposed to do?"

"No. When Percival and I were young, we and all the other knights went here and there because our minds said, 'Go this way. Go that way.' Never did it lead us to the Grail. It couldn't. It can't know about where it has never been."

The pebbles pressing into the soles of his feet were beginning to distract him. He tried to concentrate on Lancelot's words.

"As the sun rises and moves across the sky, we can see time on a sundial."

"'cept when it's cloudy," Frith said.

"Does our mind stop measuring time when it's overcast?" Lancelot said. "I don't think so."

Frith scratched his head. He admitted that was true.

"Your consciousness is like the sun, powerful and full of light. Where you shine it, things grow."

Frith looked at Alura. He could see that she was as puzzled by Lancelot's analogy as he was.

"I'm the sun?" Alura said.

"No, you are one with God. But just as the sun is necessary for plants to grow, your attention is necessary for your thoughts to grow. Your consciousness is the source of life for the mind. Because you give attention to certain thoughts they appear stronger, but that strength is derived only from your dwelling on them."

"Wait," Frith said. "Back up a little. You said 'you are one with God!'"

Lancelot waved his hand in a dismissive gesture. "Ignore that. You'll know that when you know it."

How could he ignore it? Creatures of dust one with God? That was blasphemy.

"It all becomes one when it is one to you," Lancelot said.

"One to me?" Frith said.

"Everything is already in oneness. It becomes one to you when you have no preferences to distract you."

"No preferences?" Alura said.

"I know that's hard for you to hear, but your likes and dislikes have created a... a diseased state in your mind. When you become capable of just observing the opposing forces in your mind, you will transcend them."

"I still don't understand what you mean about being one…" Frith said.

"The river and the ocean do not become the same thing when they meet. They are already part of the whole, the one. The ocean becomes the clouds, the clouds become rain, the rain becomes the river, and the river flows to the ocean," Lancelot said.

"I see," Frith said, but he didn't really. It felt as if the ground where he stood was no longer solid. "But what becomes of us when that happens? When we... flow into the sea."

"It's not that you're not still here, but the way you used to see yourself is different. Once, your self-concept fit in a tiny chalice. After you see, then what you are expands beyond even the Grail."

Frith wished he understood. But Lancelot just pressed on. "While you're engaged in mind, you are not seeing the world."

"I'm seeing the world, how am I not seeing the world?"

"You are seeing your thoughts about the world. When you let that kind of thinking go, the world will look very different. You will begin to see everything and everyone as a manifestation of the underlying spirit. When you are in that spirit, you will see the world as it is. That is seeing the Grail."

"You can show us." Alura said.

She sounded so confident that Frith worried for his own ability to see the Grail. What if she got it before he did? No, what would Lancelot think about him for thinking those kind of thoughts?

"The Grail will not be yours because I show it to you, but because you found it for yourself. On that Pentecost long ago, everyone at the banquet had a vision of the Grail, but only because we shared Galahad's experience. When I had my fourth experience of the Grail, it transformed me in ways that the earlier experiences didn't because it was my own."

Frith struggled to understand what Lancelot was talking about. "Can you better describe the actual experience? What's going to happen? What should I look for?"

"The mind changes; you discover that you are not who your thoughts said you were. The heart that was heretofore discontent becomes still. You are filled with ecstasy and know peace."

Frith looked at Alura. She was nodding like she understood. Perhaps when they were alone, she would explain it to him.

Chapter 27

Frith smiled politely and nodded as Alura and the Lady went on and on about the way women dress in some foreign land. Frith contemplated their good fortune. They were dining with nobility. Too bad no one would know it – the banquet hall was empty except for the four of them.

He had met them because he got hungry before supper. He often did. He had lifted a bit of bread and stew from the kitchen and came into the hall assuming it would be empty. Instead he had found Alura sitting with two well-dressed pilgrims.

"Oh, here is my brother," Alura said when she saw him.

His initial reaction had been to grab her and politely bow his way out. He wasn't certain she was permitted to sit with guests. He had never seen any of the other cooks do it, and he didn't want any trouble from the Abbot.

"Frith, come meet two very important guests – his Lordship and his Lady."

Frith bowed courteously to the Lord. "I am Frith, the Abbot's aide."

His Lordship nodded, but did not offer his surname or his kingdom. Odd. However, he had invited Frith to join them, and the four of them had been conversing as though they were equals ever since. It was an honor he had never imagined.

His Lordship looked bored. "We're just back from Egypt. Have you ever been?"

Frith shook his head no. He had barely been outside the walls of St. Benignus. Egypt seemed distant beyond his imagination.

"Saw the pyramids—"

If there was one thing Lancelot had taught him, it was to not pretend he understood when he didn't. "Forgive me, my Lord, but what's a pyramid?"

"Magnificent structures, shaped like this." His Lordship put his finger tips together in the shape of a triangle and stood his hands upright on the table. "Larger than your whole cathedral."

"St. Benignus must seem pretty humble to you," Frith said.

"Not at all," her Ladyship said. "Your abbot has created a fine, cozy refuge for pilgrims such as us."

"How long will you be staying?" Alura said. "I am sure the Abbot will hold a banquet in your honor."

"Not that long," his Lordship said.

Alura looked disappointed.

"Unfortunately, we have a place where we must be," her Ladyship said.

His Lordship gave her a sharp look, as if she had said too much. "But please give my compliments to the Abbot on our fine accommodations and excellent food. They are far more luxurious than a pilgrim should expect."

"I certainly shall," Frith said.

"Also let him know I shall make a most generous donation to continue the good works of his place."

"That will be much appreciated."

"Only our Christian duty."

"I must ask," Frith said. "There seemed to be something left unsaid earlier …"

Frith saw the Lord give his wife a nervous look. "You're very perceptive, young man." His Lordship hesitated. "It's just that we're going on to another… shrine. I wasn't going to mention it. Now, I'm afraid my wife has embarrassed us."

"Don't be," Alura said. "Many travelers only stop here for a night or two. May I ask your destination?"

"Sarum," her Ladyship said.

Frith's hand jerked involuntarily, spilling Alura's water. "Won't that be dangerous? I heard those were pagan lands."

"There is a Christian church at Sarum," his Lordship said. "We'll be safe there."

Alura wiped up the water with her sleeve.

"I don't know of a shrine there," Frith said. "Is it a Holy place?"

"The sacred site is actually a half day north of there," her Ladyship said.

Frith noticed the Lord looked even more perturbed by his wife's response. Maybe they should talk about something else. "Forgive our questions. Alura and I've never traveled 'cept once from Father's farm to the abbey. Is it far?"

"It's not that far, maybe a fortnight on foot or a week by horse," his Lordship said.

"Then what's the hurry?" Alura said. "Delay and sample my cooking."

"You're so sweet," her Ladyship said. "But we absolutely can't. We have to be there on the—"

The Lord slapped the table with his hand and gave her a hard look. She stopped mid-sentence and looked away. There was an awkward silence all around.

"Tell us more about Egypt," Alura said. "Frith spoke the truth, we've never been anywhere."

"Well my husband is much interested in studying observations of the sun," she said. "So we went there because it was one of the first civilizations to make a study of it."

"Yes," his Lordship said. "The early Egyptians believed the sun was a god who got into his boat every morning and floated across the sky. Of course we know better now."

"That sounds suspiciously like the old religion," Frith said.

"It's important to honor the yearly path of the sun," his Lordship said. "Is the sun not the most important thing in the natural world? Did we not find that out when it failed? These days, people depend on feast days and the celebrations of our Saints to know the time of year. But for our ancestors, it was essential to know the path of the sun to know the times to plant and harvest."

"Frith and I never learned much about that," Alura said. "I'm sure my brothers and sisters know what you're talking about, but would you mind explaining?"

The Lord answered Frith instead. "Though the sun rises in the east and sets in the west, each day the point at which it rises shifts slightly northward. It rises at the northern-most point on our summer solstice. Then it begins to shift southward again until it reaches its southernmost point –that is our winter."

After all these weeks of watching Lancelot treat them both equally, it was a little strange. Apparently this Lord thought there was no point explaining things to a woman.

"The word solstice is Latin," his Lordship added. "It means 'the sun stands still.'"

Frith felt the latest two letters pressing into his soles – L and M, for 'Lex' and 'Mater.'

"Frith is learning Latin," Alura said.

"I should hope so," the Lord said. "At the winter solstice, we have our darkest day of winter; on the summer solstice, we celebrate the longest day of summer. The equinoxes divide the day and night equally—"

"We're approaching the autumnal equinox soon," her Ladyship said.

This time the Lord gave her a small smile. "Can you keep a confidence?"

Frith and Alura both nodded. This Lord didn't know the half of it.

His Lordship glanced at his wife and she gave him an encouraging smile. "Our actual destination is Stonehenge."

"Stonehenge?" Frith said.

"Shhh, keep your voice down," his Lordship said. "During the solstice, the sun lines up directly with the gaps in the stones of Stonehenge. We intend to be there to see if it aligns with other stones at the equinox."

"But isn't that still the place of pagan rites?" Frith whispered. "Won't the equinox, of all days, be a procession of heathen worship?"

"It's a most important time of the Mysteries," his Lordship said.

This Lord and Lady seemed to have broader minds, be open to bigger ideas, than the people around the abbey. "Perhaps the time for mysteries to be fulfilled is at hand?"

Frith burned to tell them he knew one who knew the Grail, but he couldn't. He wanted to tell them that they didn't have to go all the way to Stonehenge, because salvation was only a short walk away, but he dared not. But one thing he could do was imitate Lancelot. "Imagine that you are the sun. That our consciousness is like the light rays. Beams of light shine on the objects of which you are aware—"

"You are a lad profound beyond your years," his Lordship said. "Who has taught you?"

Frith almost told him, but held his tongue. He felt pleased and a little surprised that he was doing so well. "But between the sun and the objects on which it shines, something has arisen, created by those rays, just as clouds block the sun from the earth."

"Yes!" his Lordship said.

"We may fancy there are figures in the shape of the clouds, yet when it rains the clouds dissolve. And when the rain is done and the clouds are gone, the sun rays shine without obstruction." Lancelot would be proud of him.

"Exactly what has happened in recent years!" his Lordship said. "Betrayal by those two villains nearly wiped out the sun. Now that whore is dead and her lover hiding somewhere in shame, the clouds have dissipated."

Oh. They were not talking about the same thing.

"Who?" Alura said.

"Why Guinevere and Lancelot," his Lordship said. "Arthur was too kind and it cost us all. If one of my knights cuckolded me, I'd slit him from scrotum to Adam's apple." He made an upward gesture with an imaginary blade.

"I would never—" her Ladyship said quickly.

"I know that," his Lordship said.

Frith pressed his lips together until they turned white. Alura balled her fists in her lap, her arms quivering with tension.

Apparently this Lord could not see well, for the Lord continued as if they weren't holding back their words like the mill dam.

"Though we are goodly in our Christian practice," his Lordship said. "We think the disasters of recent years have shown that we should not completely neglect the rituals of our ancestors."

"You don't mean pagan worship?" Frith said.

His Lordship looked at the ceiling. "Let us just say our interest in the autumnal equinox at Stonehenge is more than philosophical."

"But shouldn't a peer of Arthur be seeking the Grail?" Frith said.

"I judge that you are only recently a man, without benefit of our experience," his Lordship said.

Frith resented his patronizing tone. And, surprisingly enough, watched himself resenting.

"We remember the heights of Camelot and the darkness following its collapse," his Lordship said. "There are forces in nature – gods, if you will – that should not have been disrespected. There can be no harm in honoring them…" His Lordship glanced furtively around them. "…Though you can't repeat that around here."

Her Ladyship touched Alura's hand. "Just as in spring we worship the coming of new life, in autumn we give thanks for the bounty, and pay our respects to the impending dark."

"But I've heard that Sir Galahad, upon realizing the Grail, became one with God," Alura said.

"Never met the man," his Lordship snapped.

"Isn't it a higher purpose to quest for the source of one's own being, than to follow the sun from season to season?" Alura said.

"I see you are a grown woman, but very immature in your thinking." His Lordship idly tasted the remnant of his soup and pushed it away. "Bah—cold."

"Shall I bring you some hot?" Alura said.

"No, I think we have eaten enough and said too much." He stood up and his Lady rose with him. "Frith, can your sister keep our confidences?"

"I can," Alura said.

The Lord ignored her and waited for Frith.

"Better than you can imagine," Frith said.

CHAPTER 28

The next day Frith hobbled into Lancelot's garden on tender feet. Alura was already there. Able to move more quickly, she had dashed ahead of him. He immediately sat on the bench without waiting to be invited. "I think I must discontinue the study of Latin. It interferes too much with my duties."

"Giving up already?" Lancelot said. "You have but five days to go. Shall I remove my footwear and show you the calluses of many quests? Remove my shirt and show you the scars of many battles?"

Frith looked down at the ground sheepishly.

"There are painful experiences that are worth something, and there are painful memories that are worth nothing," Lancelot said. "Go through that which you must go through to reach a worthwhile knowledge. Let go of that which you have been through. Do not forget its lesson, but do not treasure the pain."

"I'm sorry, sir. Please draw for me the next two letters."

Lancelot picked up a stick and made marks in the sand. "N for 'novus' – new. And O for 'oculus' – eye. This type of learning will do you no harm. When you're attentive to the machinations of your mind that I've been speaking against, you'll see that for everything that happens your mind has an opinion about it... Doesn't it?"

Frith stooped down and began collecting pebbles. He took off his shoes and arranged the pebbles to match the letters Lancelot had drawn. "It does, sir. I have been seeing it. In snatches from time to time, but more and more often."

"The mind is full of all manner of views, opinions, desires and fears that you have accumulated," Lancelot said. "Why did they accumulate? Because you dwelt on them. If a stray dog comes, can you make it leave by feeding it? If you wash it and pet it, it will surely not go away."

Frith put his shoes back on. He winced when he stood up. 'Novus oculus,' the new eye.

"Our minds are full of pettiness because we hold on to those petty likes and dislikes. Like clouds, they obscure us from true perception. If you do not engage them, you will cease to hold them. They'll drift away on their own and that which is obscuring your view of true knowledge diminishes."

"But I haven't the willpower to stop it," Frith said.

"You have the willpower to endure stones in your shoes," Lancelot said. "Don't underestimate your will."

Frith looked pleased.

"While you can't use will to stop thoughts – they do not obey your will – you can will yourself to just let the thoughts pass."

"I'm trying, sir. I just don't understand how."

"No? Well… Have you noticed that when someone is upset you can't get them to listen until they've had their say? For example, if Alura wants to talk about something that distresses her, then there is no point in trying to do anything else until she's spoken her piece. Isn't that so?"

Frith nodded.

"Now if what's a crisis for her isn't an issue for you, then you can listen to her without being drawn into her drama, because it has no effect on you."

"Because it's her problem, not mine."

"Exactly. Now, take the same attitude while watching your own thoughts. Your worrisome self might still talk about something, but let it talk without being drawn into it, and you are freed from it. You only have to be willing to let it come and go. You're not trying to stop it, but not acting upon it either."

Frith stood first on one foot, and then on the other – novus, oculus – and finally sat back down on the ground and looked up at Lancelot. "So then what happens?"

"What happens is that you become the witness rather than the thoughts. Thoughts come and go, emotions come and go, events come and go, but you don't come and go with them. You're watching it all, but you're neither taken in by it, nor taken away with it."

"I never get taken," Alura said.

"Don't pretend that you are not following your mind when it tells you, 'I need this. I need to avoid that.' I've seen you do it, and I know you've seen it in your meditations as well."

"Sorry," Alura said. "I was making a poor joke."

"I don't think you were joking, but—"

Frith squirmed and changed the way he was seated. "Can't you give us some actual instruction?"

"You find yourself by not being drawn out of your self," Lancelot said. "It's just a question of your willingness to watch under different circumstances. The things you go through will help you let go, unless you resist."

"You don't think I am resisting?" Alura said.

Frith stood up and got between them.

"I think we keep thoughts of what we fear because we resist them instead of letting them pass by," Lancelot said. "Remember the day we went to the river? How my foot acted like a dam when I stepped in the water? Don't step in it and leaves won't gather around you."

Alura gently nudged Frith out of her way. "What if it's something you are not afraid of? What if it's something you want?"

"Wants have the same effect on your mind as fears. Stop resisting the fact that you don't have something, and it will stop bothering you."

"Because you aren't trying to get anything from it?" Alura said.

Lancelot nodded. "Most people don't realize they have a choice about how to live their life, but they do."

"That may be true for knights and nobility, but we who live at the other end of society don't have much choice," Frith said.

"In the subject I am discussing, neither do the nobility. People don't realize they have a choice because they let themselves be surrounded by their problems and desires, and the nobility have as many of those as anyone else."

"Well, a single woman certainly doesn't have a choice," Alura said.

"Not choices about what work you do or whom you marry. But you have a choice about whether or not you're happy."

Alura stuck her lip out. "Easier if you're a man."

Lancelot shook his head. "For a moment I thought you understood."

"Too well," Alura said.

"Winning a tournament or even your lady's hand doesn't ensure happiness. Wanting to change your life by changing the world outside just makes you want. Wanting isn't good because it takes you out of the now. You are only ever happy now."

"I'll be happy when I'm married."

"You don't know that," Lancelot said. "But even so, when that happens it will be the now then, won't it?"

Alura looked confused.

"Live your life from a higher point of view. Understand that you are the soul inside. Everyone and everything outside are just experiences that you're witnessing. Be ecstatic on the inside, and it will make your life outside seem good."

A tear tracked down Alura's cheek. "But I feel so lost, so abandoned."

"Frith, I believe we're seeing your flaming swords." He lowered himself until he was meeting Alura, eye to eye. "Be brave. You're never lost or alone. That's not you. That's just the mind. It spends all of time trying to use everything and everyone to make itself not feel lost. And even when it gets what it wants, when everything is all right, it begins worrying that someday it might not be."

Alura looked away.

"Most people spend their entire lives with their consciousness drawn away from God by these thoughts and emotions. When that distraction stops; when consciousness remains watching from the place within; you find the Grail. When your consciousness remains there, you begin to see the source of consciousness instead of the objects of consciousness. You begin to discover why Christ said 'I and my Father are one.' That's what the Grail shows you. You can't know any of that when you are looking at the world. You can't know that when you are lost in your thoughts. You can't know that when you are caught in your emotions. You *will* know that when you're sitting in the place of the Grail."

"Are you going to show us the Grail?" Frith said.

"Someday," Lancelot said.

Chapter 29

"What progress are you making at watching your thoughts?"

They succeeded in escaping the abbey for Lancelot's hermitage for several weeks now, though it seemed like much longer than that.

"I am sometimes able to witness my mind thinking as you describe," Frith said. "But only briefly, then the state eludes me again."

Lancelot stroked his chin. "Are you taking some time each day to sit in silence, as the monks do?"

"I sit every day with the monks Sir, but there's no silence in my head."

"That is some progress then," Lancelot said.

"It is?"

"You have progressed in that you are able to distinguish that you are unquiet. A man will not work to get well until he knows he is sick or try to find his way unless he knows he is lost."

"Oh, I'm lost in my mind," Frith said. "But I don't know it until the chime to end meditation has sounded. Only then do I realize I've spent the whole hour wrapped up in my thoughts."

"But you have spent the hour trying," Lancelot said. "That's something. When you notice that the mind is busy liking and disliking, then at least you are noticing. When you're noticing, then you're not in the midst of it. Someday you'll realize you're transcendent of it and let it go."

Frith scratched his head.

"How about you, Alura? Are you also able to find some quiet time?"

"I do. Obviously I can't sit with the monks, but I try to spend some time in stillness each night before bed."

"And your results?"

"No better than Frith's," Alura said. "I can't stop my thoughts."

"I don't expect you to. You can never stop the mind, by thought or by force of will."

"But I can't see from outside while I am trapped within it," Frith said.

"You are not outside of it, it is outside of you," Lancelot said. "Let's try to give it something to think about that you can watch."

"Are you finally going to show us the Grail?" Alura said.

"When you're ready. But for now this'll help you become more aware. After a little practice each day you'll find that you see the world around you differently."

"Is this one of Merlin's secrets?" Frith said.

"No," Lancelot said. "It's an ancient technique, simple, but not Merlin's."

"But it's a secret?" Frith said.

"I've already said that you shouldn't discuss what transpires here with others, so in that sense it's a secret. But it's not a great secret. It's just a technique to quiet the mind. Now, let me show you how. Just sit down and close your eyes."

Frith and Alura sat with their eyes closed. Lancelot spoke slowly and calmly. "As you listen to my voice, relax and watch your breath move in and out of your body."

As he talked, he held his palms above their heads, as though giving a benediction. "Now watch your mind like you have been watching your breath. It's busy formulating opinions about what I'm saying. Don't stop it, but don't become involved in it. As you witness the thoughts and feelings form, keep your attention focused on the physical movement of the breath. If the mind drifts away to other things, gently guide it back to the movement of air in and out of your body—"

"At last, I've found my way back!"

Lancelot spun to find Sir Bedivere stumbling through the gate carrying a small bundle in his good hand. "And I did it without a guide... Fortunately, the path seemed a little clearer this time. I looked for the boy at the abbey, but he wasn't to be found..."

Lancelot was standing so that he blocked Bedivere from seeing Frith and Alura. However, the spell was broken. Lancelot leaned close to them and whispered "We'll continue this later."

When Lancelot moved, Bedivere spied Frith. "What ho, there's my guide. Frith, here you are – sitting so comfortable in this place you dread."

"Sir Bedivere!" Frith said.

Bedivere noticed Alura. "What goes on now? Frith, I thought you a monk. Are you sneaking off from the abbey with town girls now? Who is this lovely wench?"

"I'm not a monk, just the Abbot's aide, remember?"

"Then why are you here bothering this great noble knight?"

Lancelot stepped between them. "Bedivere, old friend, Frith is no bother and he no longer gives in to the superstitions that once made him fear this poor hermit. As for the young woman, she's not—"

"If she's not with Frith, then with you? Sir Lancelot, have you given up your hermitage?"

"Not in that way, sire," Alura said. "I'm in this company because Frith is my brother." She curtsied to him. "I do not yet have a man. But you have a noble presence."

Lancelot sighed, inwardly. Just when he had been making progress with Alura…

Bedivere bowed to her and then he said to Lancelot, "I caught a rabbit on the way. Shall we eat?"

"You go ahead."

"Not hungry?" Bedivere said.

"No, thanks, I had communion."

Bedivere gave Lancelot a quizzical look and offered the bundle to Alura. "Here girl, are you handy at cooking?"

Alura looked to Lancelot. "May I?"

Lancelot shrugged.

Alura took the package from Bedivere. "You've not tasted roasted hare like mine. When you sample it you might see you have two fine catches in one day." Alura dashed toward the well.

"What's that about?" Bedivere said.

"She wants to show you she would be a fine wife," Lancelot said.

Frith's face betrayed his jealousy and Sir Bedivere noticed. "What's got you, boy?"

"Nothing," Frith said. "I just thought that we should leave you to knights' business. But now it seems we're waiting on supper."

"No reason you can't return to the abbey, son. They're probably looking for you after my inquiries there."

Frith shot a glance at Lancelot. "No, I shan't leave Alura behind."

"A damsel can have no better protection than two Knights of the Round Table," Bedivere said.

Lancelot made a quick jerk of his head in the direction of the well.

"I better make her a fire," Frith said and ran after Alura.

"He's a good lad," Bedivere said. "We had a nice talk on our way back to the abbey last time. You said no one would follow you, but see you have recruited a man already. Now, what's been your mind while I was on the road?"

"I'm thinking of an experiment."

"Does it involve Knights of the Round Table?"

"Not that I know of. A tremendous current seems to be flowing through me like a river – all the time now. I've been wondering what would happen if that river bisected and became two waterfalls overflowing and spilling out."

"I see you're still speaking in riddles. I've never liked riddles. Have you given some thought to our last conversation?"

"About as much as I give to breakfast or dinner."

"Good at least that's something," Bedivere said. "If you would accommodate me, I'd like to spend the night here rather than go back to the abbey. I've a bedroll on my horse. If I could camp in your yard..."

"The earth belongs to God and his creatures. I've no objection to you sleeping out here."

"Good that'll give us time to sup and talk."

Lancelot shrugged and called for Frith, who came running. "Yes, Sir?"

"Sir Bedivere is going to camp here. Would you find some more wood and build him a fire?"

Frith nodded and started for the woods.

Bedivere stopped him. "How is dinner coming?" He sniffed the air. "Do I smell it already?"

"Already started sir. She found some wild onions. It should be good."

"Excellent. Go unsaddle my horse."

"Your horse?"

"Yes, I rode him here, but I forgot there wasn't a way for him to cross the river. He's tied just the other side of the fallen tree. You'll find a jug of mead in my pack; bring that as well as my bedroll. Sir Lancelot has declined to dine with me, but you and your sister can share my feast."

"It'd be an honor to eat with a knight."

Lancelot left them. "I am going to my meditations."

CHAPTER 30

Alura sat with Frith and Sir Bedivere sat on a blanket in front of the fire sipping from cups of mead. They had eaten well and refilled their cups from his jug many times as they talked. The mead made her feel loose and comfortable; less inhibited with Bedivere than sober decorum would have permitted.

"I perceive that this is not the first time Alura has visited here," Bedivere said.

Alura looked at her brother for a sign. Should they admit it? It seemed that their secret was known, at least to Sir Bedivere.

"Perhaps Lancelot has not one, but two followers?" Bedivere said.

"Frith and I would never abandon Lancelot," Alura said. "We both know the pain of being abandoned."

Her brother was more drunk and less cautious. "Can we tell you something in confidence as his friend?"

"Of course," Bedivere said.

Frith glanced left and right, as if someone in the woods might overhear. "Alura and I have witnessed certain phenomena in his presence..."

"Oh, that isn't new with Lancelot," Bedivere said. "There are many great feats our knight has done. In years past he managed to win jousts and battles while carrying on his spiritual quest. Now he seems unwilling to leave, content with much talk and little action."

"Then do you think he is ready to settle down?" Alura said.

"You mean take a wife?" Bedivere said. "I hope not. Britain has need of him as a knight."

"Many knights are wed," Alura said.

"Most, in fact. But I'm not sure he'll ever love again after Guinevere."

"Sir Lancelot has already told her as much," Frith said.

Alura winced. Frith didn't have to tell Bedivere everything.

"Pretty women have distracted Lancelot before," Bedivere said.

He thought she was pretty? Sir Lancelot may not want her, but Sir Bedivere may. He *was* very old, but he treated his weapons and armor with care, perhaps his wife would fare as well. "Sir, have you a wife?"

"Me? No, I've lost two already, one in childbirth and the other to illness."

"But shouldn't you like another companion in your life?"

"The road is no place for a wife," Bedivere said.

"Someone to cook your meals and mend you after your battles..."

Bedivere laughed. "What are you about? Would you tear off with the first knight who passes through?"

"Gladly."

"Isn't your life at the abbey?"

"Hardly! I'm not a nun."

Bedivere laughed again. "You're not a nun or you are not like a nun?"

"Oh I'm as pure as an old maid, but I don't want to be one. What I lack is a dowry, but you, sir, are a man of wealth, without need of one. If you would dispense with that custom, you'd find here a greater treasure."

"What bargain would that be for you?" Bedivere raised his bad arm. "See for yourself, I'm half gone, already."

"I'll bet you win battles, even with one hand," Frith said.

"I can still hold my own in a fight."

"Then let us hear of your travels and cease this talk about marriage," Frith said.

"Well, yes," Bedivere said. "I've just left six of my good fellows."

"Yes, tell us about them," Alura said. If Bedivere didn't take her, perhaps there would be a suitor among his peerage.

* * *

Frith was glad Alura had given in – he found her sudden talk of marriage disturbing, as if the work they had done with Lancelot meant nothing. Of course, he could feel his own desire to be a knight surfacing as well. He picked up the jug and handed it to Bedivere. Bedivere lubricated his throat with a bit of mead and began his story.

"I heard them long before I saw them, the racing hoof beats of chargers, the sound of lance striking armor, the clang of swords upon shields."

"A battle?" Frith said.

"No, there was cheering. These were knights at sport. There was no need for me to rush to anyone's aid."

"A tournament?" Alura said. "Were there many damsels?"

"Not a tournament and no damsels, just good knights at practice. You would be surprised how much work it takes just to keep your skills sharp."

Frith poked the fire with a stick and imagined what he would have seen had he been riding with Sir Bedivere.

"As I approached in the distance, they recognized me. 'Sir Bedivere!' they all shouted. Those who were mounted turned their steeds and raced to meet me. Those who had been engaged in swordplay sheathed their weapons and removed their helmets in anticipation of my arrival. All were glad to see me and I was glad to find them, for this was the largest group of knights I'd come upon since I left here.

"There were six of them. Four young athletic knights who looked quite fit, and two more seasoned knights, like myself. The older knights, Sir

Blamore and Sir Sagremore, had ridden with me in the days of Camelot. The four younger men, I'd known when they were squires. They'd been knighted since I last saw them. They were now Sir Briede, Sir Frioc, Sir Eadwyn, and Sir Wulfric."

Frith thought about young squires being knighted and tried to remember to observe his thoughts. It wasn't easy.

"Sir Blamore welcomed me and said, 'Stay for a while.' I was agreeable and Blamore's squire helped me dismount. We went to meet their Lord, who said he knew my reputation and bid me to bide with them, to eat and drink at his expense for so long as I'd like. I accepted his offer and settled into the knights' routine, jousting and swords in the day, drinking and stories by night."

"That sounds like a life I would like," Frith said.

"I had business with the knights, but I didn't rush the process. I realized that'd been my mistake with Lancelot. Instead I simply stayed with them for several days, complimenting them on their skills and reminding them of the old days before Camelot's fall."

"Tell me about the jousting and sword fights," Frith said.

"On the field, knights on horseback hurled at each other. The men on foot hewed at their opponents' helms and hauberks; their swords ringing as they struck chain mail."

"I thought they were friends," Alura said.

"Pushing a fellow knight to sharpen his skills may save his life someday. It is the act of a friend. And no one got seriously hurt. Victory was achieved by turning the flat of the blade and smiting the opponent with enough force to make him fall down. It would then be apparent who the victor was.

"After watching them for several days I concluded that these knights, while industrious in their practice, had no purpose for which they were preparing. The young ones did it just because that is what young men do with their time. The old men were doing it to prove they were still young. It was my intention to give them a mission.

"Slowly I introduced the idea of reuniting the Round Table, and they were much in favor of it. But when I proposed Sir Lancelot to lead them, Sir Sagremore objected. 'Why should we follow Lancelot? He was not fit to walk in King Arthur's slippers.'"

"'But he already slipper'd King Arthur's wife,' another knight said. They all laughed uproariously. 'All the more reason not to follow him,' Sagremore said."

"You allowed him to attack Lancelot's honor?" Frith said.

"And Guinevere's," Bedivere said. "Sagremore has always been quick to judge. I was offended, but I didn't draw on the man, for I was trying to persuade them. I told them, 'We all concur that Lancelot should have kept his dagger sheathed, but he is a monk now. I think Lancelot will have no more women in his life.'"

Frith saw Alura frown. He hoped she wasn't going to distract Bedivere from his story to argue Lancelot's celibacy.

"But Sagremore wouldn't be pacified," Bedivere said.

"The king should've slain Lancelot as well as Mordred, for both were equally false," Sagremore said.

"Untrue!" Bedivere said. "Lancelot wasn't even at the battle of Camlan."

"So a coward as well as a traitor!"

"Do not lay the blame on Lancelot. I was there," Bedivere said. "I begged King Arthur to hold his attack until Lancelot and his men arrived."

"But Sir Sagremore says it was Sir Lancelot's affair with the queen that caused Britain to go dark," Briede said.

"Lancelot says not."

"He would, wouldn't he?" Sagremore said.

"I've spent much time in travel since the fall of Camelot and perhaps you've not," Bedivere said. "Perhaps you've been mostly living off this Lord's largesse."

"We've been practicing diligently," Briede said.

"I'm not questioning your skills," Bedivere said. "I've seen you at your best. I'm questioning your knowledge. During my travels, I've met many foreigners who have given me to know that the twilight was not limited to our isle, but spread to every kingdom on earth."

"So?"

"You know Lancelot was no sorcerer. Then how do you think two people in Camelot could cause darkness that covered over the whole world?"

"Maybe the whole world is paying penance for their sins," Sagremore said.

"Lancelot took seven of his knights and entombed Queen Guinevere with her lawful husband at Glastonbury," Bedivere said. "Can we not let that matter be buried with her as well?"

"Indeed we should," Blamore said.

"You recall that, even though Lancelot was a sinner, Arthur called him the greatest knight in the world," Bedivere said. "I think we can all agree he was that. I assured Lancelot that you would remember his great feats and overlook his flaws."

"But those are praises of his distant past," Sagamore said. "What of him now?"

"He has put on the habit and withdrawn into holiness," Blamore said.

"Blamore, have you seen him too?" Bedivere said.

"I was of the seven who helped him bury Guinevere," Blamore said.

"Withdrawn or gone into hiding?" Sagremore said.

"Lancelot would hide from no man!" Bedivere said. "No, I tell you he has found the Holy Grail."

The men's eyes widened and their mouths fell open. "You have seen it?"

"I've seen him," Bedivere said. "Those among you who remember *that* Pentecost, know the effect that I mean. He has surely realized the Grail."

"That doesn't mean ordinary men will follow him," Sagremore said.

"I am not talking to ordinary men," Bedivere said. "I am seeking to restore the Round Table, but we'll need one such as him to bring men to it."

"I imagine he's willing…" Sagremore said.

"Well… not as willing as you might think," Bedivere said.

"But the Round Table numbered a hundred and fifty," Blamore said. "There are only six of us."

"I think fifty knights would be enough to convince him," Bedivere said. "I'm willing to travel, but the Knights of the Round Table are so dispersed. Where do you advise that I seek them next?"

"I think in most realms Lancelot has few friends left," Sagremore said.

"Sagremore, when Sir Gawain died, Lancelot paid for the mourners and the Mass of Requiem for that knight. With his own hand he dealt money for the wake. Had he not taken a vow of poverty now, you know he'd do the same for any knight here, even you."

"You're right," Blamore said, "But we're too few to make a difference."

"It's a start," Bedivere said. "What other knights would you recommend?"

"Sir Galihud!"

"Sir Galihodin!"

"Sir Bleoberis!"

"Sir Clarrus and Sir Gahalatine!"

"Don't forget Sir Bors de Ganis!"

"Certainly Bors," Bedivere said.

"That only makes thirteen, counting us and Sir Bedivere," Wulfric said.

"Sir Sagremore would make fourteen," Frioc said.

They all laughed. "I think that won Sagremore over," Bedivere said.

"Those knights are scattered," Blamore said. "It could take Sir Bedivere a week or more to reach each of them – eight weeks."

"It could be accomplished in a fortnight if you rode in pairs and each pair called on only two knights," Bedivere said.

"That will still yield only a handful," Sagremore said. "I have my doubts about this, and about Lancelot. But if you're in earnest, what you need is a tournament."

"A tournament?" Bedivere said.

"There must be many knights like us who miss the tournaments," Sagremore said. "Hunting, jousting, games of swordsmanship and archery, feasts given by kings and queens."

"Yes!" Blamore said. "That would draw knights in from all over Christendom. You can use the gathering to explain our mission and to recruit them."

"Yes, but it must be a grand tournament to draw the best knights," Sagremore said.

"If Lancelot were to enter, that would draw the best knights," Eadwyn said.

"Even those who dislike him?" Briede said.

"Of course," Wulfric said. "It would be their chance to defeat him."

"If Lancelot is truly to be our leader, he must join in." Eadwyn said.

"He might become tournament champion again!" Frioc said.

"There'd be no question as to his right to lead then," Eadwyn said.

"I don't want to dampen your enthusiasm," Bedivere said. "But I must caution you, Lancelot is different now – a holy man. He may choose not to joust."

"But surely he'll attend?" Frioc said.

"I'll do my best to convince him," Bedivere said.

"Just his presence will bring his friends and foes alike," Eadwyn said.

"And if he brought the Holy Grail! That would truly restore the Round Table," Frioc said.

"This is a great strategy," Blamore said.

"This is all well," Bedivere said. "But for now, I know not who could fund such a grand tournament."

"You've never been one to back down from a challenge," Blamore said.

"Not me. But before we have a tournament, we must find a nobleman to organize it. What of the Lord of this manor?"

"No, he has neither the status nor the money for such an enterprise," Blamore said.

"Then I believe we should follow the first plan," Bedivere said. "We should set out in pairs, seeking the knights you have named. Let's leave in the morning. I'll visit Sir Bors. Your men search out the remaining six. It will be a quest!"

"A quest for men of old," Blamore said.

"No," Bedivere said. "A quest for knights of all ages."

Frith was practically trembling with excitement when he saw the cottage door open. Lancelot stepped out and looked at the sky. Bedivere stopped his story and waved to him.

"Frith! Alura!" Lancelot said.

Alura immediately stood and curtsied. "Excuse me, sir."

"Alura," Bedivere said, "Don't seek for a husband in Lancelot. I have the greater need of him."

Alura ran to Lancelot. Frith took longer. He rose, felt his head float free for a moment – too much mead – stumbled, but eventually followed Alura.

"I see you did not go back to the abbey," Lancelot said.

Frith followed Lancelot's gaze upward. The orange glow of the sunset had faded to black. "Alura, we've overstayed curfew!"

"Sir, we can't get in at this hour," Alura said. "What should we do?"

"Well, a woman shouldn't sleep out in the woods, even with a knight. Alura can have my bed—"

"You know I'm willing."

"Not like that," Lancelot said. "I'll sleep on the floor. My cottage is very tiny, but we'll squeeze Frith in there as well."

Frith's mind was thick with mead. Should he stay with his sister and lose a chance at knighthood with Bedivere just when he seemed to be gaining favor with him? True, the other day he had committed to protect her honor... but so had Lancelot. In his heart Frith knew he could trust Lancelot with his sister. But she was another matter. She had become so daring as of late, it might be up to Lancelot to keep the code of chivalry.

Earlier Bedivere had said sleeping in the wild was a normal part of a knight's journey. He'd show Bedivere he was that brave, too. "Thank you, but I can sleep out by the fire. I'm as good a man as that knight."

"This is a question of honor, not valor," Lancelot said. "What would be said of your sister spending the night without a chaperone? Alura, take blankets from my bed and make pallets for Frith and me."

"But you'll be uncomfortable sir. I don't mind sharing..."

"This body's comfort does not matter. Go in now. Frith and I'll come back after you're situated."

Alura did as she was told and entered the cottage. Frith walked with Lancelot over to the fire. Bedivere had given up using a cup and now drank straight from the jug. "There you are! Man when you go to prayers … I thought you were going to meditate all night."

"It's happened before," Lancelot said.

"Did that girl just go into your room?"

"It wouldn't be chivalrous to have her sleep out here."

"But with you?"

"Separate," Lancelot said. "Frith'll be her chaperone. I'd offer you a place but the space is really too small for four—"

"Not necessary. Nowadays, I spend nearly as many nights outdoors as in. Now that I have you, let's talk of our plans."

"Your plans – I thought I made that plain."

Frith reassumed his seat next to Bedivere and took a sip from the jug. He didn't think Bedivere would mind. He'd seen him do it.

"I didn't find a lot of knights, but those I found are willing to help find others. Sir Bors told me there are knights near the Cornish coast. I'm headed there at first light."

"Before you chase after more knights let me remind you of what Christ's disciples reported after he had sent them out. Frith, can tell us…"

"That through the power he'd given them, they were able to heal the sick, drive out evil, and make the unknown known to the peoples they met," Frith said. He caught Bedivere's look of surprise and felt pleased with himself.

"Yes that is scripture," Bedivere said.

Frith sat up a little straighter and smiled smugly.

"We who were sent on the quest, what happens when we find the Grail?" Lancelot said.

"We are fulfilled," Bedivere said. "Not myself, but certainly Galahad, Percival, and now apparently you."

"What're we supposed to do with the powers when they come?" Lancelot said.

"What do you mean?"

"Does the church want us to pretend we are submissive to the Bishop, the same Bishop who wouldn't even ordain me?"

"Careful, this could go to heresy."

"Holy power pours off my fingertips. Am I just supposed to put my hands in my pockets?"

"I… don't know." Bedivere said.

"Well it must be for some purpose. How can I make you understand that I can't go back to a time when I rode from one quest to the next looking for what I've now already found?"

"But what're you doing for we who are still lost and haven't found the Grail?"

"I'm working, teaching a few individuals, one or two at a time."

"Meaning these two? You can't sit around telling stories to servants."

"Servants?" Frith said, slurring the word.

"You've got to regain the respect of men, become the toast of tournaments again," Bedivere said.

Frith saw Lancelot smile at him. "Oh, these two toast me well enough – sometimes with a bit too much wine. They give me respect enough."

"I'm talking about making the public respect you again," Bedivere said.

"I'm not interested," Lancelot said. "Men are always seeking the mundane. Like Frith here – he's always asking if I can make him a knight. Why doesn't he ask me if I can make him a God?"

Bedivere jumped up, bumping into Frith. "What'd you say? Are you playing at god?"

"I am not."

"Good, because, you don't want to get shunned."

"I'm already shunned."

"All right then," Bedivere said. "You don't want to get burned at the stake."

"You're right, I don't."

"So while you're being a saint for two servants, what of me?"

"Bedivere, why not just keep doing what you're doing? Find the knights, restore chivalry. It's not my calling, but it may be yours."

"Without you at our head?"

"The Round Table had no head. That was its secret."

Frith saw Bedivere brighten, as though a revelation had penetrated his drunkenness.

"Yes! It was, wasn't it?" Bedivere picked up the jug, raised it to Lancelot. "Let's have a drink."

"No, that is enough for one night." Lancelot turned to leave. "Come Frith, Alura's surely settled by now."

Frith stubbornly remained seated. "Sir Bedivere is willing to talk about that which you resist. I'll come shortly. Let me listen to a bit more of Sir Bedivere's adventures."

Lancelot shrugged and left.

When Lancelot was gone, Frith turned to Bedivere. "Sir Lancelot said he made Sir Galahad a knight. Can you make me a knight?"

"A knight is more than just a title bestowed for being a good servant."

"My father is landed, if that would sway you."

"It wouldn't. Knighthood requires skills and training. You cannot just jump into armor. You must develop yourself first. You have to start by service."

"I realize that, and I am willing," Frith said. "After all, why should I be a servant to an Abbot if I can ride in service to a knight?"

Bedivere laughed. "That's good. Here fill your cup and let me tell you about the time Bors and I were…"

CHAPTER 31

Alura couldn't believe she had been allowed in his room, the place where he actually slept. She stirred the embers in the fireplace and added wood until there was a small, cozy blaze. By its light, she looked around the room, touched his few possessions – the rocks surrounding the fire pit, the small stool, the flint and steel – with reverence. She touched his bed, the straw mattress with the scratchy blankets, with disbelief. She was about to sleep there.

She took the straw mattress from his bed, fluffed it, and prepared a pallet for him on the floor as he had instructed. If she would have had any sweet flower, heather or lavender, she would have spread them around his bed to scent it.

She made a smaller bed for Frith out of a couple of blankets. When she was finished, all that remained of the original bed were the rough boards that formed the platform and a wool blanket. She laid herself on them and pulled the blanket over her for cover. It was not terribly comfortable, but what did that matter?

Still, she felt unworthy. It should be her on the floor, sleeping at his feet.

Alura waited. In the darkness, she fantasized that the separate bed might be a ruse for Sir Bedivere's benefit. Perhaps in dark quiet of the night, he might come to lie with her in one bed as her father and mother did with each other. Then she worried that if he came to her, he would find the bed too hard, for she had stripped its comforts to make up his pallet. Never mind, he could lie on her. She would be the straw in his mattress.

She became aware of an extraordinary sensitivity in her breasts. As she breathed, each rise and fall caused the blanket to drag over her nipples. She became aware of a warm moistness in her loins and ached for him more than ever.

When she had lain in this sweet agony for some time, she heard a soft creak of the door and his footsteps as he quietly entered. In her stomach there was a knot as large as his fist, as surely as if he had reached inside her and clenched it.

He did not lie down straight away. Rather – her eyes had adjusted to the darkness by then – he sat cross-legged on his blanket like he did when he meditated. Alura's body fairly quivered. He was only a few feet from her. In the still air, she could feel the heat radiating from him and knew he could feel the same from her. Yet she was thwarted. She could not move to him, and could not manage to will him to her by wishing it so.

A spicy-sweet fragrant suffused the air, as though he had thrown incense upon the coals. She opened her eyes just a peek, but there was no priest waving a censer, no cloud of white smoke, just Lancelot sitting very still. She shut her eyes and thought of him.

After a time the room lit with a saffron glow. Too early for dawn – they had just retired, and she was sure she hadn't slept. The bright light behind her eyelids was too bright to be from the fire. Slowly she opened her eyes.

The room was unlit.

When she closed them again the brightness was still there.

She realized then that her nostrils had widened. It was as though each breath blew like a clear cold wind up into the cavities of her head. The movement of air in the hollowness was almost painful, like the first, sharp intake of breath when you step outside on a winter's day. There was a tremor in her. She could feel her body shake, not from cold but from anticipation.

She felt his closeness, and the intensity of feeling increased. She felt it swell until it was like he was on top of her – not physically, for he was still sitting on his own bed some feet away. But still, that was how she imagined it. She felt him pressing down upon her, at the same time lying beneath her and on each side of her. She felt... cloaked in his presence and offered no resistance, for this was exactly what she wanted.

Then his overbearing power pressed upon her so forcefully that she came undone.

She felt him begin to penetrate her and then suddenly explode through her as if he was about to come out her throat. And yet this was all in her mind, for he surely remained sitting on the folds of his blanket on the packed earth floor. She knew that.

But throughout her were rising waves of unending joy, a joy she could never have imagined before she met it face to face. She felt a force rise up from her tailbone; pass her womb, through her entrails to her heart. There, the waves of joy came together and formed a waterfall that poured out of her chest.

It was not the kind of waterfall that gently cascades down a rocky hillside, but the early-spring, snowmelt kind that flows hard and fast. Ever widening the passage from which it rushes, pounding away the unyielding rocks below with a roar. The sound of it overcame all the night sounds around her. The crackle of the fireplace, the katydids, the frogs, the loud voices of Frith and Sir Bedivere, all were drowned in the rushing waters.

The light behind her eyes pulsed in waves. Not like the flickers of candles in church, but the way sunlight bouncing off ripples in water casts circles of dancing light.

Her body began moving in spastic jerks. Her muscles vibrated faster and faster, beyond her control. She witnessed her body do all of this, but did nothing about it, as though she was noticing it with… with the detachment Lancelot was always lecturing about. A sharp shriek escaped her throat, then she hooted like an owl and then she began to laugh merrily. Yet none of these sounds were deliberate, they were just… happening as if another girl was in the room.

Then all was still. She saw a mountain, and light rays streamed upward from it. She tilted her eyes back and looked toward the sky. She saw stars, as if the cottage roof had no thatch, as if she were lying on her back in an open field. The night was thick with stars and she wondered how she came to be outside. Yet she could feel the bed against her back.

One star in particular seemed to steal her attention. As she began to focus upon it, the others did not fade, but lost their importance until it was as if they were not there. She found herself coming closer to it. Whether she was moving toward it or the sky were coming nearer to her, she could not tell. Whichever it was, the effect was that the star became more dominant. It was all she saw and all she cared to see, so much so that a circle began to glow around the edges. The effect reminded her of when she looked at the sun and then looked away; how the sun's bright circle appeared everywhere she looked.

She heard a faint humming sound to their right. It began to form into a rhythmic rise and fall, like the sounds of the monks chanting. Had the night passed already? Was it the hour of prime, when they would be in the cathedral? No? Perhaps it was a holy day on which they would start to chant at Lauds. She couldn't recollect a saint that would have a day this month, and she couldn't make any words out of the droning sound.

As she pondered these questions, the star faded and with it, the humming sound. They disappeared so slowly, like a tree in the mist, which Alura didn't notice until they were gone.

She was caught up in trying to figure what day it was and if it was time for them to sneak back into the abbey. Perhaps they could go to the front gate and slip in when it was opened for Mass. They could mingle with parishioners making their morning devotions at that hour. Or maybe there would be pilgrims. Pilgrims occasionally arrived in the night and slept against the gate, waiting to gain admission at first light. She and Frith could enter secretly as if they were pilgrims.

She realized that she had no idea if it was still night or if the morning was at hand. From where she lay, there was no way to tell. She had heard no rooster crow, but then again Lancelot had no rooster.

If she could go out and look at the night sky, maybe she could discern the hour. She could make a pretense of going out to pee, take a quick look and steal back in. But she was afraid any movement would disturb the master. He was after all, only a few feet away. Going outside was out of the question.

But... she didn't have to pretend. Now she really did have to pee. The dilemma of disturbing him confronted her. So she settled on trying to hold it. But the more she tried to contain it, the stronger she felt the urge.

She really didn't want to leave, but when she made up the beds, she had taken no notice of a chamber pot. Not that she would dare use one in his presence. No, if she must void, she must expose her naked bottom to the night chill outdoors. That was a complication, for her brother and Sir Bedivere were out there, as well.

Wait. Frith and Bedivere were out there. Frith hadn't come to bed. It could not yet be late. All that had just transpired must have occurred in the briefest of time. She had the whole night left to spend in Lancelot's company, and she realized she really didn't have to pee after all. It was only thinking on it had made it seem so. He would probably find a lesson in that.

She opened her eyes briefly and saw him. A light around Lancelot reminded her of the shiny little rainbows on the surface of soap bubbles that floated off a wash tub into the sun.

She closed her eyes. She could feel him so clearly it was as if he were only a hairbreadth away. She could feel his pulse and she worried that he could feel hers. She hesitated to turn over or even move. She felt they were so interconnected that surely any move she made would alert him that she lay awake.

She heard Lancelot shift into a deep, slow, regular breathing, rhythmically like the waves of the sea. As the waves moved they moved over her, up and down, up and down, wave up on wave of ecstasy flowed through her.

She felt the weight of the wool blanket upon her and drifted off into its warmth, thinking, this is his blanket. Lying under it was a holy experience. She felt enwrapped in his holiness. Soon, she was the boat upon his sea and she rode him. Ocean currents coursed through her and she could not be sure if she was awake or in a dream or if that even mattered.

* * *

Lancelot had entered the cottage and in the dim firelight, he saw her lying stiffly on the bed, obviously awake and pretending otherwise. The tension between them crackled. For a moment, he was tempted to go to her... but no.

His feet brushed against something soft on the floor. He looked down and saw the pallet she had made for him. He sensed the loving care she had taken making it, that she had given him the best blanket and kept the thin one for herself. He removed his sandals, brushed the dust from his feet and sat down. He began to meditate, to go deeper and deeper inside.

Almost immediately he found the place of the Grail. As he encountered it he was surrounded by a deep clear blue light that emanated from the Grail within him. The light filled the room, but as it extended further from him it was refracted into different colors – waves of color, though as he had told Frith, he had no interest in phenomenon.

Lancelot felt Alura nearby. He sensed her state, but could not read her thoughts. Though he focused only on the Grail, in his periphery he could see Alura's light, many hues over a background of greenish-brown. At her midriff were flashes of sanguinary red.

While he was aware of Alura and her feelings, he was himself caught in a flow of energy so appealing that he was not much distracted. Not that he ceased to be aware of his surroundings. But there were so many other facets to explore.

As the stars themselves are separated by the darkness surrounding them, every atom that floated before him was separated by a subtler, inconceivably fine essence. This fineness was intermingled with the quintessence of thoughts, like the Milky Way clouds some stars, but it also illuminated the dark space between them.

Lancelot looked beyond the Grail, which itself was only a reflective instrument, like a still lake on a clear night that reflects the entire sky. Although it reflected the entire universe of stars, it did not contain any of them. It was, in fact, indifferent to the objects it reflected. He saw, interpenetrating all of the layers of creation, the light from a different star, one he could see just beyond the Grail.

The dark, clear blue light Lancelot saw around him became lighter, and then a touch of pale violet appeared. The light blue became a luminous lilac-blue. A golden sphere and then a white star appeared.

Peripherally, he noticed a saffron-colored light began to overtake Alura and brighten. The light around her became more yellow and then a deep orange. Near her heart it became the color of a crimson rose. It seemed Alura was being shown a pageant, though not of his doing. Lancelot vowed to make no effort to enlighten or affect what she was seeing. Let God show her what He would.

A ray of violet light descended into the room. The illumination around Alura became a lovely rose color, tinged with lilac and Lancelot heard the sound of rushing waters. Perhaps she was seeing the Grail indirectly as he had with Galahad.

Although he had just vowed not to intervene, he could not quite leave her alone. With an act of volition, his energy reached out and pushed hers. She emitted a sharp piercing cry, then animal sounds, finally peals of laughter. He fully expected Frith and Bedivere to burst in the door, but no one came.

Lancelot could find no justification for his meddling. He was in daily life, ever aware of the invisible, directing and accomplishing work through him. God was the only reality, transcendent – both the creator and the created, the savior and the saved. She could see or not see the divinity in her own body; that was not up to him. So why had he pushed? Had he yielded to temptation or had she pulled it from him? He couldn't tell.

The sounds of rushing water became a hum, the sound of a thousand monks chanting a continuous Amen. Each syllable blended into the next. Lancelot pleasured in it deeply and was only vaguely cognizant that the light above Alura's head had become a deeper yellow. Pale shades of diverse colors that previously surrounded her returned.

When his meditation was finished, Lancelot bowed deeply in prayer. After the *nunc dimitis* and *paternoster*, he pulled back a fold of the comforter and lay between the two halves. Alert to her presence only a few feet away, he sensed a taut force connecting them. Unable to shake it, he entered into a deep rhythmic breathing that quieted her.

What Lancelot did for the rest of the night could not fairly be called sleep. He just breathed slow, regular breaths, keeping his mind and body calm. When he felt the approach of morning, he got up quietly and went outside to meditate away from her. As soon as he was gone, Alura fell into a deeper slumber and remained therein for a long time.

CHAPTER 32

Frith was vaguely aware he was snuggled against Bedivere, who was rolled up in his blanket. It was warm by Bedivere – last night's fire was only a circle of cold ash.

Frith opened his eyes to find Lancelot standing over them. He felt Bedivere sit up abruptly.

"First light has come and I have missed leaving," Bedivere said in a groggy voice.

"I didn't want to wake you until I finished my prayers," Lancelot said. "You two looked like a cozy pair."

Bedivere pushed Frith away. "Wake up, son. You're weighing on my blanket."

Frith sat up and looked at Bedivere. The old knight was certainly grumpy in the morning.

"Sir Bedivere should go now," Lancelot said. "I'm off to morning Mass."

Bedivere hurriedly rolled up his bed roll. "No matter, I'm late to start but always ready to ride." Bedivere scooped up the rest of his belongings with the long-practiced maneuver of someone who had traveled much of his life. "I'll walk with you as far as my horse."

"Not to confession?"

"Not to church... I told you last night, I'm going the other direction."

Lancelot turned to Frith. "She still sleeps. Keep here until my return."

"But Master, Sir Bedivere asked for me at the abbey yesterday. Our absence has surely been noticed by now."

"I'll make some explanation about it to the Abbot," Lancelot said. "Watch over Alura."

"I shall. I'll keep guard, sir."

"Out here, Frith."

"Of course sir." Frith went to the door and stood stiffly, like a soldier.

Bedivere and Lancelot exited through the gate, and Frith watched until he could see them no more. It was nearly an hour before she came out, but he did as he had promised. A knight would do no less… he was beginning to learn…

Alura came out and looked around. She turned nearly a full circle before she saw him. "Good morning, sweet brother. Where are the others?"

"Lancelot to early Mass and Sir Bedivere to the Cornish coast."

She rearranged her disheveled clothes and straightened the tangles from her hair with her fingers. "Sir Bedivere left? I hoped—"

"Alura!" Frith said. "You're like a flea leaping from one dog to the next."

"My only way out is to ride the first dog that passes. You know that."

"But an old dog? With one hand?"

"Not anymore, but I wanted to—"

"What about me? While you were flirting with Sir Bedivere did you consider my needs?"

"—talk with him further about—"

"I could be a knight's squire—"

"Stop, stop, stop," she said. "We can't have two conversations at once."

She had a point. He fell silent and let her take the lead.

"I wanted to tell Sir Bedivere about last night," she said. "A wonderful thing happened. That which we once felt pour from his palms, I felt from his whole being."

"You're talking about Sir Lancelot now?"

"Ohhh yesss! Lying in his bed... I could feel him flow through my whole body and I was fulfilled."

"What? Last night you were offering yourself to Sir Bedivere; today you're back on Lancelot. You're not a flea; you're a dog in heat."

"I'm sorry. I can't help it," Alura said. "I don't have the freedom to run off. I have to bait the line and wait to be taken."

Frith stalked away. He stopped and spun back. "Well, keep it up, and the only purse you have for a dowry will be taken."

"Or freely given."

"What's that supposed to mean?" Frith knew she was trying to goad him, but that didn't stop it from working.

"You can just leave, ride off with a knight, be his squire. My only way out of the abbey is as a wife or a lover."

"Don't even joke!"

"You know I'd choose to be a wife more than anything. But that choice may not be open to me. I'm just trying to make you see a woman's dilemma."

"Well, I don't want any man's hands on you. Sir Lancelot said to me the other day that it is our chivalrous duty to keep your virtue."

"That's a strange charge for him to give."

Frith raised his eyebrows.

Alura took his face in soft hands, and looked into his eyes. "Frith, you know that one day you will have to let me go, for it is my dearest wish to find love."

It made him squirm. He felt all mixed up. Her holding him like that reminded him of home, and he liked it. At the same time it made him uncomfortable. He pulled her hands from his face, but kept hold of them. "You dream about love, but you're too young to know love... We both are."

"Oh, I'm more knowledgeable in love than you know."

What did she mean by that?

Before he could ask, Lancelot appeared behind her. "Frith, there is no one so young or so weak that their love isn't a strong force within them."

Frith let go of Alura's hands. "You're back, sir!"

"Consider the newborn. They are incapable of almost every act of self-sufficiency, yet their love is so strong as to touch the heart of everyone who comes into their presence. Some may think the mother teaches her baby love, but ask any mother, and she'll say she learned love from her first born. So you see, Alura's age has nothing to do with her capacity to love."

His sister looked happy with that, and Frith was just relieved the argument was over. "How much trouble are we in at the abbey?"

"Oh, none. I had quite an… imaginative conversation with the Abbot. I told him about Sir Bedivere's plan to reorganize the Knights of the Round Table. I said that to properly host him, I had to borrow a cook and a servant."

"He was all right with us being gone?"

"He was a little put out that I didn't ask his permission beforehand, but at least he doesn't think you spent last night in sin." Lancelot gave Alura a look.

"Certainly not," Frith said.

"Nevertheless, the two of you did put Alura's reputation at great risk."

"How so?" Alura said.

"By staying out all night. You have no idea how quickly vicious lies can spread."

"But the Abbot believed you," Alura said. "Didn't he?"

"He did. And it was a kind of truth. Bedivere did arrive unexpectedly. You did cook and serve."

"But we haven't returned," Frith said.

"I may have neglected to say if Bedivere had left yet."

Frith grinned at him and Alura giggled with delight.

CHAPTER 33

"Settle down now," Lancelot said. "We started something before Sir Bedivere came. I thought his interruption unfortunate, but last night has given me time for further meditation. I've decided to take you into the most intimate, sacred relationship."

Frith literally heard Alura purr. She sounded like a cat whose happiest wish had just been granted. Sometimes girls were just disgusting.

"Get your awareness out of your dreams," Lancelot said. "This is a serious decision for both of you."

Good. Maybe Lancelot could talk some sense into— Wait. What decision?

"I've decided this day to initiate you, to make you disciples."

"Disciples?" Alura said.

"Yes, with your coming, I see that my months of meditation and solitude have ended. It's no happy accident that you two persist in coming here, but rather that you were chosen for great things."

"Great things? Me?" Frith said. Perhaps Bedivere had changed Lancelot's mind about training him.

"Yes, I believe that," Lancelot said. "There are three kinds of men who hear of the Grail: the great, the sincere, and the fool. The greatest knight disregards all else and pursues it until he finds it. Such was Galahad. The sincere knight disregards his previous failures and remounts his quest each day anew. Such was Percival. The fool disbelieves of the Grail and scoffs at those who pursue it. You have become the sincere man."

Oh, this was about the Grail. Well he was ready for that, too. Frith nodded.

"And woman?" Alura said.

"Of course, I meant both of you," Lancelot said. "I'm going to show you a path, but you must follow that path as your own quest until you are fulfilled."

"Will the Abbot let us go?" Alura said.

"Not if you tell him."

"But he will know we are gone," Frith said.

"The path to God is not through Britain or Gaul, but through here." Lancelot pointed to his chest. "Beyond the heart." He touched his head. "Beyond the mind."

"But how'll you go with us?" Alura said.

"I am going to enter in you and awaken the Holy Spirit. She will lead you."

Frith gave Alura a wary look.

Lancelot caught his eye. "Look I'm not going to force myself on you. I haven't been pursuing you; you've been chasing me. If you decide to follow me in the quest, then you have to commit your whole self. No using the quest to get something less, like a knighthood or a husband."

"What will it… be like?" Frith said.

"Like being baptized and married and buried, all at once."

"Married?" Alura said.

"Only in a spiritual sense," Lancelot said.

But that wasn't the one that stood out for Frith. "Buried?"

"Once you know truth, your half-beliefs will be dead to you."

"Like 'know the truth and the truth shall set you free'?" Frith said.

"I see you've learned something," Lancelot said. "But here's the appropriate scripture 'If thy eye be single, thy whole body shall be filled with light.'" Lancelot looked at each of them. "I can't decide for you."

Frith looked at Alura and she nodded. He answered as she did and it came out in unison, "Show us the way."

"Yes. I'm going to show you the path your inner force follows by awakening it in you. Before we begin, you must commit to follow the teachings until the end. You can't find the Grail by following them halfway. Oh, and you must vow to keep them secret."

Finally, he was going to learn something.

"I've hidden what is going on here from the Abbot, and I've shamed Bedivere into running away. Now you must do your part. Never tell anyone what is about to transpire and never attempt to teach this to others."

They'd already held their tongue with the two noble pilgrims – of course he hadn't told Lancelot about them. "On my honor, we have kept our secret, sir. Why do you remind us?"

"To protect the purity of the teachings," Lancelot said. "Telling others will mislead more than lead them. True initiation onto the path can only come from one who is fully at its end. Most of all, it's to protect you."

"Protect us from what?"

"They killed Christ, Peter, Stephen, and most of the disciples for saying what they knew to be true. Do not think times have changed. Death at the hands of the ignorant and fearful is the reward for showing men Truth."

Frith puffed out his chest. "I'm not afraid."

"I'm not saying you are. I'm asking you to take a vow of secrecy."

"I... we... will never betray you," Alura said. Frith nodded.

"Then let's begin," Lancelot said. "You've already found you feel fear, and love and lust centered at certain places in the body. Today I'm going to awaken the snake."

"Snake!" Alura said.

"Well that's the traditional metaphor," said Lancelot. "A sleeping snake coiled at the base of a tree, when startled awake, climbs up the tree. By watching, you'll see the path she takes. You don't like snakes?"

"No," Alura said.

"Well it's just an image," Lancelot said. "Visualize instead a river which has clogged with logs. If the logjam can be broken, a great torrent of water is going to course up the river bed and burst out in a beautiful waterfall."

"I liked the waterfall last night," Alura said.

What waterfall last night? Had Alura been dreaming?

"You're going to love this one. Frith, you stand just here, in front of me. Alura, you stand behind him... Now Frith, close your eyes and begin to meditate as I've already shown you. Alura, catch him if he falls. I'm just going to pass my Self through his body, starting at the base..."

Lancelot placed his hands on either side of Frith's torso, one hand near his tailbone and the other in front at about the same height. Though Lancelot did not actually touch Frith – his hands were some distance away – Frith felt a sudden movement within. His eyes flew open and he jumped away from Lancelot.

"Whoa, I don't know what you think I am, but I don't put snakes in there!"

"Frith, Frith, calm down," Lancelot said. "Nothing physical is happening."

"It sure felt like something jumped me there."

"The Greeks have a word, *energeia*. Do you know this word? ...Perhaps the Latin, *energia*."

Frith shook his head no. He saw Alura do the same.

"It can mean the actuality or power at work in all things. When I use it, I mean that vital spiritual force that makes beings alive – *energia vitae*. What you felt was my energia flowing into you. The snake is the coiled life force. It started to untangle."

Frith tried to mask his discomfort. He must have failed, for Lancelot motioned Alura forward. "Let me initiate Alura first. Frith, you keep your eyes open. You'll see."

Frith switched places with Alura. She seemed very excited, but she'd yet to experience what he had. She would find out for herself why he had jumped.

"Close your eyes and try to relax," Lancelot said.

"Yes, Master." Her voice sounded to Frith as if she was already in meditation. How did she do that so quickly?

Lancelot extended his hands, one hand in front of Alura's pubis and one behind her tailbone. Lancelot closed his eyes. "This is the root, the beginning of survival. It stirs."

Lancelot moved his hands up, one over her tummy and the other over the small of her back. "This is the source of community, the birth of family. You can feel it stir in your womb."

"Oh Frith!" Alura said. "I can feel it tingle just as he says it's going to happen."

"Quiet," Lancelot said. "This is a serious initiation, not a ticklish amusement. Be still and experience it. As you feel each of these points know the power already within you." Then moving his hand over her spleen, he said, "Society."

Lancelot moved his hand up to her heart. "Love."

Although Lancelot's hand did not touch her breasts, Frith saw Alura's throat flush and her nipples swell. He involuntarily clenched his teeth.

But then he became aware of a powerful force that surrounded all three of them. It seemed to emanate from Lancelot. It also seemed to intensify everything Frith was feeling. Sure, Lancelot's hands could be said to be innocent, but Alura's reaction was not. His feelings confused him. Why was he so often jealous of his sister? At least Lancelot's eyes were closed so he couldn't see his face.

Lancelot moved one hand in front of Alura's throat and the other behind her neck. "Wisdom." He shifted his body so that he now stood directly in front of her. "Now I'm going to seal your initiation with a mystic kiss."

Lancelot leaned toward her, attempting to kiss her forehead, but Alura suddenly jerked her face up and locked her lips passionately on his. Frith felt a wave of fury sweep through him.

Lancelot grabbed her shoulders and pushed her away. "You silly girl! Oh, how have I been misled by last night? What vision ever made me think either of you were ready?"

Alura sniffed. "What is wrong? I could feel the river rushing up and up—"

"That wasn't supposed to happen. I'm trying to place the seal of initiation at the center of your brow – to open the eye of God."

"Oh my eyes were open the whole time!" Frith said. "Don't try to talk me out of what I saw. This isn't holy, it's hypocrisy! You gave me the 'man to man' talk about how it wouldn't be right for me to have Alura, and now you've got your hands and mouth all over her."

With no real thought other than the rage building inside of him, Frith swung his fist at Lancelot.

Lancelot stepped back seemingly effortlessly. The unexpected emptiness nearly brought Frith to the ground.

"Now, Frith, now," Lancelot said. "Look within. Who is it who sees the anger? Where is the feeling at?"

"Right here!" Frith lunged at Lancelot and wrestled him to the ground.

As the two men rolled around, Alura tried to pull him off Lancelot. "Frith! Stop it!"

But Frith wouldn't quit, couldn't quit. He didn't care where the anger emanated from or what it meant, it simply filled his entire being.

Lancelot pinned Frith's arms behind him. Frith struggled, while Lancelot restrained him. "Don't become the anger; watch it. You can awaken even in this moment by seeing. Just look, Frith."

Frith could not watch. He could only sputter, "I'm so... so... mad at you!" Suddenly, he wrenched free and pulled Lancelot's legs up forcing him to the ground.

Alura put her face right in front of his. "Frith! I am more angry than you are! At you! Now stop this!"

Frith stopped wrestling and sat on his heels. He was shocked. "Angry at me? He did it!"

Lancelot got off the ground and dusted himself off. "I think some cool water might be called for, all around." He left the two of them alone, and went toward the well.

Frith glowered after him.

"You little bully!" Alura said. "You just ruined everything."

First betrayed by Lancelot and now Alura. Why was she blaming him? "He did it. He said he was going to kiss you and then he did."

"No, I kissed him. If you want to blame someone, blame me."

"Don't defend him, I saw it."

"I didn't know what I was supposed to do. I've never kissed like that... except at play with you."

"And he dared tell me that I was wrong for that."

"Don't blame the master. I just reacted – wrongly, yes, wrongly. But the fault was mine."

"No! There's something very sexual going on here. I felt it with him too."

"No, this was something else. I just felt so much emotion come up in me ... I've waited my whole life to feel like this. This was what I dreamed last night, suddenly there it was, welling up inside me just as he said it would."

Lancelot returned from the well bearing a goblet of water. He made a sign of benediction over it and offered the cup to Frith. "Here my son, share some of this with me."

Frith took the cup reluctantly. He wasn't done being angry yet, but when the water touched his lips he felt better. He began to drink greedily until it was gone.

"You just lost your temper," Lancelot said. "That's all right. But don't lose yourself in it. You'll see that anger and jealousy are both the offspring of fear."

"You always have an answer for everything," Frith said.

"Me? The answers are within you. All that's required to overcome rage is to remain aware even when you're in the midst of its grip."

Lancelot took the cup from Frith, blessed it again and handed it to Alura. "I think we better have some more. And take some for yourself while you are at the well."

She took the cup and willingly left for the well. Frith was glad she was gone. Now he could speak to Lancelot alone. "I thought this was supposed to be some great holy experience, but you and she acted shameful. Last week you scolded me for the same thing, but it was like you forbade me so you could have her yourself."

"That's just jealousy talking," Lancelot said. "Hasn't she been saying plainly for weeks that I could have her? Yet did I? You know you cannot marry your sister, so why are you jealous?"

Frith thought about the question deeply and the answer that came surprised him, "Because I'm afraid of being left alone."

He could see that answer pleased Lancelot, but that made it worse. He looked down at the ground. "I'm a fool."

"No, you're not," Lancelot said. "At least no more than I am. I admit the situation went awry. I set out to waken her love for God, but I've only strengthened her desires."

"Alura says I have ruined it."

"No. In fact, you're now on your way. This was a battle you had on your quest."

"You mean the battle between you and me? That was just an embarrassment."

"You don't have to beat a man to be a man," Lancelot said. "Anger temporarily makes you forget yourself, but every time you remain aware during any experience, you win, even if it appears otherwise."

"I don't know how to do that while I'm angry."

"Hear your voice become loud or shrill. Notice your mind rushing to defend its position. Do this even if you see yourself lash out. Each time you can do this, you strengthen your self-awareness."

Frith continued to look at his feet. He said softly, "Will you ever have us here again?"

"Of course," Lancelot said. "And for my part, I will make this right. I see I've allowed Alura to develop too much sexual attraction. I'll try to turn her affections from the corpus to the deity. And when you become my disciples, I will treat you both equally."

Alura returned with the water. "Here, master."

Lancelot took a sip from the cup and set it aside. He offered Frith his hand and pulled him up. "I think that is enough for now. We'll try again another day."

Frith stood eye to eye with Lancelot. With all the humility he could muster, Frith said, "I truly want to master this."

"You will one day," Lancelot said. "This is God's plan. It will happen in His time, not ours." Lancelot leaned toward him and kissed him on the forehead. "Rise O Spirit!"

Frith felt a sudden upsurge overcome him.

Both men remained fixed in that position for a long time. When they separated, Frith said, "I… could feel it, master. It was like a wind blowing through each of the places you described. It was like a candle lit in each one." He paused. He still felt incomplete. "But I am afraid I did not find God."

"It'll come," Lancelot said. "It'll come. We think He's some power in a distant place, but I speak from experience. He's right here."

Alura, crowded between them, closed her eyes, and stood passively before Lancelot. Frith saw Lancelot look at her for a minute and then kiss her on the forehead. Still entranced by his own experience, Frith felt no anger, jealously, or fear.

"Seek ye first the kingdom of heaven," Lancelot said. "It is within you." At that Alura fainted very gently. Frith caught her. Lovingly, he lowered her to the ground. Softly he called her, "Alura… Alura… Alura…"

"She'll be all right," Lancelot said. "This happened to me before. Re-member the time when I saw the Grail heal the injured knight and lost my armor?"

Frith sat on the ground and rested Alura's head in his lap. "I remember all your stories."

CHAPTER 34

Alura had awakened to the sound of rain. She had gotten soaked going to the kitchen. The rain had continued throughout the morning and afternoon. Now that her work was done, she was at a loss what to do. Frith had yet to come for her, and going to Lancelot's had become such a habit that she couldn't remember what she did before. So she restlessly waited at the kitchen. That had its own hazards. Stay too long and one of the women would find more work for her, then she wouldn't be able to leave with Frith.

When Frith finally arrived, she met him at the door. "There you are, little brother; what took you so long?"

"What's to eat?" Frith said.

"Eat? We should have left already – we shouldn't keep him waiting any longer."

Frith jerked his thumb over his shoulder. "It's pouring."

She pulled him out the door, away from listening ears. They stood sheltered in the archway and watched the rain fall steadily. "What kind of disciples will he think us if we let a little rain keep us away?" Alura said.

"It's more than a little. We'll look like drowned cats by the time we get there."

"I'm not afraid of a little rain, are you?"

"No, but we meet in his garden. It'd be rude of us to ask him to stand in the rain to teach us."

"We don't have to. Maybe he'll invite us into his cottage."

"We'd never fit. It's too small."

"No it's not. It would be cozy. There is a fireplace too. We could be warm."

"We'd be standing on each other's feet."

"I know better; I've been inside. You can sit on his little stool by the fire and I can sit on the bed."

"What about Sir Lancelot? Where would he sit?"

"He'll stand. He always stands when he lectures."

"What if he gets tired?"

"Then he can sit next to me on the bed."

Eventually she got Frith to give in. He always did. He gripped his cloak with each hand and extended his arms like the wings of a great bird covering their heads. Alura held up her skirt with one hand and wrapped her free arm around Frith's waist. Soon they were slogging their way through the wet ferns. When they reached the fallen tree, the moss was slippery. They crossed carefully in single file, but only got a little wet.

When they arrived at Lancelot's, he was not in his cottage by a toasty fire as Alura had imagined. Instead he stood, comparatively dry, under a small tree whose dense foliage acted like a thatch roof.

"Good. You've come," he said and directed them to two similar trees about equal distance apart.

It was amazing; the rain fell around them, but not on them. The trees protected them as long as they each stayed under their cover. But it seemed the universe conspired against her, for under each tree the dry space was only large enough for one person. Rain could not keep them away, but rain kept them apart. Nevertheless, the ground was dry. She sat and Frith sat too. Lancelot, as Alura had predicted, chose to remain standing. Alura arranged her skirt in a circle around her like petals on a daisy. She imagined this pose made her look like a flower.

"I was wondering if you would brave the weather," Lancelot said. "That you have is a good sign."

Alura looked over at Frith. "See." It was frustrating to be forced to stay so far from *him*. "How'll we receive that wonderful experience of your energia when we're so far apart?"

"Yes, how?" Frith said.

"The flow of energia ascending is indeed wonderful, but what you experienced is already within you. You don't need me for it."

That may be, but Alura wanted Lancelot to do it again – and again.

"Yesterday," Frith said. "As I walked back to the abbey, I saw everything in a new way. The forest was alive and vibrant. I could see light emanate from even the densest tree. Today... it is less so. I long for the intensity of yesterday."

"Again, you don't need me for that. It is the movement of the energia that raises or lowers the intensity of your perception."

"What do we do if we can't stay in the state you have shown us?" Frith said.

"Once you have it awakened, don't let it go."

"But I don't know how to awaken the energia."

"Actually the energia is always flowing," Lancelot said. "But it collects or is trapped in certain places. Unconsciously the mind affects the movement of energia by its state, but you can control and move it yourself. When you do that, it will free you from unconscious control."

"Will you not bring it for us again?"

"That is your path, your quest."

It didn't sound like Lancelot was going to. She was disappointed, for now she craved the sensation of his energia almost as much as she craved a husband.

"Before the coming of the Grail," Lancelot said, "our quests were to fight evil beasts or rescue damsels; the Grail changed all that."

"But after that, the knights still rode in tournaments," Alura said. "Weren't they still inspired by the love of women?"

"Once we had seen the Grail, the inspiration was to find it. You must commit your whole being to the quest."

Alura noticed that her skirt was spread out beyond the area sheltered by the tree. Its edges were getting wet. She was forced to gather it around her knees in an unattractive bunch. Her imagined tableau transformed from a flower into a toadstool.

"I see it as a quest while we talk about it," Frith said. "But I don't see it when we're not with you."

"That doesn't mean you've failed. Being aware that you don't see it means you have succeeded. Or at least taken another step on the journey."

Alura stopped thinking about her skirt. "But now that we've been initiated, why doesn't it stick?"

"Not living life in the moment, one's eyes might as well be closed," Lancelot said. "For you're not truly awake."

"How can someone who is walking and talking not be awake?" Frith said.

Alura was glad he had asked; she didn't understand it either.

"Remember, living in your mind is like living in a dream. When you're dreaming, isn't your mind making up things?"

"Our mind makes up dreams?" Alura said.

"A few days ago when I asked you to visualize a sword, you could see it in your mind, but it was naught when you opened your eyes. Is that not so?"

"Yes."

"When you sleep, don't you see people and objects that are not there when you wake?"

Alura nodded. That was true.

"So it is when we walk around thinking about the past or thinking about the future, we miss the present."

"So living in your thoughts is like living in your dreams?" Alura said.

"Exactly," Lancelot said. "The world you see isn't the world, but our mind's reflection of it. We're busy watching the play of shadows. Focusing on shadows instead of the objects that cast them; we don't see reality."

"I thought I understood, but I guess I don't," Alura said. "What's this about shadows?"

"It is like the game children play by the fireplace," Lancelot made different shapes with his hands. "You bend your hands just so and cast the shadow of a dog. Raise two fingers and it looks like a rabbit."

She smiled, remembering nights at home.

"If you look at the shadow, you see an animal. If you look at the hands, you see how the animal is made. We try to look at the world, but instead we see the shadows of our fears and hopes, or I might say past and future."

"Why would you say 'past and future'?" Alura said.

"Reality dwells only in the now. The mind dwells mostly in the past and future. That is the elixir which produces dreams."

"Aren't I here right now?"

"I certainly hope so," Lancelot said. "But how often are you present in your duties, or when you're walking, or even alone in your bedchamber?"

She didn't know. "What did you mean by our fears and hopes are our past and future?"

"You feel abandonment not because you have been abandoned, but because you cling to it. It's not happening in the present, but taints your view of the present."

"But we *have* been abandoned."

"In the past," Lancelot said. "Try to see the present. I've given you an initiation onto the path of the Grail. Let that occupy your whole mind."

"Speaking of our initiation," Frith said. "You promised we would gain all these... qualities... love, joy, wisdom, forgiveness, and so on..."

"Yes," Lancelot said.

"But which comes first? Does a knight get these qualities when he finds the Grail? Or does he find the Grail because he develops these qualities?"

"Saint Paul said, 'Not by works of righteousness which we have done, but according to his mercy he saved us, by renewing of the Holy Ghost.' The path of the energia within you and the path to the Grail are one in the same."

"But doesn't a knight win the Grail by noble deeds?" Frith said.

"The Grail comes by Grace," Lancelot said. "It's not a reward for good deeds. But a man living in Grace will continue to do them anyway. The quest isn't the end, but the journey –persevering day after day in the effort. It's not in the deed, but who is doing the deed. Is he consciously present while performing the action, or thinking of the prize he'll win in the future?"

"And being in the present will earn him the Grail?" Frith said.

"That's like saying an archer is given an accurate shot as a prize for practicing. Keeping one's mind in the present is how one becomes conscious enough to see the Grail. You don't know where the Grail is until you look for it. When you look beyond the constant thoughts of past and future mind, you'll see it."

"Can't you give us some clearer instruction on how to work with the energia?" Frith asked.

Yes! Alura thought.

"It's much easier if you know the path it follows and work with it, not against it."

"What does that mean?" Alura said.

"It's like this. You know that when it rains, water runs to the low places. You use that knowledge when planning a garden so that water will flow where you want. Don't you?"

Alura nodded.

"Similarly, the energia collects where your mind dwells. The more you think about something, the more energia you feed it. When you take control of the flow of energia, you reduce the power of those distractions over you."

Alura wanted more, "How exactly do we do that?"

"The points where the mind traps energia are always about the past or the future. The more that you can concentrate on the present, the less power the past and future will have."

Was that true? Was that all there was to it? All her trouble caused by past and future?

"You are the source of power in this system – the sunlight that dries up the rain."

Alura smoothed the edge of her skirt where it had gotten damp. It was beginning to dry.

"You can use your power to raise what the mind thinks about by directing your attention into the now," Lancelot said. "Remember it's always now, and only now is real."

CHAPTER 35

When they arrived the next afternoon, Alura spied Lancelot in one of his flower beds. He was straightening the smaller plants that had been beaten into the mud by the rain. Frith went to watch him. Alura saw that his feet were muddy and went to the well without asking.

She had been filled with the wonder of Lancelot ever since the night she stayed here. In fact, she was even more in love with him, if that was possible. Though her desire to stand close to him had been thwarted yesterday by the rain, it had not been diminished. Today, she was bent on fulfilling it.

Alura returned with a bucket of water and led him to the bench. She insisted on washing his feet. He protested, but she did it anyway.

Alura lifted the hem of his robe and placed one of his feet in the bucket. She began to knead his sole and toes. Lancelot glanced at Frith, who rolled his eyes. Her hands moved over his ankles and calf with loving care. As her hands stroked him she felt him tense up, as if this had been a mistake. She hoped he didn't think that.

He removed his foot from the bucket, but she held onto it. She put his wet foot on her lap and lifted the other into the water. "No one has ever touched me as you did," she whispered.

"Thank you, but this is not necessary."

Lancelot took his foot from the bucket, but she clung to it. Holding both his feet in her lap, she dried them with her skirt. He withdrew his feet from her hands, stood and walked toward Frith. When there was an equal distance between the three of them he said to Frith. "I am sorry about that."

"Thank you, master but… it didn't bother me."

"That's good, but perhaps it bothered her," Lancelot said. "I promised you I'd do better at managing her feelings, but I have failed."

"Master, you have not failed," Alura said. "It pleasured me to serve you."

"I promised Frith I would treat you both as equal."

"Then let him wash your feet next time it rains."

"I'm a fool for giving in to it."

"Don't say that," Alura said. "You're wiser than any man I've ever known."

"In a world of the foolish, it's not difficult to be greater than those around you," Lancelot said. "But he who presumes to put himself above others is the greater fool."

"Are you saying we are foolish for loving you?" Alura said.

"No, I meant that I'm a fool to allow your service. It is I whose every act must serve to raise you up."

"And you do!"

"No, I don't. Not as long as I encourage you. You are too much enamored with your feelings. Now if you keep some distance between us, it'll be easier to manage. Why don't you sit on the bench?"

Alura sat on the bench as she was told. "This doesn't feel better to me."

"Have faith, it will be better for the three of us as a whole."

"I've been pondering our previous discussions," Frith said. "I have thought much about thinking. If we don't think, aren't we like the village idiot?"

Lancelot smiled. "How do we know what the village idiot thinks?"

Her brother looked befuddled. "I don't think the village idiot does think."

"Sorry," Lancelot said. "I confuse you with my jest. The real answer is that we are of two minds: one that thinks about now, and the other that lingers in the past or fantasizes the future. A farmer counts his sheep; that is useful thinking. It will help him to know if one is lost or missing. Dreaming of the money he will get when he shears them is not useful thinking and causes him anxiety."

"A man has memories," Frith said. "How can anyone keep the mind from remembering? Isn't that thinking about the past?"

"I don't want to keep you from remembering. I just want you to pay attention to the present. When you came here today, I was tending that flower bed. I wasn't thinking about your coming or what we would discuss today or what I would have to eat. I was just tending the flowers."

"Because you never eat," Frith said.

"That's just a phenomenon. It's not germane to our discussion or even to attaining the Grail. I've had a lifetime of memories. They've all happened. That's past. Which is relevant at this moment? Do you see a man more wretched for what I've done, or a man richer for what I'm seeing? Am I a man who has learned much, but lost more, or a man that does not live by bread alone?"

Alura moved closer. "I think you're a man who has known true love."

"Yes, I have, a truer love than words can speak. And I know you want me to romance you with a story of it, but it would be false."

Alura was disappointed. "Why?"

"Because clothing our highest feelings in words only profanes their true nature. To move feelings into speech requires the mind. The mind corrupts them with its opinions of how it ought to have been."

"Do you always have to speak about the mind? Can't we discuss feelings of the heart for a change?"

"You say heart because that's where you sense your emotions. Sir Bedivere would say gut, because that is where he feels things."

"But do we have the same feelings?" She hoped he could sense the depth of what she was feeling.

"I certainly hope not. But you have the same processes."

"As Sir Bedivere?"

"You might not guess it to listen to him, but yes. I've said before, the mind and the emotions are intricately linked. What you feel causes thoughts to race. What you think causes feelings to arise. In that respect, a knight and a maid are equally trapped in the mind."

"But doesn't love surpass the mind?"

"Ah, if only it would… Yes, when it is pure, before the mind gets to it."

"What does that mean?"

"The heart is chained to the mind as surely as a drawbridge is chained to a castle. As the chain is drawn up and down, the bridge moves up and down. Because the heart is chained to the mind, what the mind perceives in the world that it likes or dislikes causes feelings to react accordingly."

"But not love?"

"No, not love. When you feel love you know it."

"Oh yes-s-s"

"But what happens if you say to your beloved 'I love you'?"

"They say 'I love you' too." It seemed only logical.

"There it is," Lancelot said. "You're drawn out of the feelings of love by the need for your mind to hear the words of love. You miss the blessing of it for the coin of it. That's the mind I'm warning you about."

"I know you talk about being so awash in our thoughts that we miss reality," Alura said. "But I'm so flooded with feelings that I can't see my thoughts."

"Get beyond feelings and thoughts, both. You are the consciousness that sees them. You can watch your feelings, just like you watch your breath and mind."

"It's not... easy," Alura said. "My thoughts are so much about love, and I can't imagine living without love."

"You don't have to. Love God. Remember I said the heart is chained to the mind? Just as you can fix the problem of your mind by focusing on the now, you can fix your heart by putting your mind on God. This will raise your mind, and your heart will come with it."

Alura crossed her arms. "I don't know where to find God."

"God is as close as our thoughts allow him to be. You cannot think or breathe or feel love, but for Him."

Alura put a hand on her chest. "I don't think you realize just how turbulent it is in here."

"Oh, believe me, I do. I've had my problems with the heart in my time."

Alura uncrossed her arms and rubbed her heart with her hand. Of course he had.

"We've discussed two kinds of mind," Lancelot said, "the one in the now, which is useful, and the other, which is distracted by likes and dislikes."

"I thought we were finally talking about the heart."

"We are, but someday you'll see the heart that perceives love is overshadowed by a heart that is constructed of past pain and pleasure."

"What? I have two hearts?"

"No, it only seems so. Just as our thoughts linger because we replay them, our emotional pain leaves a bit of itself behind as well. Like the mind, the heart also becomes full of our past preferences. While you hold the past, you can't experience what you're feeling now."

"It's not that I don't know what I feel, it seems like I feel too much."

"Remember I once said that our attention was feeding the thoughts we are holding? Well, the preferences in our hearts are drawing energia to our emotions, too."

"Is that why it's so turbulent in here?"

"If you jump in a still pond and flail around, the pond becomes stirred up. When you get out, it'll settle back down and return to its natural state. When you get your attention off what you're trying to get and what you're trying to avoid – feelings you want and don't want – then the turbulence caused by your involvement will stop because you're not contributing to it."

"But if it all stops, then what? Isn't life without love cold as a stone?"

Frith came and stood next to her. She'd forgotten he was there.

"Love, peace, joy, and bliss are feelings you perceive of God. They won't go away any more than He will go away. They're being obscured by fear, jealousy, anger, and avarice. These are feelings of the mind, or I should say feelings generated by preferences: what we like and dislike, what we want and don't want. When you just experience each moment of creation, then you will truly feel love. You will be living inside of love."

Alura tried to move closer. "And will I feel that with you?"

"I don't know." Lancelot moved away from her. "You're asking about the future. I just told you, fix your mind on the now, and you'll solve the problems with thoughts. Fix your mind on God, and you'll solve the problem with the heart."

Lancelot pointed to the bucket. "Frith, your sister has brought a nice bucket of water. Would you like to soak your feet a bit before I give you today's Latin?"

CHAPTER 36

Although she still wished for Lancelot as a husband, Alura was increasingly uncertain if he would ever acquiesce to her desires. She knew that it should matter less to her – if she was truly his disciple.

She hoped someday she would find the Grail he was talking about, but did she have to spend her life in the kitchen until she did? So she remained alert for other possibilities.

When she overheard one of the kitchen boys say that Frith was going to the market, she left to look for him. She found Frith relaying the Abbot's instructions to a group of young monks.

"The next Holy day will soon be upon us. He expects it will be attended by the entire town, and a great many visitors from outlying farms. The Abbot wants there to be a procession of all resident monks, a period of chanting and prayer, after which he will say a Mass praising God for the harvest, and then we will have the distribution of the loaves."

She could see puzzled looks on the faces of the newest monks. They had not been here in previous years.

Frith explained, "In lieu of a harvest feast, it's the Abbot's custom to have the kitchen prepare loaves of bread from the new grain. During the service, the parishioners will offer a tithe to the church, and you monks will give them each a loaf and a small scroll writ with a biblical passage.

"The Abbot instructs those of you who are lettered to set aside your regular duties and report to the scriptorium to help make the scrolls. Those of you who normally work in the monk's kitchen should report to the Abbot's kitchen to help the staff there, as they have many loaves to bake. He wants the rest of you to rake, scrub, and clean every part of the abbey and grounds. Remember, we want to look our best for our guests."

While the best monks accepted this with humility, Alura imagined that some of the others wondered at Frith giving them orders. If so, they didn't comment. To his credit, Frith looked a little uncomfortable in this role. "These aren't my instructions; these are the words of your Abbot."

As the monks began to disperse, Alura pulled Frith aside. "I hear the Abbot is sending you out to the village on an errand."

"Shortly. There's a traveling iron monger in the market this week, and the Abbot is sending me to meet with him."

"Oh take me along, take me along!"

"Why? It's just a minor thing, nothing adventurous."

"Seeing anyplace other than the kitchens would be an adventure to me."

"Well, don't get your hopes up. It's a rather small market. There is not that much to see."

"I want to go. I never get out of here."

"How can you say that? Every single day we go to the woods – to Lancelot's."

"For all the good that does me."

"I don't understand."

"Oh Frith, you will never understand. I just need to get out where we will meet some new people. I am desperate."

"Well, the abbey will soon be filled with people for the harvest Mass."

"Yes, and each and every one of them is as familiar to me as you are." And she knew their wives, as well.

"Very well," he said. "Are you free now?"

"Until Sext."

Alura fairly danced beside him as they walked to the gate. No time to stop at the kitchen and let them know she was leaving. And no reason to.

They didn't need her, not really, and better to explain after she got back than risk being thwarted before she made it out the gate.

She tingled with anticipation, imagining how delightful it would be to mingle in the flow of people. It would be a respite, not just from her kitchen work but from Lancelot's dismal view of love. And he would certainly not approve of the way she was imagining her future husband waiting for her in the market, but she didn't care. She could learn to be holy later.

As she stepped through the abbey gate into the world outside its wall, she was at once dazzled with the sense of freedom and disappointed by the village. She had been six when their elder brother had brought them to the abbey. That, being her first time away from the farm, had made the town seem so urban. The intervening years being trapped in the abbey made the size of the town grow in her mind. She had often imagined it as a bustling, robust city, opposite from the sedate abbey grounds. Although only a stone wall separated the abbey from the village, it had remained a foreign enchantment to Alura until this moment. Now that she was finally seeing it, she was struck by how tiny it seemed.

There was a two-story guild hall that more or less defined a town square, along with two rows of small, shuttered stalls – maybe a dozen all told. In one stall, someone was creating a metallic clangor, perhaps a tinker rapping away at a cook pot, which provided a background accompaniment to the rest of the stalls, where the owners seemed more interested in gossiping over the counters with their neighbors than actually selling their wares. The remainder of the town was small wattle-and-daub homes, many with a goat tethered out back, one or two with a cow. Bedraggled chickens wandered at will, scratching at the dry, dusty ground and scurrying out of the way of anyone who came near.

It was at least noisier, with more commotion than the abbey. But as Lancelot had taught them, she ceased judging. And in doing so she realized that the level of activity was not the difference. There was usually just as much activity at the abbey when the monks were working. The difference was intention. The abbey state was meditative; therefore, those inside moved with intention. Out here was a bartering, clawing, more chaotic life.

That she found pleasing, the milling crowd of shoppers and merchants. It was a struggle to maintain her sense of peace because she wanted so badly to let it go and throw herself into the flow of the market. Even knowing she should keep her discipline, she was enamored by the rich harvest of men. She realized the market was a man's world. She knotted her fingers in the cloth of Frith's tunic for safety and trailed behind him.

Frith carried a roll of parchment in his hand and moved quickly through the merchant stalls. Alura wanted to linger over the displays of goods, but Frith pressed ahead toward the sound of the clanging. There, in the end stall, thick smoky clouds surrounded the noisemaker, a man in a leather apron with tremendous, bulging forearms. He was beating something on an anvil, a crimson glow reflected on his face. Behind him, two strapping lads pulled on the handles of bellows in alternate turns and Alura greatly admired their musculature.

Frith waved the parchment to get the iron monger's attention. The man saw him, but continued to hammer away. Frith motioned again, and the man answered him in beats between the clangs of his hammer. "Ye… have … to… wait… can't… let… it… cool…"

Frith nodded and they waited.

Alura got the attention of the men working the bellows and they pulled faster and harder.

"Slow… down… too… hot…"

The men returned to their previous pace, but exaggerated their biceps with each pull. So she did have this effect on men.

When the piece was the shape and thickness he desired, the man plunged it into a bucket of water and motioned for the men on the bellows to stop. He scooped a ladle of water from a different bucket and drank deeply, drew a second ladle and poured it over his head. Water ran down his face and chest.

Frith introduced himself and explained what he needed. The iron monger wiped his hands on his breeches and reached for the parchment. "Step over here in the shade and let me see what you've brought." He stepped under a small tent-like awning and motioned for Frith, who followed him.

Alura remained where she was, in the company of the two apprentices. The men also drank some water, and then took turns ladling water over each other's heads. Playfully, each man wiped the other's face clean, and then they turned their attentions toward Alura. Why couldn't she get this reaction from Lancelot?

"The hinges on the cathedral doors have cracked and the banding's broken. They no longer hold. Perhaps the design was flawed." Frith unfurled the parchment and handed it over. "I've traced them. We've added wooden straps to fortify them, but those sag, and the doors drag."

The ruddy man studied the parchment with intelligent eyes. "Nothing's wrong with the design. If I were to guess, I'd say the problem is the inferiority of the metal. These were probably made by a farrier or some local smith. But these aren't horseshoes or nails. Their iron was brittle, probably forged near Lydney or Tidenham, where they still make iron the way the Romans did when they occupied Britain. Now, my iron comes all the way from India, where they make a superior metal."

Her brother nodded his head, duly impressed. Alura smoothed the waist of her skirt.

"I'm an armorer and sword smith by trade. I don't normally do this kind of work."

"But for the abbey?" Frith said.

"For the abbey, yes. But not for free."

"Oh, the Abbot will pay, but the work must be complete this week – before the harvest Mass. We expect a lot of visitors and the doors will not bear the traffic."

"Well, it's not nothing, but it shouldn't take more than a day. How many hinges?"

While Frith was negotiating the Abbot's deal with the iron merchant, Alura flirted with his apprentices. However, she soon ascertained they were both married. Although they appeared willing to be unfaithful to their wives, that wasn't what she was looking for.

Alura liked this market very well. She looked around and it was full of men. Although some of them were old, most of them were not old-old. Anyone of them would do. Then she saw some younger men Frith's age unloading baskets of squash from a donkey cart. She wanted to wander in front of them to see if they would notice her, but she couldn't. She had to wait for Frith. No matter, they were probably married as well.

At last Frith came over to her. "That's finished."

"Good, let's stroll around the market a little bit."

"Why? You haven't any money."

"I haven't been here before. I'd just like to see it."

Frith gave in and they strolled idly through the stalls. Soon they came nearer the boys she had seen. Frith said he knew them. "They're apprenticed to some of the merchants." Rather than being about their master's work, they were loitering together and laughing.

Alura noticed them and they her. They called out to Frith, "It's the Abbot's boy!"

"Abbot's man," Frith said.

"Of course, and how is the holiness business?"

"Busy," Frith said. "We've the harvest festival—"

"And you have a new wife this week."

"Sister," Alura said quickly.

"Oh, better!"

"And maiden," she said.

"Oh a bold one!"

"My *sister*," Frith said, stepping in front of Alura defensively.

"Well, chivalry's not dead," the poulterer's son said.

"Sir Frith," said another, "or would that be Sir Peace."

Alura saw Frith start to become angry, and then she saw a most remarkable thing: She saw him master it. Lancelot was definitely changing him.

However, Frith had not mastered his pride. "It could happen someday."

"You? A knight?" They laughed.

"It could happen. You know Lancelot knighted Galahad, and then Galahad knighted Melias."

"Who's Melias?"

"A young prince of Denmark," Alura said.

They all looked at her. She looked nervously at Frith who said, "It doesn't matter. The point is a man can be made knight, even in these days."

"But there're no knights around here."

"What if there was?" Alura said. She wanted to bite her tongue clean off. Suddenly she was about to give away that which she had promised not to reveal.

Frith saved her. "A knight came to our abbey once."

"We heard about that; the liveryman told us."

"That was weeks ago – you probably never met him," said the livery apprentice.

"I might have," Frith said. "Sir Bedivere, an old knight of King Arthur's."

"At least it wasn't Lancelot," one of the apprentices said.

"Yes," said another. "If it was Lancelot, Frith'd be… I don't know… something bad would happen."

Alura realized that Frith's friends were as lost in the superstitions as anyone else. She longed to change their impression of Sir Lancelot, but she didn't dare act as Frith's witness.

But maybe there was a safe way. Everybody loved a good story. "Frith, why don't you tell your friends that story Sir Bedivere told you – the one about Lancelot and Galahad?"

While Frith spun his yarn, Alura studied one of the apprentices. She wasn't as close to him as she wanted, but as any closer might be seen as improper. She put her whole attention on his facial features and became rapt. Frith's words became background noise.

Alura noticed a soft rainbow of freckles crossed the man's nose and fanned across his cheeks, which were covered in pale fuzz. His brown eyes were focused on Frith, not her. When he laughed, his teeth were straight and his tongue was pink when he licked his lips. His lips were inviting, and she could imagine them kissing her hand.

Frith's story was cut short when one of the merchants came looking for his apprentice. He scolded the other young men as well, sending them back to their own masters. When he made a threat that their wives would go hungry, Alura realized that they were already married. Her cheeks flushed and her heart fell. As an adventure, this was an abject failure. She'd started out looking for a man, but ended in frustration. Were there truly no eligible men left?

What did it matter? She had known which man she truly wanted since she first laid eyes on him.

Chapter 37

A week had passed since Alura's failed expedition to find a suitor in the market. That disaster showed that her original plan had been the correct one; her best prospect for the life she desired was the noble knight who drew her to him daily. However, Lancelot was holding frustratingly true to his promise to Frith. He seemed to do everything possible to keep her at a distance and elude her romantic intentions. Keeping so far away, he would not sense the passions she desperately wanted him to know raced inside her.

Each day she came to him, her head filled with ruminations, and each day she left aching for him to love her more. The more romantic she felt toward him, the more distant he seemed to be. It was becoming more than she could bear.

Alura stared into swirls of soap she was stirring with a sassafras stick. Whenever the weather permitted and the butcher had accumulated enough fat, it fell to the women of the kitchen to make soap. Soap was best made over an open fire outside the kitchen. It was hot, dangerous work that stank of boiled fat and lye. And what good was it? You couldn't eat it, it didn't feed anybody. And it made her stink. It was not as bad if a hog had just been killed, and she could use the soft white fat that surrounded the kidneys. But the abbey wasted nothing, so most often soap was made from an accumulation of chunks and drippings, saved until it was too rancid for a dog to roll in, and the flies were too numerous to tolerate. Sir Lancelot would certainly stand far from her today.

Though the women did most of the work of the kitchen, young monks worked there as well. These were brawny strapping boys trapped inside a monk's habit. It seemed to her that they looked upon her as a distraction to their renunciation. She noticed that they avoided contact with her more than they did with the older women.

Yesterday they had built the fire in the pit and kept it fed as the fat was rendered. The whole process took more than a day. As the fat melted, she skimmed off bits of tissue. Once she had cleaned the melted fat as best she could, it needed to be strained. This required the boys to lift the heavy kettle and pour the hot oil through several layers of cloth. This had to be done while the fat was just short of boiling because it thickened when cool, making it impossible to filter.

Depending on the type and age of the fat, this process of heating and straining, heating and straining was repeated several times. This required the monks to remain in closer proximity to Alura than usual. It didn't bother her. She respected their decision to renounce the world and had no desire to corrupt them. She had her whole mind on a knightly man.

While Alura cooked the fat, the boys had made the lye. Ashes from the hearth had been saved and kept dry for soap-making day. The boys set a bottomless barrel on a stone slab that had a groove in it. A clay urn was placed at the lip of the groove. Straw was packed into the bottom quarter of the barrel and then the remainder was filled with the ashes. Water was then poured over the ash and allowed to seep through. In slow drips and drops, it filled the container with lye water.

The most difficult part of soap making was getting the lye just right. When enough lye water had been made, Alura would test it. She would drop an egg into the solution and see how it floated. If it did not meet her standards, new ashes would be added to the barrel, and the lye water would be poured through again to strengthen it.

But all that was yesterday. The rendered fat had been cooled overnight. This morning, clean fat floated on the water. They dumped out the water and impurities and started again, boiling the purified fat with the lye water. For six or eight hours Alura had to stand at the fire and stir it. The old woman who had taught her said it must be stirred in only one direction.

The finished product was a slippery brown jelly. It was stored in a crock or barrel and ladled out as needed. To make hard soap, salt could be added at the end of boiling, but the abbey generally did not make hard soap. The Abbot had better uses for his store of salt than wasting it on soap. "Soft soap cleans just as thoroughly," he had said. The only value the Abbot attributed to hard soap was that it traveled well. So only once or twice a year was salt added. That soap was poured into a wooden form until it hardened. Slices of soap were then cut off and wrapped in muslin. These were given or sold to pilgrims.

The only good thing about soap making was that it gave her plenty of time to think.

Alura stared into the thick, frothy, boiling mass. She reflected that the soap in the cauldron was like her life, a stew of hopes and dreams and fears and anguish and ecstasy that she was constantly stirring.

So what would Lancelot want her to do? Be in this moment – just stirring the soap. That led her into a deep peaceful serenity. When her biceps wearied, she shifted position or moved the left hand above the right. When her arms tired, she gripped the sassafras paddle with both hands and moved it by the slow undulation of her whole body.

She remembered a conversation between Lancelot and her brother:

"There are millions of events occurring in this place," Lancelot had said. "Ants are crawling, leaves are moving, birds are singing. Too much to comprehend, so the mind discards most of it and focuses on a few things, like the sound of a voice, a gesture…"

"Is that a bad thing?" her brother had asked.

"No that is the fire of discrimination, burning away what is not essential. The problem is our fire is smoky. We see everything through layers of haze."

"Haze?" her brother asked in his typical manner.

"Likes and dislikes."

Her fire was hazy, literally. She was standing in a cloud of fumes, but she saw more clearly now than ever in her life. Her solution was inherent in the problem itself. She could use this fire of discrimination that he talked about.

Sir Lancelot had told them, "We spend all our mind comparing what we see to our past likes and dislikes." She saw he was right; her mind wanted to compare... But since that was what it wanted to do, why not let it compare what it saw to the great truth: God is one!

In the slow swirl of the sassafras stick, and the meditative state it induced, it all made sense. If she made it her habit to compare everything that is One to the One that is, then there would be nothing to compare. Her mind would automatically think about truth instead of what it used to like or dislike.

Her mind was not much on soap making. But she thought Lancelot would not disapprove.

* * *

Frith came around the building, looking for Alura. He was coming to see if the soap was finished, if she could leave with him for Sir Lancelot's. He saw her staring into the pot, moving her stick, watching it boil. There was a serene smile on her face, an almost dazed look in her eyes, and luminosity about her.

The fire was now mostly red embers. Suddenly a large bubble swelled up in the thickening liquid and burst. It spewed over the side onto the hot coals, which sputtered and popped. An ember flew toward Alura, and the hem of her skirt promptly caught fire. Frith saw it and in a heartbeat leaped to his sister. Throwing her to the ground he covered her whole body with his and rolled them around.

When he looked up several of the boy monks were smirking at them.

A woman rushed out of the kitchen to see what the commotion was and found him lying on top of Alura. "Stop this foolery! Who is stirring the soap?"

Frith stood up. "You had best tend to it, Madam."

The other women came out. "What goes on here?"

"Alura caught on fire." Frith said. "Alura, are you all right?"

She fingered the charred edges of her skirt and began quaking violently. He squatted down and looked into her face. "Alura, are you burned?"

She shook her head no, but sobbed, "Who would ever want me if I was?"

He took her hands and pulled her up with him. He pulled her close and wrapped his arms around her. He didn't care what the others thought. She sobbed against his chest. He patted her soothingly.

Frith could hear their murmurs. Several of the young monks were whispering words monks should not. Holding her protectively, he turned toward them, "Have you no chivalry? Don't speak that way about a lady!"

"We see no lady," one monk said.

"Then you are no man of God."

Ethelburg, who had taken up stirring the soap, intervened. "Boys – back to the kitchen."

Frith looked at the women who had gathered around them. "Alura needs to recover. I'm taking her early today to get cleaned up. You finish the soap."

It was not a request. He had made a decision and was acting on it. It felt so completely natural that he didn't even give it a thought. He simply led Alura away.

When they got to Alura's quarters, he stopped at the door. It was not permitted for men to enter. "You better get your other skirt; this one is ruined."

Instead of doing as she was told, she slumped down by the door and fell into another fit of tears. All of Frith's confidence drained away. "Oh… come now, we'll go see the master. He'll make you feel better, you'll see."

"No-o-o-o," she cried, "I can't! My clothes are burnt, and I smell like pig fat. You go. Tell him I need to air out."

"Wait here. I'll be right back." Frith ran toward his room.

In no time he was back, carrying a small rectangle wrapped in cloth. He handed it to her.

"What's this?" She started to unwrap it and a few sprigs of lavender fell out of the muslin. "…But I gave you this last Christmas. How do you still have it?"

"I don't bathe as often as you do."

Alura looked at the hard chunk of soap, which smelled faintly of purple flowers. "I remember making this, but I have no idea why I thought it was a good gift for a boy."

"Come," he said. "Get your skirt. You can have a bath and wash your hair in the river on the way there."

"It's rather late in the season for bathing." She pressed the bar of soap to her nose.

"I think it's still warm enough."

Alura got her spare skirt from her room, and they headed toward the woods.

"You look happier," he said. "Aren't you glad we're going to see Lancelot after all?"

"I'm especially glad that I'm not going to meet him reeking of burned fat."

They walked for a while in silence. After a time he said, "You could've died."

"Or even worse."

"Worse than death?"

"I could've been disfigured. Who'd ever want me then?"

He stopped walking and turned her toward him. "Me. I will always take care of you, Alura, no matter what happens."

"Always?"

"Yes."

Alura squeezed his arm. "You know, you saved my life today. Thank you."

Frith felt his cheeks flush a little. He turned away and resumed the trek toward Lancelot's.

CHAPTER 38

Frith kept one arm around his sister as they made their way through the shadowed woods. Alura clung to him, shivering, both of her arms wrapped around his waist. Her hair wet his shirt where she pressed tightly to his shoulder. Her teeth chattered and her clothes stuck to her body. The river had not been as tepid as he had predicted. While she had bathed and changed into her spare skirt, he stole away and buried the burnt one. He reasoned that it'd only remind her of the incident.

They came upon two fawns nestled asleep in the bushes, who startled awake and stood swiftly, but didn't run. A brother and sister, Frith thought. Nearly grown. He was surprised they didn't dash away at the sight of two humans. Instead, they paused for a long moment to look him over. Frith looked back at them and wondered that they were alone. Perhaps they were orphans, abandoned by their mother.

Then the one Frith thought was the brother gave a short bark that sounded like a dog, flashed a signal to the other, and made a frightened flight. In a fraction of a second the sister followed. They disappeared into the forest as if they had never been.

"That was amazing," Frith said.

"Do you think they were afraid of us?"

"They didn't seem to be, not at first."

When they reached Lancelot's gate, Frith saw him watering his flowers in a most peculiar way. Cupping his hand in the bucket, he scooped water out, and then let it trickle off his fingertips. He had a look in his eyes similar to Alura's when he first saw her stirring soap at the cauldron. They exchanged greetings, and Frith waited for Lancelot to ask why Alura looked like she had come through a rainstorm, for her hair hung in long wet ropes that trailed water and made wet streaks on her clothes. But Lancelot made no comment on her appearance or their late arrival. Instead he began immediately with the day's lecture.

That wasn't like him. He noticed everything. But then again, no one was the same today. Instead of following Lancelot around as she had been wont to do, Alura stayed close to Frith. And Frith was not as attentive as usual. In fact he was not listening to Lancelot at all.

He was still absorbing the way he had ordered everyone around at the fire. He had acted like a man, like a knight. No, he had been a man. He no longer had to pretend. The transition that once looked so difficult had been so instantaneous it passed without his noticing. But now what were his responsibilities?

Obviously he needed to take things more seriously. No more grousing about his studies. Also Alura should not be left alone; the world was too dangerous and he could lose her. He needed to give up his plans to run away, needed to stay and protect her, needed to tell Lancelot to help her.

"Sir," he said, "forgive me for interrupting. But Alura may have need for healing like you did for Sir Urre."

"Sir Urre, there is a name I've not heard in a long time…" Lancelot cocked his head and paused for a moment. "I don't recall having told you about him…"

"You didn't. Sir Bedivere told me the story."

"Ahh, Bedivere…"

"He said you healed that knight."

"Did he? That's rather like saying the streambed creates the water. Still, Alura doesn't seem injured. In fact, I don't believe I've ever seen her in such a calm state."

Frith looked at Alura. No she didn't look hurt. Her face was all shiny, but her eyes were kind of glazed.

"So Alura, how are you injured?" Lancelot said.

"She was nearly burnt to death!"

Lancelot softened. "I'm glad you are still with us."

Then everything changed. He noticed a shift in Lancelot's demeanor. Then the garden changed. It was as though every flower and plant became empathetic with Lancelot's empathy toward his sister. Was that really happening or was it his imagination? After all, how could a stupid plant know Lancelot's thoughts? Still, things that didn't seem logical seemed to keep happening around Lancelot.

Alura stroked Frith's cheek with the back of her fingers as a mother would a child. "Frith saved me."

Frith pulled away. He usually liked when she did that, but not this time, not in front of Lancelot.

"Instead of listening to me natter on," Lancelot said, "Why don't you tell me what happened?"

"Well, she was making soap, and the cauldron bubbled over onto the fire. Her skirt burst into flames."

"How tragic," Lancelot said. "My grandmother died like that."

"She did?" Frith said.

"Yes."

"I'm so glad that didn't happen to Alura."

Alura related her version of the story. Frith felt gratified at the way she told the story, yet a little embarrassed. He kept his eyes on Alura, feeling too shy to look at Lancelot. He rubbed Alura's arm affectionately.

"So you have burns in need of healing?" Lancelot said.

She lifted the hem of her skirt and showed the men her bare legs. Certainly a bold and improper act among strangers, but he was family, not a stranger. And if Lancelot was to heal her, Frith supposed it must be allowed. Frith studied her bare calves. They were crimson, but there were no blisters. In fact, the soft downy hair on her legs showed no sign of being singed.

More likely the redness was from the cold water. Alura rubbed them self-consciously with her hands.

"You can put your skirt back down, dear," Lancelot said. "Your body has escaped harm, but it is elsewhere we must prevent scarring."

Frith expected Lancelot to begin the healing, but he didn't. He began a new lecture instead. "Where's the balance between being more cautious because you've learned from an experience and being afflicted because you're holding on to the fear of a past experience? Consider also that the mind may try to use the experience to justify why you shouldn't have to do what you dislike. For example, you dislike soap making..."

Frith knew that to be true, she'd said it often enough.

"The mind will pit what it likes against what it dislikes. It'll tell you it's perfectly safe to work around fire to cook because you like to cook. It'll tell you it's dangerous to work around fire to make soap because you already don't want to make soap. Instead of the experience making you a stronger person, it can be something your mind uses to get its preferences. The problem is, that's not the way to grow."

Now Frith was listening. "So how does Alura fight that?"

"By letting it pass. The experience wants to pass through and become the past, but as I've said many times, it is we who are holding it. It's the leaves against the dam, again." Lancelot looked into Alura's eyes. "You cannot hold onto this fearful experience or it'll affect not only your soap making, but everything that you do. You need to let it pass, to let it go to the place it wants to go."

"Where is that?" Frith said.

"That place is wisdom. Let it move from the place of fear to the place of wisdom. It's wisdom to use your past experiences to navigate your future without coming to harm. It's fear when you treasure your bad experiences. Each of those we cling to is a link in a chain that holds us, and when enough of them have been forged, we are fettered. Alura mustn't allow the pain which is the memory of this ordeal to take up residence in her body. She must let it go so it can transform from fear to wisdom."

"Will you now begin her healing?"

"Why don't you do that?"

"Me?"

"Yes, I'll show you how. You have to learn to depend more on each other and less on me."

"Why is that?" Frith said.

"I've told you, I'm near the end of my journey; yours is just beginning. I don't want you to depend on me for your healing, but on each other. It's not my goal to make you my own, but to free you."

Frith felt Alura tense when Lancelot said that. He knew Alura still wanted Lancelot to make her his own. And for just a second, he understood her pain. It was hard being a woman.

"Let's begin your instruction. There's a connection between the movement of the energia and breathing. So imagine that you can make breath flow in and out through your chest, instead of your nose. Similarly, imagine breathing in and out of the place on your forehead between your eyes."

Frith tingled at the knowledge that Lancelot was giving him personal guidance, but when he actually did the breathing he felt a soft melting inside of him. Maybe this was one of Merlin's secrets.

"Frith, this is neither magic nor Merlin's incantations," Lancelot said. "It's just Alura learning to be open enough to let her problems drift away and you making energia available to help them float away."

Frith knitted his eyebrows and concentrated on his breathing.

"Don't try, Frith," Lancelot said. "When I do this, I'm not trying to do anything at all. To try, we must use our willpower, and what happens then is almost never the right thing. The less I try, the more things are able to flow the way they're supposed to flow."

After Frith had practiced the breathing a few times, Lancelot said, "Alura, I would just tell you to go make another pot of soap, sort of like Frith getting back on a horse that threw him. But that is not practical, for it will be many weeks before you'll make soap again, and by then the memories will have set their patterns of fear and pain."

How had Lancelot known he was thrown by a horse? And, wait, how did Lancelot know he was thinking of Merlin's magic?

Let it go. Questions for later. Let them go.

"Close your eyes, both of you," Lancelot said. "Frith, you don't need to see Alura to know what you're doing to her. See within yourself something moving with the breath. Allow it to flow in and out with the breath as though there were an opening in your heart."

Frith tried not to try.

"Alura," Lancelot said. "If you can breathe as I just taught Frith, it'll increase the effect more than double. However, that's not a necessity. You need only to remain passive and watch it flow through you. Let go of the drama and painful memories of the experience."

Frith extended his arms and moved them around in imitation of what he'd seen Lancelot do.

"Just let it flow," Lancelot said. "You're not trying to push anything into her. Just relax and let her draw out what she needs from you. Her feelings are more fragile than butterflies. If you try to grab a butterfly, you'll ruin its wings. You must hold your hand open gently and wait for it to land of its own accord. It's the same here. Gently breathe and allow her energia to rise of its own accord.

"Alura," Lancelot said. "You can't carry this around with you forever. You're going to be around fire every day. You're going to carry pots of boiling water. You're going to carry caldrons of stew and gruel. You can't let your fears stay in you. They'll pass if you just let them go. The past just wants to float away. and it's we who're holding it back."

Frith felt compelled to embrace Alura. Something flowed between them. It was different from the passion that stirred so hard within him during the play. Instead this was like a warm merging.

"Good," Lancelot said quietly, his voice sounding distant. "But Frith, don't dwell in her heart. You don't want her fear to tarry there. Take another breath in through the heart and breathe it out at the point between your eyebrows. As you breathe in and out of those places you're actually transmuting them – changing their state."

The clouds parted and the garden lightened. Frith could sense it on his eyelids. He opened his eyes slightly. The flowers turned their blossoms toward the sun. Frith saw orbs of light floating upward in the streaming sunbeams.

Lancelot did not scold him for opening his eyes. He was again talking to Alura. "Think of them as bubbles of soap."

Frith felt her stiffen, as if she remembered the bubbling cauldron. Surely Lancelot could see into her mind for he said, "No, not the bubbles when making the soap. Think of the bubbles that are formed when you wash with soap. You pour the soap into the water, bubbles form and float up out of the washtub... Those are the bubbles which I'm speaking of... light iridescent bubbles that rise in the air burst into nothingness.

"Alura, imagine those bubbles are the memories of this experience, and as Frith makes them lighter they are floating away. You're just letting them go. You're not holding on. They pop, are gone, and will never trouble you again... Take one more breath." He clapped his hands, once. "The healing is done."

Frith and Alura parted. Lancelot picked up the bucket of water and told Frith to extend his hands. Lancelot started to pour water over his hands.

"They're not dirty," Frith said.

"No, but perhaps they're tingling. Are they not?"

They were. Frith nodded.

"Running water will neutralize the effect. A stream will do, but you're not always near a river, so, here, I'll just pour this."

When Lancelot had emptied the bucket, Frith shook his hands vigorously and water droplets flew about his feet.

"I think that is enough lesson for today," Lancelot said.

"But we interrupted your lecture," Alura said. "You never got a chance to finish it."

"Experience is always better than words. I think the experiences you had today have taught you far more than I could ever say."

Alura gave a little tremble. "If you are sending us away early, will you not give us a blessing?"

"Today you've given each other your blessings." Then Lancelot did a very unusual thing. He put his hands on each of their shoulders and walked between them to the gate.

Frith could feel his cool touch and a spark from Lancelot entered his body. He sensed that Alura could feel it too. As if they were connected and that he should know what she was feeling.

Frith opened the gate and let Alura go first. Lancelot didn't come through. He stayed in his yard. Yet as they walked away Frith could feel Lancelot's hand as though it was still on his back. It was so real, he turned and looked behind him, but the master remained standing at the gate, smiling.

Alura, as affectionate as when they came, put her arm around his waist. "Frith, you will forever be my heroic knight." She paused for a minute then added, "But I'm still determined to get Lancelot for a husband."

"I understand."

They walked a ways in silence.

"You only have one skirt now," Frith said. "I'll tell the women in the kitchen to get you another. It may not be new, perhaps one from their thinner days, but at least you'll have two."

"Do you think they'll listen to you?"

Frith smiled. "I'm certain of it."

CHAPTER 39

The week passed. The Holy day came, and the baking was finished. The kitchens were closed so that the monks who worked there could participate in the services and the women could attend the celebration with their families. Lancelot did not attend. Neither did Frith and Alura, who took advantage of the holiday to slip away earlier than usual.

Lancelot moved around the garden as he talked, always managing to keep himself equally distant between Alura and Frith. Alura's displeasure with this was evident. Most of the past week, she had sat on the bench, scuffing her feet on the hard-packed dirt. Today, she remained standing and followed him about while he taught, trying to maneuver ever closer.

Alura wrapped her hands in the pleats of her new skirt and swung her arms in semi-circles, making it swirl around her. Her ploy to capture his attention was transparent to him. She did not appear to be paying attention to his lecture, so he used an example he knew would catch her interest.

"Walking through the woods, a damsel spots something coiled in the brush. She jumps back. Is it a snake? No, it's a discarded piece of rope. But her fear of the rope is the same as if it were a snake."

"Maybe the rope just reminded her of how women are bound," Alura said.

"Maybe. But the point of the story is that we do not see what we see. Every event is shown to us through a fog of hopes, dreams, wishes, fears, wants, and beliefs."

"A girl has to have dreams."

"A girl has to eventually wake up."

"You know I'm not talking about that kind of dream." Alura moved even closer, finally positioning herself where it was difficult for him to move away.

"I know exactly what you're talking about."

Lancelot could feel her vitality. She may not know of love, but she had discovered that women could stir something in men, and she was playing with it. He needed a pretense to leave, and his body responded. His voice suddenly weakened, his throat became scratchy.

"Excuse me while I get a drink," Lancelot said.

"I'll get you some water," Frith said.

"Thank you, no, I want to go myself." With that he walked briskly away, leaving them alone.

Alura stuck out her lower lip. "This feels very cold."

"You're not speaking of the fall frost, surely."

"Don't be dense. The frost I feel is not on my toes, but as though Jack Frost reached out and touched my heart."

"You don't mean Jack 'Lancelot' Frost?"

"Oh, Frith, he freezes me out as surely as autumn kills what we fail to harvest."

"But isn't today the equinox of two seasons? The master is just trying to balance equally between two disciples."

Alura's voice cracked. "But he's felt so distant ever since that night we stayed here." A tear fell. "Frith, I don't know what to do."

Lancelot returned from the well, but kept his distance from her. "Sorry, something in my throat—"

"Are you against love?" Alura said.

"Never, love is an ideal through which we find our best selves."

"Then how do I find my best self?"

"That is what we are about," Lancelot said. "Stop worrying about that. I shall be the one to take you."

Alura ran to him and wrapped her arms tightly about him. "Oh Sir Lancelot, you have kept yourself so distant of late—"

Lancelot tried to pry her arms from him. "No, no, no. I mean, I can help you rise above your desires."

"I thought I would never be loved."

"You are loved, Alura," Lancelot said. "But I love you and Frith equally. You are both my disciples."

"But you finally said you would take me…"

Lancelot gripped her arms and held her far enough away that he could look directly into her face. "That does not mean to take you to wed."

"But you admit being attracted to me."

"In my youth, I'd have grown weak to my knees before such as you."

"But no more?"

"My knees do bend in your presence, but only before the divine dwelling in you."

Though he tried, Alura would not let him go. "Is that all you see when you look at me?"

"Alura… I wish it were only that. My mind, my heart, my soul wants to see only your soul, but the truth is, my eyes see also your fair features. I wish for all the world it were not so."

"And I wish for all the world you would make me a wife."

Lancelot finally freed himself from her grasp. "I want not to cause you anguish. I only want to awaken you. But you continue to press me to pain you. Plainly spoken, I can never take you to wife."

"Is it because you'll never marry? Then just let me live here. Take me away from the abbey and we'll stay as we did that night."

"We can't do that. That one night has already put us in a compromising position, and Sir Bedivere knows it. I told you not to fall in love with me."

"How do I help it?" Alura said, openly in tears. "I've tried to hide my feelings from you, but you've entered into me and raised me up. I've tried to release my feelings, to watch them, to let them go, but the more I try, the stronger they grow. If not your wife, then take me for your bed. I don't care about propriety; I only want to share—"

"Alura, Stop!" Frith shouted. "Your impropriety shames us all."

She put her lips next to Frith's ear. "If he sleeps with me, then will he not marry me? His code of honor should command it."

Frith made a face.

Alura wheeled on Lancelot. "Is chivalry dead? Are women nothing more to men than chattel who can bake good loaves and breed a bushel of sons? I don't want that for my fate. You have brought me to life, and it's ruined me for ordinary men. I need a husband who is as you are. And there are none."

Lancelot walked to Frith's side and put his arm across his shoulders. "Would you leave Frith alone at the abbey? Haven't you both suffered abandonment by your family?"

"Can't we all live here together?" Alura said.

Lancelot slapped his forehead. "What do you imagine? Frith builds a hut, you build a hut, and we start our own little monastery?"

"No, that you marry me and our brother comes to live with us."

Lancelot threw up his hands. "These are the machinations of mind I have been teaching you to ignore. You let it control you."

"Control me?" Alura shouted. "This whole week, I've felt as if you were controlling every movement, trying to control my every feeling."

"Calm down. My only intention has been to help you rein your passions."

Alura clenched her fists. "Well I shan't be a spinster, slowly drying up in the abbey kitchens until they put me in the ground. I am a grown woman. My mother and sisters were married and had babies before they were my age. If you won't have me, then send me to Sir Bedivere; he'll find me a man." She unclenched her hands and extended her open palms, "I know you can persuade him."

"A single woman in a company of knights?" Lancelot said. "Chivalry or not, your virtue is not assured."

"I don't care," Alura said. "Let them all take me."

"Alura, don't speak such words!" Frith said.

"Once proffered, I see no reason to take it back. I'm not a little girl. I am made a woman who now wants to be loved like one."

"That's not what you'd become," Lancelot said. "Stop running after men. You're not a cow to be traded for some beans."

"But have a life of drudgery ahead of me?" Alura said.

"You don't know that."

"I would at least like to know love before it ends."

"Life could end with your next heartbeat. Don't fixate on what may never come."

Alura's face turned an angry red. "Fixate? Isn't your resistance to me because you're fixated on a lover who's dead?"

"I assure you it's not," Lancelot said.

"Then what is it?"

"It's the Grail. Alura, I promise you, the love you will live in daily if you find it will be greater than anything you imagine with a husband, even with children. Your situation at the abbey frees you from the need for you to wed and gives you time to seek your Grail—"

"I don't want to become a nun."

Lancelot shook his head. "I'm not talking about the nunnery. There is but an obsession with rules. You've already attained something holier than all their priests, yet they'll never let you become one."

"Then I don't understand what you want me to do. You don't want me in a nunnery, you don't want Frith to want me, you won't send me with Sir Bedivere, and you won't take me yourself—"

"Maybe the obstacle you must overcome is that want for a husband."

Alura began to cry. "You treat my problems as though they are not real."

"They're not. That's what I've been trying to tell you."

"You don't know what it's like to be a grown woman and have everyone treat you like… like a child simply because you're unmarried."

"They're fools," Lancelot said. "They're trapped in the mundane. I'm trying to show you that the experience of exploring what *is*, is greater than the experience of trying to get it the way you want it to be. Besides, maybe a husband will come when you no longer think you need one."

Alura slumped down and covered her head with her hands, "Oh, you vex me, dangling that which I've always craved, then telling me to give it up."

Lancelot gripped her arms and raised her up. "The universe brings us exactly where we need to be and sets up circumstances the way they need to be."

Alura still looked unhappy. "You promised me that God would give me everything I want. Then why is it that what I want is a husband and God hasn't given me a husband?"

"When comparing us to the lilies of the field, Christ promises to give you every good thing you need—"

Alura took a step back. "Don't quote me scripture. I speak with my heart."

"I'm not trying to defeat you with some obtuse scripture. Surely you know the beatitudes. What is the sixth? 'Blessed are the pure of heart, for they shall see God.' I ask only that you purify your heart. Alura, to see God! Is that not worth it?"

Alura started crying again. "I can't defeat you with words. I'm not learned, except for what you've taught me."

"Having a thicket of words in your head is not *knowing*. Someday you'll lose what you know, but you cannot lose what you are. If you actually get the things you want, they too will pass from you. But the essence that knows you as you... when you become that... it's the treasure that moth and rust can't corrupt, that thieves can't break in and steal."

"The only thing I know is that my heart hurts when I think that you don't want me," she said sobbing. She dashed out the gate, into the forest, back toward the abbey.

CHAPTER 40

Alura dashed out of the yard, leaving the gate ajar.

"You'd better go after her," Lancelot said. "See she goes back to the abbey. Stay there and keep her from running after Sir Bedivere."

Frith followed, but she was too far gone. By the time he crossed the bridge, she was already through the woods. By the time he could see the hedge, she was already pushing through it, not caring how the thorny bushes snagged her clothes. By the time he cleared the hedge himself, she had entered the abbey gate.

The harvest Mass had ended. Outside the church, nearly the entire town was milling about, holding their little loaves of bread and talking. It was a feast day, and they were reluctant to return home to their daily duties.

Alura burst through the back gate weeping and looking disheveled. She ran straight through the crowd without the slightest care for stealth. The throng parted like the red sea in the swath of her careless flight. Some of the kitchen women recognized her and reached out for her, but she ignored them and rushed on. She was a mess with a dirty, tear-stained face, tangled hair, and damaged dress. She ran straight for her room and locked herself inside. The women followed her.

Frith arrived too late. By the time he reached the holy mob, the path of chaos Alura had cut was already closing up. A group of women stood outside her door. Frith circumvented the crowd and went to the monks' kitchen, which was empty. He hoisted himself to one of the clerestory windows and watched her door, out of sight.

Women he recognized from the kitchens called to her, but she refused to come out. Soon, others he only recognized from the village had gathered too. They could hear much sobbing inside. They were not above putting an ear to door, but this was unnecessary, for Alura's plaintive cries carried well.

"What is the virtue of virtue?" she moaned "Does it win me my man?"

"A young woman that age ought to be married," said one of the cooks. "Dangerous not to be."

"She's unmarried?" asked a woman who did not know her.

"Yes, and out in the woods on her own. It's not safe."

"Not with you-know-who living out there."

"Oh, I am undone!" Alura wailed.

"Did she say her virtue is undone?"

"Shhh, I can't hear."

"Lancelot said he was above that, that he would protect my virtue," cried Alura.

"Lancelot?"

"That's what I heard."

"Me too," said another.

"No doubt it was him; you saw where she ran from…"

Frith started. This was spinning out of control, and quickly.

"Do you think he forced himself on her?"

"What difference does it make? If a woman keeps company with Lancelot, it's irrelevant; the result is the same, isn't it?"

"Well, I certainly wouldn't let my daughter around him."

"But she hasn't a mother here, has she?" said a cook.

Frith looked around. He was tempted to set fire to the kitchens, if only to create a distraction. But the cooking fires were long since out.

"My husband said he saw her in the market just the other day, flirting with a group of married men."

"She'd best not be around my husband!"

Alura cried out in despair, "Oh! I am undone, and I can't bend him to my will."

"So Lancelot's where she's been idling…leaving me all the work."

"Well, what of the vile rake?"

"We should tell one of the monks; they'll know what to do with him."

"Ha! The monks, they welcome him every morning. They're too meek. All they'll do is fast, pray, and do nothing. No, we tell our own men. They'll get the depraved debaucher."

"And what shall we do with this wench?"

"There's nothing to be done with her; she's under the Abbot's protection."

"You're not implying…"

"Of course not. I'm only saying as long as she lives here she's untouchable."

"Except by Lancelot…" That made them all laugh.

Slowly Alura grew quieter and less interesting, and the crowd at her door began to leak away. When it became clear that she would not be threatened, Frith dropped to the floor and sank against the wall.

The worst part was, he had no one to blame. He really did feel for Alura and her pain and wished he could heal it the way he healed the fear of getting burned. But it ran too deep, and he was too inexperienced.

He didn't know what would come of the women telling their husbands, but it would not be good. He should warn Sir Lancelot. He glanced around outside. The courtyard seemed clear; he started to run for the back gate, but then he stopped. Lancelot had definitely told him to stay here. What if he left Alura and she ran off while he was gone? It would be his fault and he would have failed both Alura and Lancelot.

CHAPTER 41

When Bedivere went to church the next morning, the Mass was relatively poorly attended. The monks were there, of course, and a few visitors who had not left after the harvest celebration, but very few town folk. He suspected that many felt yesterday's celebration was enough religion for the week and returned to their daily affairs.

Bedivere had hoped to find Lancelot at communion and thus save a trip to the woods, but Lancelot must have slipped out before he could find him. As Mass ended, Bedivere overheard too many whispers about Lancelot. The monks of course were stoic, but the townspeople who came to church that morning were murmuring.

Bedivere had almost skipped Mass that morning. He'd arrived yesterday, exhausted from a long trip, and taken a room in the abbey. He had, of course, attended yesterday's harvest Mass. Being a guest of the Abbot, he could hardly do otherwise, but afterward he chose not to mingle and retired as soon as it was over. He had taken off his boots, put up his feet, and taken a nap. By the time he awoke, the crowds had gone home and the kitchen was closed. Feeling groggy, he went back to bed.

He awoke this morning refreshed and very hungry. He went to the Abbot's kitchen for breakfast, but Alura was not serving. Perhaps she was cooking in the back. When he finished, he inquired after Frith, but did not find him. Since Frith didn't know he'd returned, perhaps the boy had already left for Lancelot's. It didn't matter. Bedivere could find his own way now. However, he must first see about his horse. He had ridden straight to the stable when he arrived yesterday, but the liveryman had already left for the festival. Bedivere had no concern; he left his horse tied there, thinking the man would surely recognize the animal was his. Even so, the livery would be his first stop this morning.

After arranging for the care of his horse, he decided to stroll through the market. It was there that he began to hear talk against Lancelot. Outright disrespect was being bandied about openly in the street. Bedivere's first instinct was to speak in Lancelot's defense, but then he wily joined in their conversations, hoping to find the cause of their discontent. But the more he participated the more concerned he became. He'd seen mobs before, and this crowd was on the verge of becoming one.

Once he perceived that the victim in their gossip was Alura, he felt it was his duty to put her under his protection. It also seemed likely that Lancelot would need defending as well. He was angry at Lancelot for getting them into this mess. How could an enlightened man be so stupid? Still, he couldn't abandon him.

Bedivere headed back toward the livery. He was torn. He could see that one knight was not going to be able to be in two places at once, but he was reluctant to ride for help, for that would mean leaving both Alura and Lancelot unprotected.

Fortune smiled as he approached the livery. He chanced on a rider who was just leaving town. Reaching into his money pouch, he pulled out a handful of silver and pressed it into the rider's hand saying, "Take a message to Sir Bors! Ride your horse hard, and with this money feed him well at the end of your journey. He will have earned it." Grabbing the first thing he could find, a scrap of leather, Bedivere scratched a message to Sir Bors asking him to bring a company of knights with all haste. He rolled the piece of leather into a scroll, tied it with a thong, and thrust it at the rider.

Slapping the man's horse on the rump he shouted, "Go man, you are on a knight's business."

CHAPTER 42

This autumn, for the first time in years, Britain was not cold. The sun was warm. Green foliage was plentiful; very few trees had changed colors. But the abbey gardens had been harvested, and the ground lay barren except for some beets. Monks were digging up the last of those today.

Frith did not cut across the garden this time, but followed the long path around. He preferred not to be seen by the Abbot again today. It seemed the Abbot was paying more attention to him since he started meditating with the brothers. And the other day, when Frith had recognized some writing in a breviary open on the Abbot's desk, the Abbot had been thrilled. The Abbot apparently had decided Frith had a calling and was trying to pressure him into taking vows. He was certainly giving him more tasks to do lately, and most of them involved religion. But Frith had no intention of becoming a monk.

They hadn't gone to Lancelot's yesterday, and it looked as if he might not get to go today. He wanted to go, but Alura was being difficult. As badly as he wanted to go, he couldn't unless he could persuade her to join him. Lancelot had charged him to keep her from running off, and if he left her alone, that was a real possibility. Even after he told her that they needed to warn Lancelot about the trouble resulting from her outburst yesterday, she continued to resist him.

Alura needed to recognize that their sibling relationship had been transformed. He was now the head of their little, two-person family. Frith decided he would be as the master. He would remind her of what they'd learned from Lancelot. With this plan in mind, he headed to the Abbot's kitchen.

Frith would have preferred to wait until they were alone. But Alura had become reclusive and reticent. She retired to her room as soon as her work was finished. Frith wasn't allowed in her quarters, so he had no choice. He would have to talk to her in the kitchen. He had warned Lancelot that teaching a woman was going to bring trouble.

Frith reached the herb gardens. They too had been cut bare. Balm, betony, lavender, mint, marjoram, and rosemary were tied in bunches and hung drying on a rack. Thyme, yarrow, parsley, coriander, and cicely were already dried and put away. These and other herbs would flavor the Abbot's banquets throughout the coming winter.

He entered the kitchen from the rear door. A variety of cooking smells commingled in a delicious bouquet. Frith still had a voracious appetite – knowing Lancelot hadn't changed that. His higher Self might be waking up, but he still had to satisfy his body's demands.

Alura was making a pudding. The other women greeted him cheerfully, but Alura kept her attention on her bowl. Ethelburg pulled on his sleeve. "It's good that you've come. After that horrible man… Well, you need to get her to talk."

Frith went over to Alura and gave her a little pat on the head. She looked up and smiled, but turned back to her work. He could see she was making a marrow pudding they called Whitepot.

"I missed seeing you yesterday," Frith said.

Alura nodded. She began grating leftover biscuits into a bowl.

He lowered his voice to a whisper, "Shall we go today?"

She shook her head no. She went to the fire and began boiling milk and cream in a pan.

Frith followed her, staying close so that his voice wouldn't carry. "The master says people pursue relationships because they believe it'll make them happy, but they're really hiding from their feelings of lack, or fear."

"Why wouldn't I want to be free of loneliness and fear?"

"You would, but if you free yourself by wanting, the satisfaction will be short lived."

Someone spanked him from behind, affectionately. "Frith, where do you get such ideas?"

It was one of the cooks, who had wandered close without his noticing. Frith waited until she left. "Once you have true love flowing inside you, nothing can take that away."

"*He* has taken that away."

Under Lancelot's tutelage, Frith had learned to see that the turmoil in him was also going on in everyone else. He felt compassion for everyone, but especially Alura. "You know the master's lessons aren't just talk; they're real. You are causing your own grief, or rather your mind is."

She didn't answer him. When the milk and cream were boiled she took the pot to the table and poured it over the biscuit crumbs.

Frith followed her. "Sir Lancelot says the thoughts will just flow by if we let them."

In another bowl Alura beat eight eggs with a spoon. She added a little rosewater to make them sweet.

"Remember what he said about the river? When you step into it something *is* going to happen, not *nothing*."

Alura poured the beaten eggs into the biscuit mixture and added a little salt. "I don't want to think about it."

"Sir Lancelot says when we live in fear of our past experiences, or in hope of our future, we stop the now."

"Sir Lancelot says this, Sir Lancelot says that, I don't want to talk about him," Alura said loudly.

Everyone in the kitchen stopped work and listened intently.

Alura hung a pot of water over the fire. While she waited for it to boil, she began scooping marrow out of a beef bone. She stirred the bits of marrow into the pudding.

Frith stayed close to her. "Alura, you know that avoiding pain is not the answer, either."

Alura had thoroughly cleaned a number of small intestines. Taking up the first of them, she inserted a funnel and began filling it with pudding.

Normally he would never have spoken about these things in front of others, but Frith forgot himself. "We must be willing to go through a momentary pang, to be through and done with it. It is like Adam and Eve and the fiery swords."

"No," Alura said. "If he has given me up, I have given him up. That's not momentary."

"But I will not give up on you," Frith said. "Be willing to watch from a place of peace. Don't give up!"

"I can't find that place anymore," Alura said. "I just want out."

"There's only one way out," Frith said. "Not being in."

"Or not being here." Alura put the pudding-filled intestines into the water to boil.

Frith glanced around the kitchen and saw confusion and concern on the faces of the women. He quieted his voice. "But while we are here, we need to be somewhere."

Alura kept her eyes on her pudding. "Then go to him."

"I can't. He'd be… displeased if I came without you." He couldn't tell her he was essentially keeping her under guard.

"What do I care if he's displeased?"

"I was scolded last time you sent me ahead."

"Well, don't let that stop you. Go!"

"I… I can't leave you. Sir Lancelot has told me to make sure you don't run off—"

"Well you can be sure I am going to… with the first man who will have me!"

One of the cooks rapped her knuckles on the table. "But what kind of man will take you now missy?"

CHAPTER 43

Neither of his disciples had come for their lessons for several days. Lancelot had not gone to morning Mass today, but he didn't usually see them at church anyway. The townspeople, who were never particularly warm toward him, had become even colder. He was being shunned, and for what? Guinevere, still? She was in the grave.

Finally, on the fourth day, Frith arrived, looking and feeling as agitated as he'd ever seen him. A month trying to teach peace – wasted. "Frith! I've missed – well not missed, but I'd become accustomed... It's been days. Have you been practicing your meditations?"

"Yes master, but the Abbot has kept me very busy, and it's been near impossible to get away."

"You seem unduly upset," Lancelot said. "And where's your sister?"

"I know you said not to leave her... but she's what I am upset about."

"I thought you were past that."

"It's not that. She's put you at the greatest risk."

"There's nothing in this world worth giving up your peace for—"

"I know, but please, hear me out," Frith said. "The whole village – the whole church – has turned against you."

"I don't remember them being for me."

"No, I mean this is serious. If she doesn't speak for you soon, I fear a mob will come to harm you."

"Fear's a powerful emotion…"

"Alura was devastated by your rejection of her."

"I've not rejected her. I embrace her and uplift her."

"Oh, I know, but when she went back the other night, she was angry with you. Someone heard her say that you behaved improperly with her and led her on."

He was beginning to see the problem. "And that someone told someone, who told someone else – gossip flows like dogs wag their tails."

"Well, the wags in town have blown it out of proportion, and she's not saying anything to stifle it."

"So like mad dogs they bark on…"

"While she sits mute."

He sat down and gestured for Frith to do the same. "They already call me an adulterer, and truly. So what if they add licentious monk, or libertine, even if it's false."

Frith remained standing. "And if it's rapist?"

"No! Surely your sister hasn't said rape!"

"Of course not. But that's where the gossip's headed, and she hasn't given them reason to think otherwise. You remember how she was talking crazy, about giving up her virtue?"

"Just desperation, nothing more. Someone overheard?"

"She ran right through the crowd as they were leaving the harvest Mass – carrying on about you as she went," Frith said. "Now she's just closed up. She won't answer any of their questions. They assume it's a sign she's been deflowered."

"Oh what nonsense," Lancelot said. "You once thought I wanted her, but now you know better. This too will pass."

Frith shook his head. "There is a new force giving it strength."

"What is that?"

"Sir Bedivere has returned. When he heard the town aflame with rumors of you and Alura, he added fuel to the fire."

"How high are the flames?" He was joking, but Frith didn't seem to see the humor.

"Sir Bedivere's been telling people you also had an affair with some woman named Elaine."

"I did. She was Galahad's mother."

"I trusted and admired Sir Bedivere," Frith said. "But now.... Why isn't he rushing to your defense – a knight for a knight?"

"Sir Bedivere has a very judgmental nature," Lancelot said. "And he's not above intrigue. He may believe what he's doing has some greater purpose."

"Well, he's not acting how I thought he would."

"Frith, I can't say what he's up to. Of course he doesn't think I'm a rapist. But Bedivere may think stirring up an angry mob will compel me to join him."

"I don't see what good that does if the mob gets you first."

"Bedivere is an experienced strategist. He's probably already sent for re-inforcements. But he may intend to let this play out far enough to force me away with him."

"He wouldn't!"

"I could be wrong. Maybe that isn't his strategy. Bedivere is judgmental and self-righteous. Maybe he feels justified in telling men I am a de-baucher."

"No, he told both Alura and me that he needs you for his cause."

"He may want me for his cause, but still not be able to resist judging me for my past. The mind, when it judges others, almost always gets it wrong."

"If he really believed this about you, why would he still want you?"

"Bedivere is a true believer. Not in a religious sense, but in this plan he's made up. He's willing to go forward even if he thinks I've slipped back into my old ways, because for him, the end justifies the means."

"And you're willing to just let him say whatever he wants, do whatever he wants?"

"Bedivere's going to do what he's going to do. I can't be concerned about him. But I am concerned about your sister."

"Alura's just angry. You said yourself she'll get over it."

"She's still my disciple. I'm in pain for her pain."

"I know. I… kind of am myself. But it's not your fault. This is all her doing."

"I wish I could say that I was better with women, but I was betrayed by Elaine, Guinevere sent me away, and now it seems I've mishandled Alura's feelings as well."

"You were only trying to keep your promise to me."

"I tried to placate everyone, and it made no one happy."

"I'm happy. Well, except for this. I don't know what you could do to make her happy 'cept marry her."

"Getting married is no guarantee of happiness; most likely it gets her the opposite."

"I defer to you on that. I know I'm not ready to marry. But at last, I see her point. Marriage gets her out of the abbey kitchen and gives her a life as someone's missis."

"I want her to find her own life as Alura, not someone else's. The same for you, when you reach the Grail, where you live won't matter a whit."

"What about the immediate problem? If she won't speak to clear your name…"

"I'm more concerned about her reputation than mine."

"Hers?"

"Vicious tongues can be sharper than wolves' teeth. She's like a sheep at their feast. She doesn't realize what will happen. No matter what they do to me, no matter what they think I did, they will label her a whore."

Frith clenched his fists, his whole body shook. "They can't say that!"

"It doesn't matter what a man has done, or perceived to have done. The same villains will turn twice as fiercely on the woman."

"Oh, poor Alura."

"Now you understand."

Frith paced back and forth. "Alura must go home to Mother—"

"Will your father permit that once he hears the rumors?"

Frith shook his head. "No. He is a hard man."

They were quiet for a time. Finally, Lancelot said, "Frith, you must reach through her pain and get her to come back to me. I can show her how to disregard the useless noise of sabers rattling along the quest."

"I don't know if I can do that."

"Sure you can. I can help her... I can help both of you." Lancelot paused for a moment. He'd been happy in his habitual solitude, but now he felt responsible for them. "You must let me take you onward."

"Oh, I haven't lost faith in you," Frith said quickly. "But I don't know if I can bring her here again."

"I think you can," Lancelot said.

"Sir Bedivere guards her constantly. I don't think I can get her away from him, even if I can convince her to see you."

"I'll take care of Bedivere."

"Are you going to fight him?"

"No, if I fight him, then he has won before we begin. Even if I defeat him, he will hold to his belief. No, I've got to convince him that what his mind is telling him is worth less than what is true."

"I believe you have some power over truth that other men don't. Tell me what I should do."

"You persuade Alura. Be ready to come at my word."

"How will we know when?"

"If this works, Sir Bedivere will bring you a message."

Frith looked dubious. "But he's against you seeing Alura; why would he do that?"

"I foresee it."

Frith's eyebrows went up. "And do you foresee the message as well?"

"'It is the hour to reconcile.' When he brings you that message, bring your sister at once."

"If I can…"

"I have faith in you," Lancelot said. "Go now. Convince your sister to be amenable when Sir Bedivere asks if she will come."

Frith left and Lancelot sat down. He closed his eyes, quietly seeking guidance and direction from within.

CHAPTER 44

A few hours after Frith left, Bedivere arrived. Lancelot was still sitting with his eyes closed, just where Frith had left him, but opened them at the sound of the gate.

"Sir Lancelot, how good to see you again."

"Sir Bedivere, I heard you'd returned."

"And I heard quite a bit about you in the village, but that is trouble enough. Tell me how you've been otherwise, and I shall tell you how it goes with the Round Table."

Lancelot decided the best approach would be the overly-formal language of the old court. It might remind Bedivere of the way Arthur conducted himself. "Dear noble knight, I'm sure you are pursuing your fellows with all diligence, I'm just at my prayers, and not in a mood to relive the old days. Please forgive me."

"Of course, I understand," Bedivere said, "You must be distraught with the ill winds that blow from town."

Lancelot let the remark go. "I am like a leaf. Winds are neither good nor ill. They're just what they are."

"But these winds seem most injurious."

"The nature of man is like all things in creation, just an outcome of what has passed before."

"You don't have to hide behind philosophy with me. I've known you years longer than anyone here. Why don't you confide in me? What really went on with Alura?"

"Nothing we can speak of."

"We can speak of anything, you and me. We are fellows of the Round Table."

"Stop with this. There's been more than enough talk already."

"But give me some details," Bedivere said. "I know more than most."

"What do you suppose you know?"

"Come, old friend, I saw that girl enter your quarters that night."

"She could hardly sleep with you," Lancelot said.

"But she could with you?" Bedivere said. "I question that reasoning."

"Bedivere, I slept on the floor."

"Well, only two of you know the truth of that. If she doesn't say it, who will be your witness?"

"Then I shall be as lost as her chaperone Frith was," Lancelot said. "He was found in your bedroll in the morning, drunk as I recall."

"You're not inferring something unmanly?"

"Your circumstances are as innocent as mine, I'm sure."

"There's a big difference though."

"What's that?"

"I don't have the licentious reputation that you do."

"Ancient news," Lancelot said.

"Lancelot, the whole kingdom knows that you carried on with Queen Guinevere right under King Arthur's nose. That doesn't lend credibility to your claim when another young woman says you seduced her."

"Did she say that?"

"She didn't deny it."

"But I didn't," Lancelot said. "You don't really believe the rumors of rape, or you wouldn't be here."

"Seduction is another matter." Bedivere said. "If just the boy had been coming here, that would be one thing. People might have thought it noble that you were training him. But what possible excuse could you have for having a young woman here so often, even overnight?"

"I was doing the work of God," Lancelot said. "I thought the work was so important one night wouldn't matter. Surely, everyone would understand."

"Apparently not," Bedivere said. "I arrive back and find the whole town talking about it. How can I defend your honor when I know about the other damsels?"

"Word is that you have said quite a bit about that."

"It's my duty to protect maidens. It's part of the code."

"What part of the code involves spreading gossip like an old alewife?"

Bedivere struck his thigh with his fist. "The fact is, you have lived a wanton life for twenty years – and a few years living in the woods by yourself doesn't wash that away. Then, just when I thought you'd reformed, it appears you have done it again."

"But I've told you I haven't," Lancelot said. "I freely confess my sins with Guinevere. I not only betrayed my king, but my spiritual mentor as well. What could be fouler?"

Bedivere shook his finger in Lancelot's face. "Betraying your spiritual achievements for a maidenhead."

Lancelot pushed his hand away. "What she wanted to give away I did not take. I swear to you."

"In that oath you are likely suspect," Bedivere said. "Can you swear you never touched her in any way?"

Bedivere sounded as though he was prosecuting a trial. Touched her in what way? Familiar little pats of affection or reaching into her with his energia? What about the initiation gone awry? He wasn't going to lie even to assuage Bedivere. "That I cannot swear."

"Good God, man! Then what are you confessing? The town grows angry. You could be murdered. If I'm to guard your flank, you'd best tell me."

"I cannot reveal the secrets of initiation."

"More secrets?" Bedivere said. "I saw enough of that at court – secret conversations, secret initiations."

"You misunderstand," Lancelot said. "I cannot reveal them because you cannot understand them. They only make sense to an initiate. Do not be outraged."

"I've been outraged since your affair with Queen Guinevere. People blamed Guinevere, but she was harmless. You were the great seducer. Is this girl's case a repeat of the same lustful actions that brought about the fall of Camelot?"

The degree of anger seething in Bedivere was unexpected. He really thought all of this was just Bedivere's ploy to get him to leave. "I do not deny feeling lust," Lancelot said. "That may arise in any man. I deny the action."

"You think that I can't conceive the temptations even the greatest of saints might fall to?" Bedivere said. "I don't know the certainty of her chastity, but I know the certainty of your past mistakes."

"Which I do not deny," Lancelot said, "but Alura is a victim of gossip gone wild, not of my mistakes."

"We are all victims of your mistakes. Accept the fact that your mistakes brought down Camelot. Now your mistakes ruin the lives of two young people."

"You are so hardened in this blaming me for the world's woes—"

"Because your newest mistake threatens our plans to restore the Round Table. But I will not have that. I vow to protect your escape and I will."

Ah, here it was. "What do you mean?"

"Your time here is up," Bedivere said. "I will hold off the mob for tonight. Go to the coast, gain a ship, and sail away. Leave your mistakes behind, and when this crisis has passed, you can rejoin me with your life intact, if not your reputation."

Lancelot took a deep breath and rolled his eyes. "Escape to some far foreign place or wander the oceans for however many days?"

"Yes. For surely by morning, they will come to take you. If you are still here..."

Lancelot wasn't sure what to do about Bedivere. He had anticipated this strategy, but he had kept his mind on the present and tried not to make up a future. Now it was here. He waited to see how it would unfold.

He was quiet for a long time with his eyes turned toward heaven. Bedivere shuffled his feet but didn't interrupt his thoughts. Finally, Lancelot spoke slowly, in a soft voice, "You've been a great help in clearing my vision. I see you're right; my time in this place is nearly over."

"Good. Then you'll disappear before dawn?"

"I will. You remain here. I'll go where very few can follow."

"Good plan," Bedivere said. "But how'll *I* know where you've gone?"

"Alura will show you."

"Her? You can't take her with you! She's the source of your trouble... Unless you marry her—"

"No, that's not our destiny."

"Good, we don't need a wife tagging along," Bedivere said. "Just leave on your own. Don't take her with you."

"No, I won't," Lancelot said. "Still, I cannot leave with things as they are. The two of us must be reconciled. Do me one final service, and I will leave."

Bedivere gave him a suspicious look. "What is that?"

"Bring them to see me one last time before I go"

"That's preposterous! You can't delay to dally with that girl."

"That's not what I'm proposing. Think of it as making restitution – straightening out a bad situation before I leave."

He saw Bedivere hesitate. "I don't know if the girl will see you, sir. She is under protection."

"Under your protection."

"My chivalrous duty."

"I'm sure, but I think she'll come," Lancelot said. "Go through the brother. Give Frith a message to bring his sister... without your hindrance."

"Without protection?"

"Frith will be her chaperone."

"That apparently hasn't worked so far."

"Then… accompany them, if you must."

Bedivere stuck out his chest. "Of course, I would be satisfactory protection."

"But don't tell them I'll be leaving," Lancelot said. "Just give Frith this message: The hour to reconcile is now."

Bedivere looked puzzled. "That's a very strange message, sir."

"Frith will understand it," Lancelot said. "He will see to Alura."

Bedivere still hesitated. "It is not a difficult thing, to say a simple message, but it is a morally questionable thing."

"Morals? You still don't think I—"

"I'm not judging whatever this sordid affair may have been. But isn't it enough for me to hold the mob at bay while you escape? You expect me to bring your victim back to you again?"

"She is not my victim."

"So you say, but you also say that this is your condition for leaving. It doesn't seem to me you're in a position to be giving conditions."

"It's not a condition," Lancelot said. "It's a boon I am asking of you. Will you not grant it to me? For old friendship?"

"You know I'm willing to help you," Bedivere said. "It is your wrong attitude that has prevented you from receiving my help."

"Bedivere, I assure you it's vitally important that I see Alura and Frith. Will you do it or not?"

Bedivere sighed. "Yes. I'll pass the boy your message, but I'll not promise the results. And you must agree to go whether they come or not. Do I have your word?"

"You have it. I'm certainly going."

"Good. I'll bring you my horse. You can leave straight from here and avoid town."

CHAPTER 45

After Sir Bedivere departed, Lancelot went to the stone altar and knelt there, praying for a long time in silence. Finally he began to speak aloud to a star only he could see:

"I see now my hour soon comes.

"Let not the mob destroy the good work I have done. I pray that the Holy Grail which has quenched me shall pass to my disciples that they may too drink deeply until their cup runneth over.

"If it be thy will, let thy will, not my will be done."

Then Lancelot was silent for a long while.

A look of anguish slowly came over his face, as though he had heard an answer he did not want to know. Again he gave voice to his prayers.

"Forgive me. I see my errors are many, but the greatest may be that I have presumed upon the spiritual gifts you have lent to my enlightenment and used them to create disciples of my own, but the fault is mine, not theirs …

"I avoided the world, but the world brought itself to my door and I have fallen for its enticements. As I was once attached to the attentions of the public, so I have become attracted to the affections these two brought.

"I have allowed them to make of me an idol, and I have worshiped at the idolization of myself.

"I see now that my Grail shall not pass. Let me step aside that they may receive from you all that was transmitted to me. I surrender them unto you.

"I pray that the cup of knowledge be given unto these two, that someday you grant them their Holy Grail."

After Lancelot was again silent for a long time, he had a final realization and blurted out, "Oh my God, have I become as the Fisher King?"

With his hands still clasped in prayer he laid them upon the stone. He rested his head on his clasped hands and discarded all thoughts of himself. He remained in that penitent position until the hour of their coming.

CHAPTER 46

Evening was nearing when Alura followed her brother down the path, now better worn than it ever had been. Sir Bedivere walked behind her, leading his horse.

When they came to the place that the horse could go no further, Bedivere made to tie it to a tree, but Frith stopped him. "Forgive me, sir, but would you mind waiting with your horse, so that we might see Sir Lancelot privately?"

Sir Bedivere turned to Alura. "Are you sure?"

"Yes." Alura said. What did she care? Of course she would be safe. That was the problem.

"Call out if you need me," Bedivere said, "I'll be within earshot."

"Have no concern," Alura said.

Bedivere led his horse to a small break in the forest where some wet grass grew. The horse bent his head and began to graze. Frith was already across the bridge, waiting for her. She was in no hurry.

When they reached the gate, Alura saw Lancelot with his head pressed to the stone altar. Frith hesitated. She looked at him, waiting for him to make a decision. This was his idea; he shouldn't be afraid to disturb the master.

She saw Lancelot opened his eyes. He stood up slowly, as if in a daze. He motioned them forward, and Frith pushed her through the gate.

"Thank you for coming. I'm so glad to see you."

Alura felt him direct the full measure of his charisma at her. His voice was warm and soft, but she wasn't going to allow herself to fall for that again. She was determined to remain cool and aloof.

Lancelot smiled at her. "Alura, I must beg your forgiveness."

Alura gave him the briefest acknowledgement and then looked away.

"I am afraid I misled you, inadvertently, not fully realizing what was transpiring between us."

She looked down at the ground, feeling quietly pleased, but still said nothing.

"You asked in our first meeting if I were the Fisher King, and I denied it. I see now that I very may well have become like him."

This was not the apology she was expecting. She looked at Frith. He seemed equally lost by the direction of the conversation. "So what does that mean?"

"Earlier in our acquaintance, I told you only a little of Percival's story, the part I needed to explain why you couldn't live here. I didn't appreciate the depth to which you both would eventually be able to comprehend. Today I'm going to tell you the whole story. You're both far more capable of understanding it fully. I think you'll see why I fear that I've repeated the Fisher King's error."

CHAPTER 47

Lancelot pointed to the bench, "This will be a long tale – you may as well be comfortable."

Frith sat down on the seat, upright and alert. Alura slumped down beside him. She was bored already.

"You will recall that Percival rode a whole day across a wasteland until he came to a river he could not cross," Lancelot said.

Alura drew a line in the sand with her toe; a river between them she could not cross.

"There he met the men who were fishing. One of them was very old. He lay upon a litter covered with fine cloth instructing his son where to cast the nets."

"The Fisher King," Frith said.

"Indeed. The king invited him to his home and said 'I will send word and you will be received warmly.' The king was true to his word. When Percival approached the castle, he saw the drawbridge already lowered. He crossed the bridge and found that he truly was expected. Attendants came to greet him. One took his horse; another helped him remove his armor and took charge of it. Others came to lead him to his rooms. Percival reposed in his rooms until two attendants came for him.

"Now Percival was a relatively new knight at that point in his life and traveled light, without retinue or even a change of clothes. With his armor removed, he was rather shabby and dirty from the road. The attendants took note that he was ill prepared to be received at court. So they brought him basins of water, and when he had washed, another brought him a splendid robe. The robe was made of fine wool and beautifully embroidered, the sort of thing a royal personage would wear. He was given to know that it had been loaned to him by the mistress of the castle herself.

"Thus attired, he was led into the great hall. When he had been seated, there entered an assembly of knights bearing the crippled king on a litter. They helped the king onto a luxurious couch near to Percival. The king was much beloved by the people in his domain, like a father. He wore a crown of sable and a robe of the same rich fur. He spoke graciously to Percival. 'Please take no offense if I do not rise to greet you, for I can move only with great pain.'

"Tables were brought in and set before them. They entered into good conversation and there was much feasting, but the king did not partake of the food."

"You've already told us this," Alura said.

"Never in such detail," Frith said, "Do not break the spell with your mood!"

Her mood? So what? She had agreed to come, not to like it.

"During the celebration, a wondrous pageant ensued," Lancelot said. "A procession entered the hall, each bearer carrying a mystical object. The first, a youth, carried a white lance, the tip of which emitted drops of blood that ran down the lance. Next came two squires who carried a golden candelabra with ten branches that filled the chamber with light. Thereafter followed the queen herself, bearing a grail from which streamed such a brilliant light that the candles which only moments before had illuminated the chamber were now overcome as the moon and stars are by the morning sun. The grail was wide and somewhat deep, large enough to serve a pike or a salmon, but it contained only a bit of bread – the Eucharist.

"When the king saw it, he bowed before it saying, 'mea culpa' and all those present did the same. Although women are forbidden by the church from acting in a priestly capacity, the queen served the Eucharist, the king received it, and no one present objected.

"Percival saw all these mysteries and did not comprehend them. He burned to ask their meaning but was afraid doing so would show his ignorance – he was *very* young at the time. So he kept silent.

"The fact was, he was having his first encounter with the Holy Grail, for that was what appeared in that hallowed chamber. As each course was served, the Grail appeared again and again, completely uncovered, that he might see its nature. But Percival did not inquire about it. If he had, he would have achieved it himself, then and there. Instead, he told himself that he would definitely ask someone in the morning when he was ready to leave, when the revelation of his ignorance would no longer matter. So he kept eating.

"Percival's failure became apparent to the king and it made him very sad. He said to Percival, 'If you don't mind, I must go to my bed. Please stay in the hall as long as you wish.' Four stout knights came and carried the king away.

"After the king had retired, Percival continued to puzzle over all the things he'd been shown. The lance that bled and the Grail to which the king and all his kin had bowed were beyond his understanding. Trying to figure it out made him very weary. He went to his bed and slept soundly until morning.

"When he arose, he dressed and went down to the court. He looked in the yard; he looked in the great hall, but found no one. The empty castle filled him with sorrow. He had fully intended to ask about all he'd witnessed the previous night, but he came upon nary a soul. He did come upon his armor laid out for him, and found his horse in the livery already fed, saddled and ready to go.

"With no other recourse at hand, he put on his armor and mounted his horse. He was surprised to find the castle gate open and the drawbridge already lowered for him. He thought perhaps the people had gone into the fields and that he'd find them there. As he crossed over, the drawbridge began to rise while he was still on it. His horse had to jump the last few feet in open air. He looked back to see the castle now sealed against him.

"He rode through the valley without finding the castle occupants. He thought perhaps they were in the woods, harvesting nuts or fruits or gathering wood. He turned from the valley meadows into the forest, but rode until evening without finding a man or woman who he could ask. It was very sad. He eventually learned that if he had asked the appropriate question, he would've healed the king and his kingdom."

"Because he would have understood the Grail," Frith said.

Lancelot nodded. "He would have fully experienced it."

Alura was not satisfied. "So you lied when you told us that Percival found the Grail."

"No, Percival did find it eventually," Lancelot said. "But he missed his best opportunity and had to quest many more years before he was ever to find that castle or see the Grail again."

"You say his failure was not asking questions, and you say you've become like the Fisher King. Then am I like Percival?" Frith said.

Lancelot laughed. "Don't worry, Frith, no one would fault you for not asking enough questions." He smiled at Alura. "Why do you think Percival didn't ask the right questions?"

This story had failed to resolve her issues with him. As far as an apology went, it wasn't much of one. She didn't see why Frith had insisted that she come. "I understand exactly why Percival kept silent," she said. "You've no idea what it's like to be in the presence of a bunch of men who all know more than you do. You dare not speak. If you ask about something you don't know, you display your ignorance. And in my case, if I speak wisely they'll ask me, 'How have you learned such a thing?'"

"Of course I know what that's like," Lancelot said. "I was once an ignorant, young prideful knight – even worse than Percival. But believe me, neither Percival nor I was as advanced at that age as you already are. Percival told his story many times over the years, that being his first experience of the Grail. As he grew more enlightened, more honest with himself his explanation changed.

"At first he blamed his mentor Sir Gornemant, who had trained and knighted him. Sir Gornemant, in the course of his instruction, had tried to stifle Percival's tendency to chatter insipidly by telling him a proper knight doesn't ask so many questions. Percival wanted to be seen as proper by the Fisher King's court.

"In another telling, he said that he was afraid he'd be thought rude if he asked questions during the ceremony. Finally, he confessed that instead of focusing on the events before him, he was feeling self-conscious that he was wearing the queen's cloak.

"But in his final telling, Percival was being shown a wondrous pageant, every phase of it was filled with sacred symbols and deep meaning. Again and again he was shown the Grail, yet his mind dwelled on the shallow and unimportant."

"Sir," Frith said, "are you telling me this story because like Percival, I'm obsessed with knights while I'm in the presence of something greater?"

"Don't be ridiculous," Alura said, "he's telling me I am like Percival, because I'm obsessed with husbands instead of his pretty stories."

"Neither of you is like Percival," Lancelot said. "I'm not retelling his story because I think either of you lack understanding. It is I who was lacking. I first told you of the Fisher King in a simplistic attempt to discourage Alura's attentions."

"Well, it had the opposite effect," Alura said.

"I see that now," Lancelot said. "But the real story of Percival and the Fisher King was a pageant being played out by the universe to bring Percival to his destiny. When you near the end of your quest, you see a synchronicity about you, everything cooperating toward your realization. Every element has meaning. Why is the king a fisherman?"

All right, he had drawn her in. "Is it… biblical?"

Lancelot smiled and nodded. "When Percival meets the king casting his net on the water, he's being shown that it is the enlightened man's duty to draw men into realization."

"But the king was crippled. He wasn't really casting the net, his son was," Frith said.

"The king's mission was to draw men from the old ways," Lancelot said. "He hoped his son would be his spiritual successor, but it was failing. He had to keep instructing the men where to throw the net. They weren't getting it on their own."

"The old ways meaning the old religion?" Frith said.

The answer seemed obvious to Alura. "Not the old religion, the old ways men think of the world. Their souls are drowning. With his net, he's trying to draw them into his boat."

Lancelot looked pleased with her answer. And she was pleased by that.

"The king was like a father to his whole kingdom," Lancelot said. "It was his responsibility to guide them on a spiritual path to their own realization."

"But he was ill," Frith said.

"That's why the king invited Percival to the castle," Lancelot said. "He knew his force was diminishing. In Percival, he saw hope."

"Was the king going to make him his disciple?" Alura said.

"The king was not looking for disciples. He and his entire kingdom were looking for a successor. When Percival arrived at the castle, he was welcomed by everyone. The queen herself gave him her cloak."

"Surely, when the Grail appears to a man, it doesn't care how he's attired," Frith said.

"Certainly, the manner of his dress was not important, but thinking about it distracted him whilst he saw the Grail," Lancelot said. "The kingdom had prepared for him, but he was ill-prepared. A great ceremony was laid out for him to experience the Grail and bring about a new order, but he didn't grasp what he was being shown."

"Men!" Alura said. "Percival wasn't the last man to miss what was being laid out for him."

"Don't judge Percival," Lancelot said. "He was young and inexperienced."

"But how is one judged who rejects the opportunity at hand although he is neither young nor inexperienced?" Alura said.

"Percival missed the opportunity, but he did eventually find his Grail," Lancelot said. "No, I want you to look at the king. It was he who, anxious to pass his knowledge on, took Percival to his home. It was he who tried to make of Percival what he wanted him to become. He who put upon him a procession of holy relics that Percival wasn't ready to comprehend."

"But he had to, to save his kingdom," Frith said.

"Did that make it right?" Lancelot said. "Was the king not meddling in the natural course of Percival's destiny because he felt his own failure pressing upon him? Because his own time to leave was coming?"

CHAPTER 48

Frith jumped up from the bench. "Is that why you said that you've become like the Fisher King? Is it because you're leaving?"

This was the first Alura had heard of it. "What?!"

"I've come to think of the Fisher King because like him, I've tried to force you out of your inexperience to a revelation that you're not ready for yet. When the king saw his mission failing, he put his hopes on passing his Grail to Percival. The failure was not Percival's, but the king's. I feel sure the king realized later that Percival would find the Grail at the appropriate time. For the Grail is greater than all of us, even we who think we know it well."

Alura wheeled on Frith. "What leaving?" A crowd of emotions she couldn't sort out coursed through her. Anger was no longer among them. Her brother was focused on Lancelot and ignoring her.

"Sir Bedivere told me you were leaving," Frith said.

"Sir Bedivere says too much. That's not the message I gave him to bring you."

"Is that why you retold the story?" Frith said.

"Bedivere also says the village is coming in the morning to exact their justice."

He said that as if it were nothing. The pain, anger, and frustration that had kept her distant these several days was completely gone. Breaking her resistance, Alura ran to him, crying "Oh No! Master, don't leave."

This time he didn't push her away, but let her hold onto him. "Alura, my dear Alura, why didn't you tell them what really happened?"

"You forbade us to speak of what transpires here. We took a vow of silence."

"Good God girl, that doesn't mean stand silent while they call you a slut or me a debaucher. I meant don't tell them what I teach you."

She knew that. "I guess I was a little… mad."

Lancelot stepped back, but she continued to hold on to his arm. He looked into her eyes. "Well no matter, you have no blame in the wicked tongues of town gossips and small minds."

She scanned his face for signs of anger and saw none. "You're not mad?"

"There's such a thing as destiny," Lancelot said. "We are all arrows in God's quiver. Our lives go as the archer aims, too swiftly for us to change the course."

Alura felt like she was being swept downstream in rushing river of emotion. "Please don't leave. I'll tell them, I'll tell them nothing happened."

"It will not be enough. They'll believe what they want. A young girl in love with an older man suddenly denying he's her lover. That's not going to convince them – especially when he already has a ruined reputation."

"But… this is so unfair!"

"Yes, it is," Lancelot said, "but life has a knack for equilibrium. The most painful of events often turn out to be the force that dislodges the log that's blocking the stream."

What could she do? "If you must leave, can't I just go with you?"

"Me too," Frith said.

"Where I'm going, I'm afraid you cannot follow."

"We will!" they said in unison. "Wherever you go!"

"Your destiny lies elsewhere. Mine is at hand."

That sounded so final. Her initial anxiety was replaced with a greater one. Her stomach was in a knot. "What are you saying?"

"I see it is time to join Merlin and Arthur, to see my beloved Guinevere–"

"No!" She tightened her grip on his arm.

"But Sir Bedivere said you were only leaving..." Frith said. "He brought you a horse."

"Tell him to take his horse to the livery. I won't need it."

She was stunned. "You cannot mean to end your life. Not because of me."

"The church says suicide is the unforgivable sin," Frith said.

"Oh, my death won't come by my own hand," Lancelot said.

Frith clenched his fists. "Surely not at the hands of the mob!"

"Bedivere assures me the crowd comes for me. But when they come, they'll find an empty corpse."

Alura began weeping uncontrollably. "How can you say this?"

Lancelot spoke calmly. "Don't be afraid. Saint Paul said, 'I die daily.' I have been to death's threshold and back so many times, it's nothing for me to simply step over it."

"Not being afraid of death is not the same as being dead," Frith said.

"Frith, the lower self dies to the higher self, until there's no more to die."

Alura felt like she might throw up. "But I don't want you to die!"

"Death doesn't want anyone except those who don't want it," Lancelot said. "Those who want death can never have peace."

She blamed herself. Her obstinacy had kept him from Mass. "Are you dying without your Eucharist?"

"I'm not lacking of a bite of bread. It's not necessary to actually eat the Host to have communion. I can have communion in any moment with just a breath. Haven't I taught you that life comes from the mouth of God?"

"If that's so, why have you been going to Mass when it only agitates the men who are against you?" Frith said.

"To participate in the ritual."

"Even when you no longer have need of it?"

"When you dwell in spirit more than in the world, continuing to honor sacred rites keeps the soul from drifting away."

Alura moaned. "Then attend Mass at the abbey! Why say you will go away?"

"I've talked with God, and he has shown me my end."

Now her tears turned into anger at God. "What kind of God would take your life for my mistake? I should've told the truth." She sobbed. "I should've told the truth."

Lancelot embraced her again, patting her on the back. "You've made no mistake. It's I who made mistakes."

It felt good to be held by him, just not for this. "But why must you die for them?"

"It's not a mistake to die. I thought you were a mandate I was given – to transfer my spiritual linage so the line would not end with me."

"And you've succeeded," Frith said.

"No I haven't. My cup cannot be passed. I cannot give you Lancelot's Grail, but perhaps I've helped in some way."

Alura sniffed. "I feel I've harmed you, not helped you."

"I've learned from you both, as I hope you've learned from me."

"What could you learn from me?" Alura said.

"I've learned that the real courage is to stand guiltless, facing the predicament in which you find yourself because it is God's will."

"Death doesn't seem like the courageous way out," Frith said.

Maybe, just maybe, her brother could talk him out of it.

"No man or woman who comes onto this earth leaves it by any other means than by death," Lancelot said. "But we are not our bodies. The soul leaves our bodies like the threshers leave the husks from grain."

This explanation did not make her feel any better. "And where does that leave those of us who are not taken by the threshers?"

"To continue to grow in the fertile soil where you've been planted."

"But I don't want to be left. I feel more discarded than planted ...abandoned again." She wept harder.

"We're all caught up in circumstances of a universe so vast we will never untangle them, but it's our duty to play them out."

Alura knew any remaining hope of marrying Lancelot had shattered on his impending tombstone. The idea of marriage was suddenly unimportant compared to losing her teacher. "But how can we do that without you?"

"It is lucky that you've even done it with me. I've come to realize that I let my own false sense of pride take on a task that I never should have."

"What task was that?" Frith said.

"I began with the best of intentions, thinking to impart what was imparted to me, but now I see that I should've never been so presumptuous as to make you my disciples."

"Master, don't say such a thing!" Alura said. "It's me. I've been a bad disciple. I've run away from you. You've been my greatest teacher."

"Our greatest teacher," Frith said. "When I look back at who I was when we started, I just…"

"I tried to change the way you see the world, or rather the place you see it from. But I see now that isn't enough."

"You freed me from my fear of being alone, my jealousy, and so much more," Frith said.

"And you've opened my eyes to so much," Alura said. "I've been such a fool, but I know better now—"

"It's not your fault. And you have both grown much; I'm very proud of you. But I am not my son. I can't give you the experience of the Grail the way Galahad could. But don't lose hope. The teachings I've given you are the Truth. They can themselves bring you to the light."

"Don't think you've failed," Frith said. "What you've started here in us isn't going to stop. Energia is moving in me like the tide of the sea, rising without explanation."

Alura wiped her wet cheeks on his robe and lifted her face so she could look into his eyes. "Me too. Even when I kept myself away in anger, I practiced as you taught us."

"Well, what I've said in the weeks we've had together may not have been enough, but it will have to suffice. You'll succeed on your quests, on your own."

"We will?" Frith said.

"I've seen it. I am assured by a vision this night that, if you persist, you will be guided by real saints to your own Holy Grail."

"You're a real saint," Alura said.

She felt his body stiffen. "Avoid my mistake of trying to be a saint for others. Remember your vow never to reveal these teachings?"

She nodded, so did Frith.

"Don't let yourselves decide you're ready to break it. Don't listen to your own counsel on this."

"Yes, Master."

"I have a plan for you, so before we part—"

"Let us not part!" Alura cried out. She couldn't help herself.

"Don't be afraid," Lancelot said. "Through daily practice, the soul learns you are not the body. The body is like a cart that you ride in, but you are not a prisoner in a cart. You are free to get off at any time."

"A man can do that?" Frith said.

"The moment you're comfortable with all of creation, you're free to come and go at will. I will this night make a fully conscious exit from this body, as I have done many times before. But this time I will leave it behind."

"Oh please… No!" The reality of it was just too harsh for her to accept. She would gladly give up marrying him. But he couldn't give up his life. Who would ever teach her now?

"Calm yourself, my dear one." Lancelot rubbed her back soothingly. "I have a plan for you to follow. But let me say it quickly, for we've been too long in retelling Percival's story, and Sir Bedivere is surely getting anxious. Let me instruct each of you before he grows impatient and bursts in on us."

Lancelot parted a little from her embrace. "Frith since we met, you often wondered why I wouldn't dub you a knight. In truth it was because I loved you, and I was afraid it would be your death warrant."

"How so?"

"Without any training or practice, you would suddenly be subject to challenges by battle-hardened men, who could kill you without raising a sweat. You were trying so hard to be a man, you'd have thrown yourself at them out of sheer pride. Instead, you are now more nearly a realized man than any knight."

Alura saw how this pleased Frith. Lancelot turned his eyes back to her. "Alura, you were once convinced that a man was your only way out of a life that drags on you. But do you now see that, if you had a husband, that husband would be making demands of you. If you had children, those children would be making demands of you. You would wind up far more constrained than you would even be in the abbey kitchens. Within a short period, any time you might have for your spiritual practice would be gone."

"I surrender," Alura said, and she meant it. With those words, the notions she had been raised with fell away. The idea that marriage was the best life a girl could hope for dissipated. She did not have to do what everyone else did.

Lancelot walked over to the altar and picked up a scroll. "The world's entering a dark and dangerous age, and you need time to find your own Grails. Until you reach that exalted state, you need somewhere to stay together during your inner quest."

"Where's that?" Frith said.

"Make your den within the abbey, living like foxes where no one sees you quest."

"Within the abbey?" Alura said. "But you told me not to become a nun."

"And I'm not telling you otherwise now," Lancelot said. "Continue your service, both of you. Your low positions are an advantage because people don't notice you as long as the work is done – unless you create a spectacle."

Alura felt herself blush.

"You have free time, and the opportunity to pursue the Grail quite unnoticed by everyone around you. Has it not been so these many weeks?"

"I can accept that fate," Alura said. "But don't hold Frith back for my sake. I see he's a man now. If he needs to ride with Sir Bedivere, let him go."

"He doesn't. Frith knows where to look for the Grail," Lancelot said. "Frith, if you told Sir Bedivere you are on a quest for the Grail, he'd think you needed to charge back and forth across the countryside on a horse. You know from what I've taught you that the quest for the Grail is—"

"Within."

Lancelot nodded. "Living at the abbey, you'll be able to support and cover for each other. The world will see only an unwed sister and her doting brother."

"What of Sir Bedivere?" Frith said. "He knows too much about this, and he doesn't seem likely to hold his tongue."

"He'll not be trouble much longer. Here's a letter for him. Keep it until tomorrow morning."

"May we know its contents?" Alura said.

"It binds the knight by an earlier oath to put aside his judgments about what he's seen and asks him to send a company of knights to transport this body to its burial place."

This was becoming far too real for her. Alura broke down again. "Oh, I can't bear it!"

Lancelot bent down and picked some flowers. "I was distraught near to death when Guinevere gave up her body. After long fasting and prayer, I realized that to be with the Lord is to be with those who are also with Him." Lancelot handed her one of the blossoms. "Have no fear when I leave you, for at the end of your quest, when you find the Grail you shall know – not intellectually but in every fiber of your being – that we are one."

"If we might keep you here a bit longer," Frith said. "One thing I must know..."

Lancelot smiled. "Yes, Frith."

"What was the question Percival *should* have asked?"

"Whom does the Grail serve," Lancelot said.

"Who *does* the Grail serve?" Frith said.

"The Grail is within you. When you find the Grail, ask, and it shall be known to you." He handed Frith the other flower.

Frith furrowed his brow. "If Percival had asked, would he have become enlightened and healed the king?"

Lancelot pulled both of them to him and embraced them. He kissed each of them at the center of their forehead. "May you become beings of realization. True saints. This is my final blessing. No tears now. Take that letter and give it to Sir Bedivere at dawn. Go now, in peace." With that he pressed them toward the gate.

A force she could not explain made her feet to move with a lightness she did not expect. She and Frith made their way to Sir Bedivere.

"Isn't Sir Lancelot with you?"

She shook her head and saw Bedivere's body tense. He snorted like a bull about to charge Lancelot's gate. "He gave me his word."

Frith blocked his way. "Sir Lancelot is definitely leaving as he promised, but he said he won't need your horse."

"Oh." Bedivere gave a whistle and the horse came to him. He patted its neck and took the lead rein in his good hand.

Alura pulled Frith to her and began to walk toward the abbey with her arm around his waist. Bedivere, following, tried to engage them in conversation, but she was unwilling to speak. She found herself experiencing a curious mixture of pain and bliss. Perhaps something similar was happening to Frith, for he was also mute in Sir Bedivere's company.

The three of them walked back to the abbey in silence.

CHAPTER 49

The Abbot fell into bed exhausted and was soon fast asleep. It had been a difficult and trying day. The Bishop had arrived unexpectedly and a feast had to be organized. It was not an ideal time for the Bishop to visit. The kitchens were closed and the cooks had the day off. There also was the uproar over rumors about Lancelot and one of the kitchen staff. There was no need to involve the Bishop in that! Just when the Abbot thought he had everything managed, a group of knights arrived. They too had to be feted, and so were joined in banquet with the Bishop. It proved to be a long night.

The knights said they'd been summoned to the abbey by Sir Bedivere, but when they arrived, neither Bedivere nor Frith could be found. The Abbot assumed Frith was with Bedivere, guiding him to Lancelot again. It was not the first time that Frith had disappeared that day. The Abbot had noticed his absence when he needed help with so many unexpected guests.

The Abbot was sleeping soundly when he was startled awake by great peals of laughter. His first thought was that the knights were engaged in some drunken reverie inappropriate to a house of God. As his sleep-dulled senses cleared, he realized the noise was coming from the Bishop's quarters. Desiring to ascertain what was going on without personally confronting the Bishop, the Abbot sent a young monk to the Bishop's room.

The boy returned to the Abbot almost immediately. "Come quick, Holy Father, the Bishop is having a fit."

The Abbot rushed to the Bishop's room and found clustered about the open door the entire fellowship of monks and knights. He pushed past them into the room and found the Bishop in great mirth, though sound asleep. Perhaps something had seized possession of him. He approached the Bishop's bed and, seeing a sweet smile on his face, changed his mind. Possession rarely left someone so peaceful. Perhaps it was just a loud dream, and the laughter not unlike someone talking in his sleep.

The Abbot touched the Bishop several times to no avail. Finally, he shook him firmly until he woke. "Your Grace, what ails you?"

"In Jesus' mercy," the Bishop said, "why did you wake me? I was never in all my life so ecstatic."

"Your merriment was so boisterous that the monastics thought you were possessed," the Abbot said quietly.

"I am not bewitched," the Bishop said. "It was truly a vision, heaven sent. There was Sir Lancelot with me, and more angels than ever I saw men in one day. Then I heard Sir Lancelot say, 'Bishop, give me last rites, for now is my hour.'"

The monks and knights in the doorway began to edge into the room. "It cannot be. We saw him yestermorning at Mass, and he was in good health."

"Nonetheless, this is what I saw," the Bishop said. "I was about to satisfy his request for last rites when I saw he had no need of them, for the angels heaved up Sir Lancelot unto heaven, and the gates of heaven opened for him."

"Perhaps this dream was simply the result of too much rich food tonight," Sir Bors suggested.

"I want to be dissuaded," the Bishop said. "This is a strange doing. But we can know for sure. Go to his hermitage and disprove my vision. I shall be glad if I'm wrong and Lancelot is still with us."

Although it was not yet daylight, Sir Bors dispatched several knights to Lancelot's hut.

CHAPTER 50

It was nearly dark when Bedivere, Frith, and Alura returned to the abbey. He left the siblings to enter the back gate, and when it shut, he mounted his horse and rode around the abbey perimeter to the livery. He entered the abbey by the front gate and went straight to his bed. He needed his rest for the coming battle. He fell into a deep, deep sleep.

It was not until he heard the sound of armored men on the march that Bedivere awoke. Thinking his knights were just arriving, he hurriedly pulled on his breeches. He threw his surcoat over his nightshirt and dashed into the courtyard to greet them. However, they had already departed. Seeing the Abbot's house illuminated by numerous candles, he went there and learned the disastrous news. The Bishop had seen a vision.

* * *

Morning dawned grey and a wet drizzle fell. Bedivere clung to the hope that the Bishop's nightmare was only an effect of indigestion. Then Frith arrived and handed him Sir Lancelot's letter. Bedivere read the letter and pressed his lips together until they were white. His eyes raced over the words again and then he rolled up the scroll. He saw Frith watching him.

"I am awaiting the return of a dispatch of knights. When they've made their report, I'll meet with you and your sister. Can you arrange it?"

He had somehow sensed it would be unnecessary to defend Lancelot from the mob, for when he dressed this morning, he went unarmed. Lancelot's letter confirmed it, but there was no reason to disclose its contents just yet. It was only just light. He would hold out, against hope, for Bors' men to return.

When the knights returned with the fearful confirmation, he instructed them as to Lancelot's wishes and bade them Godspeed. He felt some comfort knowing the mob had been cheated of its vengeance, but he knew it was now his dreadful duty to deliver the blow that would strike down the boy and girl. He'd have preferred to face the mob, sword in hand.

He sought out Frith and asked him to find his sister. When they came, the happy countenance on their faces made him fear to lay the terrible tragedy upon them. Yet there was hope in his dire message if he could find a way to say it, but that was not his forte. He was not a man of the cloth; better he should have left it to the Abbot to tell them. Then again, Lancelot's letter had been addressed to him. This was knights' business, and he was, if anything, a man respectful of his duty.

They found a small unoccupied niche, and Bedivere plunged into it. "His body has left, conveyed by nine knights to Joyous Gard to be buried there, as he requested." He was circumventing the words he could not bring himself to say: Lancelot was dead.

"That corpse was not the essence of the Master," Alura said.

Bedivere was taken aback. This was not the reaction he'd anticipated. Perhaps the girl was not willing to accept that he was gone. "The Bishop would agree."

"The Bishop?" Alura said.

Perhaps it might help if he revealed some of the details. "Yes, last night as Sir Lancelot left his body, the Bishop was shown a vision."

Frith grew wide-eyed.

"His Grace said that he saw angels take Sir Lancelot into heaven."

"But not his body," Frith said.

"No, not his body, Sir Bors dispatched several knights to verify the Bishop's vision. They found him in his garden where he lay... dead." There, he'd said it. "They say he smiled with a sweet sense of peace about him."

"Did his body give off a light?" Alura said in a voice filled with wonder.

"What a strange thing," Bedivere said. "Why would you ask that?"

"Because he often quoted us the scripture 'If thy eye be single, thy whole body shall be full of light,'" Alura said. "And his eye was surely single."

"Um… when Sir Bors returns from Joyous Gard, I'll ask him," Bedivere said. "Now, what should I do about you two? Frith, you still want to ride with me in service to the knights?"

"Thank you, sir; that's most kind. I once dreamed of it, but no more. Now I shall do as Sir Lancelot has asked."

"What, stay at the abbey?"

"Yes, I'll stay here and watch out for my sister."

"Indeed, she needs a man's protection, but only until she is wed." Bedivere turned to address Alura. "I will not marry again, but I'll bring you a husband if I find one along my travels."

"No, thank you," Alura said. "Sir Lancelot has set my feet firmly upon another path."

Bedivere was astonished. "And what is that?"

"To live in humble quietude at the abbey, to take communion daily with the me who is not of this world, at a place in myself that is not in this world."

Her convoluted words made his head swim – she sounded just like Lancelot at his worst. He shook his head like a man with a fly buzzing his ear. But her voice had been filled with spiritual power. A soft light seemed to surround her. He glanced at her brother to ascertain if he was also witnessing the phenomena, but Frith too seemed to glow from within.

Bedivere was not a sensitive man, yet he could feel something emanate from her. It reminded him of a time long ago, a Pentecost banquet with Galahad…

Bedivere took a deep breath, preparing to make a decision. Then he found the decision had already been made.

"I see Sir Lancelot has changed us all," he said. "Since hearing the Bishop's tale, I've taken to mind that if I can't get the knights to reorganize, I'll come back here, myself. I understand there's a hermit's hut that's vacant."

Alura smiled. "I am sure he would like that."

> *'…And Sir Bedivere was there ever still, hermit to his life's end.'*
> —*Sir Thomas Malory, Le Morte de Arthur, Book XXI, Chapter XIII*

READ THE SEQUEL

Lancelot's Disciple

Sequel to *Lancelot's Grail*

by Richard Gartee

Frith, Alura, and other characters from *Lancelot's Grail* are back as their story continues in the compelling sequel, *Lancelot's Disciple*.

When Lancelot's spiritual mantel consecrates Alura, Frith is left wondering why the same didn't happen to him. As she becomes established in her seat of Self, Frith resigns himself to remain at the abbey and watch over his sister.

Then, Jacob, a Jewish merchant sent by their father, comes to take Frith on a journey along the ancient Silk Road. A reluctant Frith leaves the Christian abbey he has always called home to sail with Jacob to the Mediterranean city of Tyre.

With four knights for protection, the men caravan to Samarkand, the Central Asian capital of the silk trade. There they meet the Sultan, a wealthy collector of Oriental holy men.

Frith is invited to study at the Sultan's newly formed mystery school, where he is tutored by a Taoist, a Buddhist, and a Hindu Swami. Overwhelmed by metaphysical experiences he receives from them, Frith becomes nearly catatonic during the journey home, causing Jacob to consider revealing hidden Jewish mysticism to set Frith right.

Once back in Britain, Frith must sort out his confusion, attain the Holy Grail, and reconnect with his saintly sister waiting at the abbey.

Available in paperback and ebook from the same bookseller where you purchased *Lancelot's Grail*.